TERROR IN THE MIST

C.G. MOSLEY

SEVERED PRESS
HOBART TASMANIA

TERROR IN THE MIST

PROLOGUE

August 28th, 1992
New Orleans, Louisiana

Claire Hutton became a resident of New Orleans thanks to her husband's job. Gavin was an attorney from a small town in Arkansas and though his practice was growing, higher aspirations eventually brought him and his family to the Crescent City. There was resistance from Claire at first, but once she became acquainted with her new home, she quickly decided there was no other place she'd rather be. The rich history and colorful buildings the city boasted were very charming and there was never a shortage of things for a family to do.

Claire and Gavin's oldest daughter, Samantha, had just gotten over a nasty bout with the flu and was more than eager to get out of the house to get some fresh air. As soon as she'd felt better, Sam had practically begged her mother to take her out shopping in New Orleans's French Quarter Market. There was some jewelry that she'd had her eyes on for quite some time and she had finally saved up enough money to purchase it. Claire was so pleased to see her daughter feeling better, she happily drove them over to the popular shopping venue as soon as she got off work.

The sun was beginning to set as they arrived and Claire noticed that there were more people than usual on a Thursday night. She suddenly remembered there was some sort business expo occurring downtown and thus parking in the area was scarce. They left the car a couple of blocks away and made the short walk toward the market. It was a brisk night and Claire suddenly found herself wishing she'd brought a slightly heavier coat. She glanced over at her sixteen-year-old daughter and pondered if she'd made a good decision bringing the girl into the cool evening air immediately after she'd been so sick. As if she'd read her mind, Sam looked over at her mother and smiled. It was enough of a reassurance to erase any guilt that may have been creeping into Claire's head.

"Is there a particular piece you're interested in?" Claire asked, pushing away a strand of brown hair that had blown across her face.

Sam nodded eagerly. "Yes, there is a charm bracelet that Kate's boyfriend bought her from over here," the girl replied. "She showed it to me at school the other day and did her best to make me feel bad that her boyfriend buys her things."

Claire frowned and looked at her daughter, puzzled. "Well, why would she do such a thing like that?" she asked.

Sam looked back at her mother and her blue eyes sparkled. Claire took a moment to admire her beautiful daughter. As much as she hated to admit it, Samantha was the spitting image of her father. Blonde hair, blue eyes, and a smile that could instantly alleviate any sadness or sorrow in any situation.

"She's trying to make me feel bad because she has a boyfriend and I don't," Sam explained. "I'm going to buy the bracelet so that she knows I don't need a boyfriend to have it."

Claire smiled. Though her daughter may have gotten her looks from Gavin, clearly her personality and independent spirit came from her.

"Good for you," she said, pulling her daughter closer as they walked. "And you keep your money, I'll buy the bracelet."

Sam beamed. "Really?"

"Really," Claire replied with a smile.

When they finally arrived at the market, Claire allowed Sam to lead the way. The young girl knew exactly where she was going and led her straight to a corner booth surrounded by tables draped with green cloths. On top of the tables, there were wooden cases adorned with hundreds upon hundreds of various pieces of jewelry.

There were two middle-aged women that ran the booth and Claire thought they looked so much alike that they must be sisters. She refrained from asking and just politely waved as Sam began to scan over the wide selection. One of the women was slightly taller than the other and her brown hair was put up in a bun. She wore red-rimmed glasses that looked a lot like the ones Claire had seen Sally Jessy Raphael wear on her television talk show. The other lady wore her hair down but wore similar glasses.

It's the glasses, Claire thought. *They look related because they're wearing the same glasses.*

"May I help you find something, sweetie?" the woman with the bun asked Sam.

Sam looked up from the case she was standing over. "Yes, ma'am," she replied politely. "I'm looking for your charm bracelets."

The woman motioned for Sam to follow her over to the other end of the booth and Sam eagerly followed. Claire stayed where she was at. A pair of earrings had caught her eye.

"Anything I can help you with?" the other lady asked her.

Claire looked up and smiled. "Oh no, I'm just looking," she replied. "I'm here because of her," she added, nodding toward her excited daughter.

The woman's face softened substantially as she returned a smile of her own. "She's lovely," she said. "I know you must be proud."

"Oh yes, I am," Claire answered.

"You enjoy her and take good care of her," the woman said in reply. Claire picked up on a bit of sadness in her words.

"I most definitely will," she replied. "There's not a lot a mother won't do to take care of her child."

The woman nodded, seemingly happy to hear Claire make the statement. "I'm so happy to hear you say that," she said. "I had a daughter like her many years ago."

"Oh, you did?" Claire asked. She didn't like the way the woman used the word *had*.

The woman nodded. "Yes, but she died in a car crash," she said somberly.

Claire felt a knot tighten in her stomach. "Oh my," she whispered. "I am so sorry."

She looked on as the woman looked down toward the ground. "She was about the same age as your daughter," the woman added. "Looked a great deal like her too."

Claire could hear the hurt in the older woman's words and she felt a lump in her throat. It seemed as if her and Sam being there had opened an old wound the woman had been dealing with for many years.

"I'm so sorry for your loss," she said, reaching out and holding the woman's hand.

The woman smiled at her and seemed to shake off the hurtful memories. "Enough about that, dear," she said apologetically. "I noticed you had your eye on those earrings. Would you like for me to retrieve them so that you can see them up close?"

Truthfully, Claire didn't want the earrings. She liked them, but she just didn't think they'd look right on her. However, since the woman had gotten so emotional about her deceased daughter, Claire almost felt like she had to buy the earrings out of sympathy.

"Sure, I'd like that," she replied after considering it a moment.

The lady carefully handed the earrings over to Claire and she stared at them with forced interest.

"They really are beautiful," she said finally. "I think I'll take them."

The woman's face brightened and she seemed to have forgotten all about the conversation concerning her daughter.

"That's a good choice, dear," she said. "I'll go wrap these up for you and we'll wait on your girl to pick out her bracelet."

Claire nodded as the woman hurried away and, except for the busy folks strolling from booth to booth behind her, she suddenly found herself standing alone. She was thinking about what the woman had said about Sam looking a lot like her deceased daughter and it gave her a chill. The unsettling thought was depressing and she again felt a deep sadness within her returning and swelling to the point she thought she was going to cry.

She surveyed her surroundings in an effort to shake off the unsettling thoughts. All she saw around her were people smiling and laughing. Everyone seemed to be having a genuinely good time and enjoying each other's company. The outdoor pavilion that housed all the booths was long and wide enough to allow a heavy flow of people to navigate the lengthy corridor between them. Claire found herself standing at the very end of the pavilion, so she had a good view of the heavy traffic of happy people throughout the entire market.

As she looked on and pondered which booth they'd visit next, she heard a loud commotion coming from somewhere near the riverfront. The mighty Mississippi River ran parallel to the French Quarter Market and the water was just a short walk from where Claire was standing. She heard screams and whatever was going on seemed to be originating from somewhere near the water.

"Mom, what's going on?" she heard Samantha ask.

Claire looked over to find her daughter standing nearby with a worried look on her face. "What is all the screaming about?"

The woman with the bun in her hair looked worried too. "You two better get out of here and get to some place safe," she urged. "I'll hold your jewelry for you and we can continue this transaction later."

Claire nodded in agreement and grabbed Sam's arm as she turned to run in the opposite direction from the commotion. As she did so, she locked eyes with the other woman that had lost her daughter.

"Take care of her," the woman said, pointing at Samantha.

Suddenly, without warning, Claire and Sam were overcome by a mob of panicked and fleeing people. The people were still screaming, and some were crying. Claire heard someone say something about a man getting eaten alive. She felt a cold chill run up her spine. As the sea of scrambling people continued to rush past them, Samantha was suddenly knocked to the ground. Claire looked on in horror as her daughter was trampled on, unable to get up.

"Get away from my daughter!" she screamed as she tried desperately to push back against the flow of the crowd. It seemed that the harder she pushed, the further she was swept away from Sam.

Despite the growing distance between her and her daughter, Claire did not relent. She continued to push through the crowd to make every effort to get Samantha to safety. As her lungs began to burn from all the screaming she was doing, finally the crowd began to thin a bit and for the first time it allowed Claire to see exactly what the source of all the commotion actually was. The sight horrified her.

In the middle of the corridor, there was an enormous crocodile unlike anything she'd ever seen before. She estimated the animal had to be at least forty feet long. The crocodile's snout was slick with blood and the animal was surrounded by numerous body parts and other gore that Claire was unable to identify. The visual made her scream again, probably louder than she'd ever screamed before, and for a moment, she became frozen in terror.

Samantha was finally visible again, but Claire could immediately see that she was injured. Her daughter's ankle was twisted oddly, and she was sobbing uncontrollably, but Claire was at least relieved to see that she was alive. The giant crocodile seemed to notice her too, and to her horror, Claire noticed the vile creature began to hobble in Samantha's direction.

Claire's heart began to beat so intensely she could feel the vibration of it in her ears. With the crowd finally out of the way, she started running back toward Samantha. The crocodile continued its approach and it seemed as if Claire would get to her daughter at the same time as the animal. If that happened, Claire knew there would be no way to avoid disaster. She pushed forward as fast as her legs would carry her, but as the enormous animal seemed to burst forward with more speed, she knew her efforts were futile. She was about to watch her daughter be eaten alive and there was absolutely nothing she could do about it.

"No!" Claire screamed as the crocodile opened its large maw and lunged for Samantha. She fell to her knees in defeat and wailed with her eyes closed, unable to watch the nightmarish scene play out in front of her. She heard Samantha scream and the mother in her would not allow her eyes to remain closed. When she opened them, she was surprised to see that Sam was somehow still alive and crawling toward her. It was then, that she noticed that the crocodile had chosen another victim instead. It was the woman that had helped her with the earrings. The woman that had told her the sad story about the loss of her daughter.

As the crocodile devoured the screaming woman, Claire ran for her daughter and dragged her away.

"She pushed me out of the way," Sam screamed while sobbing. "The lady pushed me out of the way!"

Claire eyed a nearby streetcar. She saw the horrified driver watching the scene unfold. He was wearing a purple button-up shirt with an even darker shade of purple colored tie. The man was staring at the chaotic scene with a blank stare.

"Can you walk?" she asked Samantha.

"I think so," Sam replied, struggling to get to her feet. She was clearly trying to hold back tears.

With Claire's help, she managed to stand and the two of them gingerly made their way to the streetcar.

"Where does this track go?" Claire asked the driver.

The man looked over at her and said nothing. He was apparently in shock.

"Where does this track go?" she asked again, this time yelling the question.

The man seemed to snap out of it. "Woldenberg Park," he mumbled. "To the ferry," he added, almost as an afterthought.

"Alright," Claire said, pushing past him and onto the streetcar. She realized they'd parked relatively close to the ferry. "Get us to the ferry terminal."

The man nodded, but said nothing. He continued to stare toward the enormous prehistoric-looking crocodile as it devoured another screaming victim.

"Now!" Claire screamed, and she slapped him.

The man looked over at her, wide-eyed. He seemed to be in disbelief that she'd hit him.

"I'm sorry," Claire explained. "But unless you want to end up like those people you're so enthralled to watch die, we need to move now!"

The man slowly nodded and took a deep breath. It seemed he'd finally gotten the point. Within seconds, the streetcar was moving away from the carnage.

CHAPTER 1

The drive from Jackson to New Orleans took only two hours and ten minutes. Jonathon Williams had broken every speed limit along the way, but it was imperative that he made it to New Orleans as quickly as possible. Once he arrived at the edge of the city, he pulled into a convenience store parking lot and made his way to a payphone.

He reached into his pocket to retrieve some change and Mr. Cold's business card. He dialed the number on the card and after one ring, there was an answer.

"That was a fast drive," Mr. Cold said.

"It must be nice to have one of those mobile phones," Jonathon quipped. "How did you know it would be me calling?"

"No time for questions," Mr. Cold replied. "Make your way toward the French Quarter. You will find me behind the Aquarium of the Americas. There is a makeshift command center there. When you arrive, tell any authorities you encounter your name and show them identification. They will allow you in. If you encounter any local law enforcement along the way that tries to delay you, have them call me directly. Do you understand?"

"Understood," Jonathon replied, and he immediately hung up the phone and returned to his Jeep.

As he motored further into town, he noticed a steady stream of vehicles heading the opposite direction. He couldn't remember seeing that many cars leaving New Orleans since the last hurricane had been in the vicinity. Jonathon navigated most of the trip down Interstate 10 until ultimately taking Canal Street toward the aquarium.

He pulled the Jeep onto a curb, grabbed his fedora, and frantically made his way toward a large gathering of soldiers and New Orleans policemen at the rear of the aquarium. As expected, Jonathon was stopped, but just as Mr. Cold had promised him, once he showed his identification, he was allowed through. As he jogged toward a large covered structure at the rear of the aquarium, he scanned his surroundings for any sign of Mr. Cold. He didn't see him, but there was another familiar face that he did see.

"About time you decided to show up," Glenn Hardcastle grumbled.

Hardcastle was dressed better and appeared much cleaner than he had been the last time Jonathon had seen him. He was wearing a white button-up shirt, khaki pants, and brown boots. The only thing he wore that Jonathon *did* remember was his hat. Hardcastle's hat was made of leather and the band was decorated with raptor claws.

"I'm really surprised you're not dead," Jonathon said, offering a handshake.

Hardcastle looked down at his hand and then back up to Jonathon.

"You think after everything that happened between us on that barge that I'm going to shake your hand?" he asked, narrowing his eyes. "You know, you've got a mean right hook that cost me a couple of molars."

Jonathon pulled back his hand and wasn't sure how to respond. He just stared at Hardcastle for a long awkward moment.

Finally, the dinosaur wrangler allowed a smirk and offered his hand.

"No hard feelings," he said with a wink as Jonathon shook his hand.

Jonathon looked around at the chaotic scene. "So where is Cold?" he asked.

Hardcastle turned and pointed toward a cluster of men in suits. "Over there," he said. "He and some of his C.I.A. buddies seem to be having a disagreement with the National Guard on how to proceed."

Jonathon was confused. "A disagreement? What is there to disagree about?"

"Well, it seems that the National Guard was to destroy the croc, but Cold is more interested in capturing it and keeping it alive," Hardcastle explained, annoyance in his tone.

Jonathon's mouth dropped open from astonishment. "You've got to be joking," he snapped. "Catching that thing is not an option—it must be destroyed before someone else gets killed." He looked around as another thought occurred to him. "Speaking of the *Sarcosuchus*...where is it?"

Hardcastle smiled. "I thought you'd never ask," he said. "When the animal came ashore, it immediately attacked the French Quarter Market just past the park over there," he explained, pointing in the direction of Woldenberg Park. The park, as well as the market, bordered the Mississippi River and it was Jonathon's understanding that the crocodile had entered the river from the Gulf of Mexico, swam a short distance into the city, and climbed out to search for food.

"It killed a few folks in the market before moving into the park where it finally settled down," Hardcastle continued. "It remained there until the National Guard arrived"

"And they didn't kill it when they had the chance?" Jonathon asked, still astonished.

Hardcastle nodded and stared back in the direction of Mr. Cold and the soldiers he was arguing with. "Oh, they tried," he replied. "But Cold told them to take it alive instead."

Jonathon shook his head in disbelief. "I'm not believing what I'm hearing. How utterly stupid can he be? Is anyone going to learn from the mistakes of Angus Wedgeworth and Eric Gill? These animals can't be controlled and we can't coexist with them. They must be left alone." He paused and seemed to ponder the situation a moment. "Is the animal still in the park?"

Hardcastle smiled and seemed to be amused by the question. "I'm getting to that," he said. "You see, Cold brought me along to put a couple of darts in the croc and knock it out like we did on the island. He had me take cover behind a park bench along the Riverwalk so that I could take a shot when the Guard drove the croc toward me."

"Something tells me this plan didn't work," Jonathon said.

Hardcastle shook his head. "Of course it didn't," he grumbled. "They tried to drive the thing at me by shooting the ground in front of it. All that did was scare the hell of it and drive it back into the river. It was a stupid plan."

Jonathon looked toward the river. Now that the sun was set, it was hard to see the water, much less anything that happened to be *in* the water. "So it's still in there?"

"We think so," Hardcastle replied, peering toward the water himself. "It's probably on its way back into the gulf by now."

"Good, you made it," Mr. Cold said suddenly.

Hardcastle and Jonathon had not even noticed that he was approaching.

"Yeah, I made it," Jonathon replied, holding out his hand.

As Mr. Cold shook it, he said, "I trust that Glenn has gotten you up to speed with everything that is going on?"

"Yeah, you could say that," Jonathon replied with a bit of a scowl. "He tells me that you're interested in catching the animal and keeping it alive?"

Mr. Cold nodded. "Yes, that's right," he answered, and there was obvious confusion on his face. "I thought you'd agree with that sentiment," he added. "But your tone is telling me otherwise."

"Look, I'm all for the preservation of these animals," Jonathon explained. "But only on the island. When these animals get on our soil— or any civilized soil—then the safety of human beings should take precedence."

Mr. Cold bit his lip and lowered his head. He placed his hands in his jacket pockets and strolled a few steps away from Jonathon, gazing out toward the river. "You're right," he said. "Lives were lost today and don't for one second think that I take that sort of thing lightly." He suddenly spun back in the direction of Jonathon and Glenn. "For the record, not one life has been lost since we arrived on the scene. If we get into a situation where I feel the animal is endangering lives again, trust me, it will be destroyed."

Jonathon took a step toward him. "Any efforts you make to try and catch this animal will be endangering lives," he replied, poking a finger into Mr. Cold's chest.

Mr. Cold looked down at his chest and smoothed out the fabric on his shirt where Jonathon had just poked him. "The opportunities that these animals present to this country are tremendous," he said. "There is no telling what we can learn from them. If we could figure out how they've managed to survive extinction, it may unlock secrets that will ensure the ultimate survival of our own race."

Jonathon looked away as he thought of the fountain of youth. It seemed that Mr. Cold was still unaware of its existence and the role that it played in keeping the dinosaurs alive. "Look, I see your point," he said finally. "And trust me, I get some of the reasons why the United States is interested in studying the animals. Keep in mind that I showed you where that island is so that you can do all the things you're preaching to me about. Why do you have to have this particular animal?"

"They want to weaponize it," Hardcastle said, unexpectedly.

Jonathon snapped his head around to look at him. "Did someone tell you that?" he asked.

Hardcastle shook his head and looked past him to Mr. Cold. "No one told me that," he replied. "It's just a hunch. It's the only feasible reason I can come up with. That animal should be killed, period."

Jonathon glanced over at Mr. Cold. "Look me in the eyes and tell me that's not what's going on here."

Mr. Cold took a deep breath through his nose and looked Jonathon straight in the eyes. "The truth is, I'm not at liberty to say exactly why we want this animal alive. You both were brought here for very specific reasons," he snapped. "Glenn, you're here to tranquilize the animal as you've clearly got experience with that. And Jonathon, you're here due to your expertise and experience dealing with these animals as well."

"What neither of you *are* here for is some sort of authoritative role. That's why *I* am here," he growled, pointing at his own chest. "Now both of you please do what is asked of you, and nothing more. If I want to be lectured on how dangerous the animal is and what all can go wrong, trust me, I will come straight to the two of you."

Jonathon smiled and shook his head in clear annoyance. "My God, you people never learn," he whispered. "So since you're calling all the shots, what is the next step?"

Mr. Cold paced in front of them for a moment. "Well, truthfully, we've lost the animal for the time being," he said, almost sheepishly. "We've got eyes all over the river and searching for any sign of it. When we find it, the plan remains the same. We will hit it with a tranquilizer and once it's captured, we will ultimately return it to the island where it belongs."

"And if you *don't* find it?" Jonathon asked with a raised eyebrow.

Mr. Cold clenched his teeth and slightly cocked his head to the side. "Then I suppose you can continue to lecture me on why I should've had it killed immediately."

Jonathon was about to argue the point further when something caught his eye in the river. It got Hardcastle's attention at almost the same moment.

"Cold, I thought you told me no one was to be permitted in the river?" Hardcastle asked.

"That's right," he replied, and then he caught sight of what they were looking at.

"Then why the hell is there a ferry crossing it?" Jonathon asked.

CHAPTER 2

"Do you think they are in real danger?" Mr. Cold asked as he squinted his eyes trying to get a clear view of the ferry.

Jonathon shrugged. "I suppose it depends on where the *Sarcosuchus* is," he replied. "If it is in the vicinity, then I'd say absolutely there is a real danger."

"I know that like the crocodiles of today, they are definitely attracted to splashing and unusual movements in the water," Hardcastle chimed in. "When we were trying to catch one of these things, they always came when something got in the water making a racket."

Jonathon looked behind him to where the soldiers were standing. "I think it would be best to get these guys ready just in case," he said. "There is probably no sense in trying to call the ferry back since it's already halfway across."

Mr. Cold shoved his hands in his pockets and rocked on his heels as he watched the ferry intensely. He was growing increasingly frustrated and seemed conflicted on what his next move would be. It wasn't helping when he came to the realization that Jonathon and Glenn Hardcastle seemed to have different ideas on how to handle the *Sarcosuchus*.

"What is that?" Hardcastle said, taking a few steps closer to the river.

"What do you see?" Jonathon asked, suddenly alert and very concerned. He squinted and quickly saw what had gotten Hardcastle's attention.

Directly behind the ferry, the waters began to swirl and bubble furiously. Clearly, something was chasing after it just below the surface.

***

Claire Hutton and her daughter Samantha had taken a streetcar to the ferry terminal in hopes of finding their car and making a quick escape before things got any worse. Much to her dismay, Claire quickly discovered that the lot where she'd left the car was now surrounded by the National Guard and it appeared that Canal Street had been closed off too. She and other citizens that were unable to get to their vehicles were advised to remain in the parking lot near the ferry terminal until it was safe to leave. Claire looked back in the direction of the French Quarter Market and wondered where the enormous crocodile was now. The nightmarish images of the unfortunate patrons being eaten alive were etched in her mind and made it impossible for her to feel completely safe until she and Samantha were back at home.

"How is your ankle?" she asked Sam.

Samantha winced and did her best to put on a brave face. "I'm okay, Mom," she said. "I'm just ready to go home."

Claire held her daughter close and decided that the best thing for them to do was to hunker down and wait on the National Guard to handle the situation. Sam's ankle was swelling, but Claire was pretty sure it was not broken. She wondered if Gavin was aware of what was going on and knew that if he did, he would be extremely worried about them. Claire noticed a payphone at the edge of the parking lot but unfortunately there was a line of people waiting to use it. Just as her pulse was beginning to slow down back to a normal rate, gunfire began to ring out from the direction of Woldenberg Park.

"What is going on?" Samantha asked, her voice cracking with fear.

"I'm not sure," Claire replied, unable to hide the worry in her tone. "Maybe they're killing it."

Suddenly, several people came running from the direction of Woldenberg Park. They were screaming and as they ran near Claire, she pleaded for them to tell her what was going on.

"The soldiers are shooting at that thing!" a woman with tears in her eyes screamed. "But they weren't even trying to kill it—it's like they were forcing it to come in our direction!"

"What? Why would they do that?" Claire asked, confused. The woman never responded; she was pulled away by who Claire thought may have been her husband.

Claire looked around to see what the soldiers nearby were doing and suddenly realized they were headed toward the gunfire.

"Something is wrong," Claire told Samantha. "Get on your feet, we can't stay here."

As she pulled Samantha off the ground, she then noticed that a crowd of people were making their way onto the ferry. She figured that must have meant the killer crocodile was indeed heading straight for them and their only real escape was to cross the river.

"We've got to get to the ferry, Sam," she said as she threw her daughter's arm over her neck. "Come on, I'll help you...we've got to hurry."

With Claire's help, she and Samantha made it to the ferry just as the captain was ready to leave. The lower deck was usually filled with cars, but now there were only people. Everyone was seated near the center and most of them were visibly scared.

"Mom, what was going on?" Sam asked once they'd found a spot to sit.

"Someone said the soldiers were shooting at the crocodile and it was headed for where we were," Claire explained. "I guess the captain of the ferry decided he had to get everyone away from the danger."

"Thank goodness for that," Sam said, sounding relieved and pleased that they'd just escaped another close call. Then she looked up at her mom and tears began to form in her eyes.

"What's wrong, Sam?" Claire asked, clearly worried.

"This is my fault," Sam said, trying to choke back tears. "If I hadn't wanted to come here, we'd be at home safe right now."

Claire kissed her daughter's forehead and held her tightly. "This is in no way your fault," she said reassuringly. "I wanted to come just as much as you did. Everything is going to be fine so just relax…okay?"

Samantha nodded but said nothing; she just stared out into the black water of the Mississippi. Claire wanted to console her further, but decided it was best to just be quiet. They'd be on the other side of the river in a matter of minutes. Once over there, she'd find a phone and call Gavin. He'd come get them away from here and his job afforded him people in high places that could assist him if need be. Suddenly, once again, there was more screaming.

Claire stood up abruptly to see what was the matter. To her horror, she saw the water behind the ferry swirling violently. The people around her suddenly began to panic and frantically scramble toward the stairs that led to the upper deck.

"Okay, come on," Claire said, pulling Samantha to her feet yet again.

Samantha moaned and was clearly in pain, but she was too scared to complain. Unfortunately, her injury slowed them down enough that they found themselves at the end of the line of people trying to get up the stairs. Claire looked over her shoulder and what she saw terrified her. The giant crocodile's massive head was out of the water and it was touching the rear gate of the ferry with its snout.

"Oh my God," she said. "I'm scared it's going to try and climb on board."

***

"We've got to do something," Jonathon muttered, his voice a mixture of panic and determination. He could now clearly see the

Sarcosuchus's head rising out of the water behind the ferry. It was going to board…there was no doubt about it.

"Darn right we do," Hardcastle said, throwing his large rifle over his shoulder.

Mr. Cold threw up his hands up as if he were trying to persuade the men to remain calm. "I'll get a team of soldiers headed over there," he said. "It hasn't boarded yet. Glenn, there is a tiny fishing boat docked near the edge of the park," he added, pointing. "You and Jonathon take that boat and get into position where you can safely fire the tranquilizer."

"You've got to be kidding," Jonathon groaned. "You *still* think you can take that animal alive?"

Mr. Cold glared at him. He seemed to be agitated. "Mr. Williams, I'm not going to debate this with you any further. If you want to help those people, then do as I say. Take Glenn out there and get him into position to stop that animal."

He turned away without another word and began to jog back toward the soldiers waiting near the rear of the aquarium. Jonathon then looked over at Hardcastle, unable to hide his disgust.

"He's nuts," he said. "Why don't these people ever learn?"

Hardcastle shrugged and began sprinting toward the boat. Jonathon followed and once they arrived, he was a little disheartened with what he saw.

"This is suicide," he said, staring wide-eyed at the tiny boat. "If you miss and that thing comes after us, it's over."

Hardcastle climbed in the small aluminum boat and began yanking on the outboard motor. "Just get me close," he said between pulls. "I won't miss."

"Alright," Jonathon said, climbing aboard. "But for my own peace of mind, do we have any lethal weapons at our disposal?"

As the boat roared to life, Hardcastle looked down at his tranquilizer rifle and then back to Jonathon. "Well, we have that," he said, pointing at the large hunting knife on Jonathon's belt.

Jonathon looked down at the knife and then back to Hardcastle. Jonathon was unable to see his eyes thanks to the shadow the brim of his hat was creating. But there was no mistaking the smirk Hardcastle was giving him.

"Let's go," he said, crouching down at the bow.

Jonathon maneuvered the little boat toward the center of the river and released the throttle once they were approximately fifty yards away.

"It's so dark," he said. "I don't know how you plan to hit that thing in the right spot."

Hardcastle was aiming the rifle at the *Sarcosuchus* through the high-powered scope. "Well, it's a lot easier when it's quiet and I can concentrate," he quipped.

Jonathon bit his tongue and looked back toward the aquarium to see if the soldiers were moving yet. To his utter surprise, they had remained in the same spot. He squinted hard and scanned the area for Mr. Cold. He finally found him and could clearly see that he and whoever was in command over the soldiers were having another heated disagreement.

"I don't believe this," he said with exasperation.

"What?" Hardcastle asked, still concentrating on the dinosaur.

"They're on the shore arguing," he replied, still staring with disbelief.

Hardcastle lowered the rifle and peered over to see for himself. He sighed. "Looks like one too many chiefs," he grumbled. "I'm assuming the National Guard probably shares your point of view. Everyone seems to want this animal dead except Cold."

"I don't get it," Jonathon said. "Why is he so hell-bent on keeping it alive?"

"I told you," Hardcastle replied. "They want to weaponize these things."

Jonathon was about to reply when he suddenly heard screaming from the ferry. He and Hardcastle looked over just in time to see the *Sarcosuchus* pull the front half of its body onto the lower deck of the ferry. The entire rear of the vessel sank lower into the water due to the added weight.

"We've got no time to wait on them," Jonathon said. "Can you take the shot?"

Hardcastle again raised the rifle and used the scope to zoom in on the enormous animal as it pulled itself further onto the ferry. The animal began thrashing wildly as it appeared to be struggling to get the rest of its body on board. Hardcastle hoped that it wouldn't, and not just because of the unfortunate souls that would probably become a quick meal. He also feared that if the animal got any more of its body on board, it would probably be enough to cause the vessel to sink. As he scanned the lower deck with the scope, he soon noticed a woman and a teenage girl that were getting much too close to the prehistoric crocodile's snapping jaws. It appeared that the young girl was injured, and as the weight of the *Sarcosuchus* shifted the rear of the vessel lower, the girl seemed to have lost her footing and slid toward the animal's snout. He pulled the gun down.

"We've got to get on board," he said, looking back at Jonathon.

"What? Why?" Jonathon asked. "Why can't you just shoot it?"

Hardcastle shook his head and laid the gun down. "Those partitions on the lower deck are blocking my shot for one thing," he explained. "Also, there is a young girl that is mere feet away from that thing's jaws. Even if I got a dart into it, the effects are not immediate. We've got to get over there now or that girl will die."

Jonathon clenched his jaw and immediately revved the tiny boat's engine. He had no idea what they were going to do once they got there, but if they didn't act fast, more people were definitely going to die. The small vessel was moving so rapidly that both Jonathon and Hardcastle had to place a hand on top of their heads to keep their hats from blowing off. The air was somewhat chilly and Jonathon shivered, although he couldn't tell if it was from fear or the cool air. As they drew nearer, he had a much clearer picture of what was going on. The young girl was screaming as she continued to slowly slide down the slope of the weighted-down ferry. Her mother was screaming in a panic and clearly wanted to go after her daughter. In fact, the only thing stopping her seemed to be a couple of male passengers that were holding her back against her will.

Jonathon steered the tiny boat alongside the ferry and both men immediately jumped onto the deck. "Get her up the steps!" Jonathon yelled to the men that were holding back the girl's mother.

"NO!" she screamed. "I will not go without my daughter!"

The woman thrashed violently and clawed at the men so severely she drew blood. Yet somehow, they managed to drag her up the stairs as her daughter screamed after her.

Glenn Hardcastle quickly scrambled down toward the girl, but as soon as he did so, his feet slipped out from under him on the wet deck. As he slid fast toward the open maw of the *Sarcosuchus*, he managed to reach over and grab one of the partitions near the edge of the deck. The rear of the ferry seemed to slope even further as the large animal managed to get a little bit more of its body on board. Jonathon grabbed the stair railing to keep from sliding. The young girl slid dangerously closer to her death.

"Reach for my foot!" Hardcastle shouted at her. "Grab my foot!"

The girl looked up the slope at him, her eyes filled with terror. When Hardcastle first looked into her eyes, he thought she was surely going to die. Her eyes seemed to suggest that she'd given up and accepted her fate.

"Come on, girl!" he yelled. "Dig your nails into the deck and claw your way up here!"

The girl looked back at the snapping jaws of the *Sarcosuchus*, only mere feet from her now. She then did as Hardcastle suggested and dug her nails and the toes of her shoes into the deck in a desperate attempt to climb up the slippery incline.

"That's it," Hardcastle said excitedly. "Keep it up, you're doing it!"

Jonathon watched the scene unfold and felt a terrible sense of dread. In his mind's eye, he could see the injured girl *almost* make it to Glenn only to lose her grip at the last moment and tumble into the jaws of the *Sarcosuchus*. He could then picture Hardcastle going after her, only to be eaten alive as well. And all of this would occur while he stayed clutching tightly to the railing of the steps.

"This isn't going to work," he said aloud. He'd intended to only think it, but somehow he spoke the words before he knew what was happening.

Hardcastle glared up at him with fury. "Shut your damn mouth!" he growled. "She's doing it!"

Jonathon looked past Hardcastle and noticed the girl had probably moved a grand total of two feet since she'd begun her ascent. One slip and it would all be over. Jonathon had studied alligators and crocodiles for a couple of years early in his career. After all, they were probably the closest living animals to dinosaurs that existed today. He'd spent a lot of time in the bayou of Louisiana and had once gone on an alligator hunting trip. During the months of August and September, alligator harvesting is permitted in the state to control the population. Desperate for a chance to see the animals up close and in the wild, Jonathon joined an alligator hunter and gotten more than he'd bargained for. The old man had been hunting alligators for years and knew all the tricks of the trade. On that particular day, he and the old man managed to bag three alligators. The old hunter had taught him about a "kill spot" on the back of the alligator's skull. Supposedly, if a bullet or knife was projected into the quarter-sized kill spot, it would provide a direct route into the animal's tiny brain, disabling it instantly.

As Jonathon watched the young girl struggle to make her way up the deck, he remembered Hardcastle jokingly suggesting that his knife was their only means of killing the animal once and for all. As he thought back to the old hunter that showed him exactly where the sweet spot was on the back of the alligator skull, he realized there was really only one shot at getting everyone off the ferry alive. And it was all up to him.

Jonathon looked above him and scanned the environment for something to grab onto. The only thing he could see was the conduit for the fluorescent lighting and, though he wasn't confident it would hold him, he decided it was his only option. Once he climbed high enough up the stairs to leap for it, he did so successfully and immediately felt it bend under his weight. Although the conduit bent with each grasp forward he made, it held together and soon after he'd shimmied into position above the thrashing the crocodile.

As he's suspected, the girl had made no more progress since he'd made his decision to try and kill the dinosaur. He also noticed that Hardcastle had spotted him and was staring up at him with astonishment. He said nothing, and Jonathon couldn't tell if he remained silent to keep from breaking the girl's concentration or if he was truly shocked speechless at the feat.

Jonathon held onto the conduit with one hand and retrieved his knife with the other. He placed it in his teeth and bit down hard. He knew that if he dropped the knife, the consequences would be deadly. For a brief moment, he thought back to the last time he'd used the knife to kill a dinosaur. It was the first time he'd ever arrived on the island. A *Dromaeosaurus* attacked him and he'd been forced to stab the dinosaur in the skull.

You can do this, he thought.

Once he was satisfied that he was in the best possible position, Jonathon dropped from the ceiling and landed onto the back of the *Sarcosuchus*. The animal immediately noticed his presence and instinctively tried to turn its head back toward him. Unable to reach him, the animal then began thrashing wildly and, much to Jonathon's dismay, it began to retreat back into the water.

"Oh, no you don't," Jonathon growled through his teeth still clenched on the knife blade. He dug his fingernails into the slippery back of the animal but every time he tried to free one hand to grab the knife, he was unable to do so for risk of falling off. The animal continued to shimmy backwards and was beginning to make rapid progress back into the water. Jonathon decided if he was going to kill the prehistoric crocodile, it was now or never. He knew if there was any chance for success, he'd have to be quick.

He eyed the "kill spot" on the back of the animal's skull and with one quick motion, he released the animal with both hands, grabbed the knife, and plunged it deep into the dinosaur's flesh. For the first time, Jonathon heard the animal let out a roar that he didn't think the animal was capable of. It flailed backward through the air, throwing him off of it.

Jonathon estimated he'd flown about thirty feet through the air and had landed in the river. He was now treading water, and though the water was bitterly cold, his adrenaline was running too high to notice. Immediately, he realized his knife was still plunged into the back of the animal's skull, but to his horror, the creature was not dead. His mind quickly contemplated what his options were as the *Sarcosuchus* began to swim rapidly in his direction. Jonathon quickly decided the only option he had left was to flee.

Although in the back of his mind he knew it was useless, he began to swim with all the speed his adrenaline-fueled body could muster. He estimated that the river bank was another 150 feet away. He wasn't going to make it…there was just no way. Though his mind had given up, his body refused and he kept swimming. He began to feel some turbulence in the water behind him and he knew at any second he'd be swallowed whole—or bitten in half at the very least.

Suddenly, as it seemed all hope was lost, Jonathon heard an eruption of gunfire behind him. There was frantic splashing behind him as well and he suddenly realized that the animal was being shot. Jonathon didn't stop swimming until he heard the gunfire and the splashing cease…only then did he dare to look back. When he did, he was pleased to see that the National Guard had finally made their approach by boat and quickly disposed of the *Sarcosuchus*. The large animal had become shiny with blood and had rolled over onto its back…but somehow it was still floating.

Jonathon breathed a deep sigh of relief as he slowly turned and continued his swim toward the bank. *Cold is going to be pissed*, he thought.

***

"How is the girl?" Jonathon asked, his teeth chattering.

He was seated over the rear bumper of an ambulance, his clothes still dripping wet. An EMT draped a heavy gray blanket over and around his shoulders and, though it helped, he was still unable to keep his teeth from chattering.

"The girl is fine," Mr. Cold said, his gaze focused on the lifeless body of the prehistoric crocodile that had just been pulled from the river. "Her father is apparently some big shot lawyer here in New Orleans," he added, finally turning to look at Jonathon. "He'll probably sue us for every penny he can get."

Jonathon's eyes narrowed. "Well, I can't say that I would blame them," he replied, annoyed. "You had multiple opportunities to stop that thing sooner and didn't. It's an absolute miracle that no one else got killed."

Mr. Cold put his hands in coat pockets and bit his lower lip. "You still fail to grasp the importance of what we're trying to do," he said defiantly. "There is a wealth of information that we can get from studying these animals…information that can be used to—"

"I know, I know," Jonathon interrupted, holding up a dismissive hand. "They could hold the key to ensuring the future survival of the human race. I heard you the first time," he groaned.

"And yet you still question our motives?" Mr. Cold asked.

Jonathon shrugged. "I said I heard you…I never said I *believe* you."

Mr. Cold took a deep breath through his nose, anger clearly welling up in him. He stared at Jonathon for a few seconds before finally shaking his head and casually strolling away.

"Are you trying to make him snap your neck?" Hardcastle asked, stepping out of the shadows.

Jonathon grinned and shook his head. "Nah, I'm just letting him know I'm not buying the load of B.S. he's trying to sell me," he answered.

Glenn Hardcastle leaned against the rear corner of the ambulance and crossed his arms. "Well, just keep in mind that Cold is in the C.I.A.," he said. "I'm pretty sure if he gets tired of you, he can have you killed."

Jonathon laughed, although part of him thought Hardcastle was very serious.

"What you did back there took guts," Hardcastle continued. "I didn't know you had that in you."

Jonathon pulled the blanket tighter around him. "There's a lot you don't know about me," he said, turning his attention to the dead *Sarcosuchus*. "What do you think they're going to do with it?"

Hardcastle shrugged, removed his hat, and ran his fingers through his sandy blond hair. "Probably send it to a lab and cut it into a million pieces."

"That's what I was afraid of," Jonathon replied. "I'm starting to regret showing them where the island is. There's no telling what they've got planned for those animals."

Hardcastle shook his head. "You don't regret it," he countered. "Your wife may not be here if you hadn't shown him."

Jonathon sighed and knew Hardcastle was at least partially right. He had agreed to show Mr. Cold where the island was in exchange for a cure for his wife Lucy's cancer. What Hardcastle and Mr. Cold didn't know was that Jonathon had brought back a small vial of water he'd taken from the island. The vial of water had been taken from the fountain of youth and, to his knowledge, neither of the men knew of its existence either. Had they known, they would've been aware of how the dinosaurs had managed to escape extinction. If Cold hadn't made the deal to give

Lucy the cure for her cancer, Jonathon was fully prepared to cure her with the vial of water—even if it meant immortality for her.

"You're right," he said finally. "I don't regret doing what I had to do to keep Lucy alive."

"He's not done with you," Hardcastle said. "You know that, right?"

Jonathon's eyes narrowed as he looked up at Hardcastle. "Well, I'm done with him," he said flatly.

CHAPTER 3

September 13th, 1994

"It's been two years since the government got involved. I'm just asking you to consider it, that's all," Silas suggested, a hint of desperation in his voice.

Jonathon thought he sounded as if he were practically begging. He sighed and said, "Look, old friend, I'm not saying no...I'm just saying not right now."

Silas leaned back in his cushy office chair, a look of dejection on his face. "That's easy for you to say. You're still a young man. I'm not only aging, I'm broken," he grumbled. The older man was dressed in his trademark cargo shorts along with a brown button-up shirt. For the first time since Jonathon had known him, he wasn't wearing a hat. His hair was now entirely gray and thinning.

Jonathon smiled and glanced over at the cane leaning against the wood-paneled wall. Silas had narrowly survived the injuries he'd sustained from the gunshot he received during their last trip to the island. Unfortunately, the bullet that Glenn Hardcastle had fired into his leg had caused permanent nerve damage and shattered part of his femur. Doctors had told him he'd never be able to walk without the assistance of a cane again.

"You're not broken," Jonathon argued. "You're the strongest guy I've ever met. I mean that."

Silas took a deep breath and allowed himself to smile slightly. "Well, I appreciate that, pal."

"Sooner or later, the public is going to find out about the island," Jonathon said. "And when that happens, I say we go all in on the book you're suggesting. But until that happens, if we tell the world our story, it's going to bring a lot of unintended consequences."

"Like what?" Silas asked, clearly not buying it.

"First off, how do you think Cold and his cronies are going to respond to it?" Jonathon asked. "They've made it clear that they want us to stay tight-lipped about it while they do whatever the hell it is that they're doing over there. If we talk, they're going to come after us, and I don't trust that guy."

Silas arched an eyebrow. "Are you suggesting that you think he'd have us killed?"

Jonathon shrugged. "I'm saying I'm not sure what he would do. And to me, it's just not worth the risk. He's already pissed at me for refusing to take part in any of the experiments they're performing on the island."

Silas eyed him suspiciously. "And you don't know what they're doing?"

"Of course I don't," he replied. "When the incident was going on in New Orleans with the *Sarcosuchus*, I can remember Glenn Hardcastle telling me rather adamantly that he thought Cold's interest in the dinosaurs had something to do with weaponizing them."

Silas nodded. "I could see that," he said. "Do you think that's what is going on?"

Jonathon sighed and shrugged his shoulders. "I certainly hope not," he replied. "Even if that is what's going on, I don't see how it could work. Most of the carnivores are nothing more than killing machines...a lot like sharks really. Have you ever seen them train a shark at Sea World?"

Silas shook his head and then stared off toward a window that provided a nice view of the large fountain in front of his home. He seemed to be thinking hard about what Jonathon had just said.

"Silas...what is it?" Jonathon asked, noticing his strange change in demeanor.

Silas looked back over to him and Jonathon could see that something was troubling him. "Did you ever ask your dad what we went through to get that vial of water from the fountain?" he asked.

Jonathon furrowed his brow as he considered the question. "I don't think I've ever thought a lot about it," he said. "We've never discussed it."

"Well, there was so much going on, I can see why it probably never crossed your mind," Silas said. "Do you remember the time that we went into the cave to stop Angus Wedgeworth?"

Jonathon nodded. "How could I ever forget that crazy lunatic?" he said. "Yes, I remember there being a few *Troodons* in there..." his words trailed off as he thought back. He could remember the *Troodons* surrounding them and Osvaldo, the man that had been cursed with immortality, sacrificed himself so that they could escape. Suddenly, he found himself wondering how his father and Silas managed to get the vial of water all alone.

"How on earth were you two able to get the water out of the fountain and get out of there alive?" Jonathon asked.

Silas smiled. "Well, I've been waiting two years for you to ask me that question," he replied. "When we arrived at the cave, I warned Henry about the *Troodons*. I told him that you'd said they were some of the most intelligent dinosaurs on the island and that they'd been aggressive the last time we'd encountered them."

"And yet you went in anyway?" Jonathon asked.

Silas seemed offended by the question. "If it was the only option we had to save Lucy's life, then there was nothing to think about," he replied, leaning across his desk.

"So what happened?" Jonathon asked, now intrigued.

Silas's eyes twinkled as a wide smile spread across his face. He slowly leaned back into his chair again and took a deep breath before speaking. "Well, we quietly slipped into the cave and everything seemed just as it had been the last time you and I were in there," he explained. "There was a beam of sunlight that shone through an opening in the cave ceiling and it seemed to come down directly onto the pool of water in the center of the chamber."

"And what about the *Troodons*?" Jonathon asked anxiously.

"At first, they were nowhere to be found," Silas replied. "I tossed Henry the vial and told him to fill it up quickly while I kept my eyes on our surroundings. The moment your father scooped out some water, I noticed movement in the shadows."

Jonathon leaned forward in his chair. He couldn't believe his father had never told him any of this.

"As you can imagine, it was a *Troodon*," Silas continued. "Immediately, I thought back to what those things did to Osvaldo. It stalked out of the darkness and stepped into one of the shafts of light that was piercing through the cave ceiling. Just as before, the top of its head was covered in feathers, but this one was bigger...much bigger. It stopped and stared at us for a long minute as if it were trying to figure out what we were doing."

"It didn't attack?" Jonathon asked.

"No, and it was just one," Silas replied. "I pointed my rifle at it and it growled at us and took a step back. I told Henry to take the water and start heading back out of the cave. As he started walking toward the exit, I began walking backwards behind him, but I kept the rifle pointed at the dinosaur. To my surprise, the darn thing followed me."

Jonathon crossed his arms and continued to give his undivided attention. "So once you got outside, did it continue to follow you?"

Silas shook his head. "Once we got outside, there were more of them waiting for us," he said. "They were lined up in a semi-circle around the opening of the cave. There were probably ten of them and they just stood there watching us. I looked back to the big one that had followed. It just casually strutted out in front of us and began making the most unsettling guttural sounds at the other *Troodons*."

"Guttural sounds…what do you mean?" Jonathon asked.

Silas paused a moment and stroked his beard as he pondered the question. He shifted in the office chair and it squeaked in protest. "I don't know how else to describe it," he said. "Jonathon, if I didn't know better I'd say it was somehow speaking to them."

Jonathon scrunched up his face from bewilderment. "What do you mean it was *speaking* to them?" he asked. "You mean it was communicating with them. I mean, most animals have their own ways of communication."

Silas shook his head. "No, it wasn't like that," he said adamantly. "This thing sounded as if it were speaking to them somehow…with its own sort of language. It emitted strange sounds that seemed to come from deep inside its chest and the inflection and cadence with those sounds made it seem like the dinosaur was talking to the other ones."

"That's ridiculous," Jonathon said as he shook his head. "It couldn't have been speaking…animals don't speak."

Silas smirked and seemed to be slightly annoyed. "I was there and I know what I saw," he replied. "And there is a lot of evidence that seems to suggest that dolphins may have their own language, so it's not so far out of the realm of possibility as you seem to think. You yourself went on and on about how intelligent those things were."

"Well, they were very intelligent as far as dinosaurs go," Jonathon replied defensively. "But I wouldn't go so far as to say that their intelligence level is like that of dolphins."

Silas rolled his eyes and again shook his head. "Well, after the *Troodon* that followed us spoke—or barked—whatever you want to call it…the others backed off and let us through. It seemed as if they'd been ordered to let us go. There was something very unsettling about it."

Jonathon considered what he'd just heard for a moment before standing and pacing the room a few times. "I'm not sure what to make of that," he said finally.

"Well, I only bring it up because, as both you and I have witnessed before, those animals are dangerous," Silas said. "And they are highly intelligent."

Jonathon stopped pacing as he suddenly caught on to what Silas was suggesting. He looked over at him and asked, "You believe they are intelligent enough to train?"

Silas nodded. "You can debate how intelligent they are with me all you want," he replied. "But, I know what I saw, and I saw those animals communicating in a way that I've never witnessed before. And I don't have to tell you how many animals I've watched over the years. *If* Cold were looking to use any of the animals on the island in the manner that you're suggesting, the *Troodons* would be his best option."

***

"So what did he want?" Lucy asked as she piloted their family sedan away from the airport and back toward their home.

"He wants to write a book about the island, and everything that we've experienced on it," Jonathon replied.

Lucy glanced up at the rearview mirror and peered at their one-year-old daughter, Lily, as she cooed and played with a tiny stuffed bear within the confines of her car seat.

"Oh my," she said, somewhat surprised. "He wants to go public about the island?"

Jonathon leaned over and rested his forehead on the passenger side window. He watched the pine trees zip by as they motored down the interstate and into Bienville Forest.

"I think he's getting frustrated," Jonathon replied. "And I get it...truly I do. Mr. Cold and whatever government operation he is working with is doing God knows what on that island and the people in this country don't know a thing about it. Something tells me it's all going to come back and haunt me one day."

Lucy pursed her lips as she contemplated a response. Finally, she said, "Well, maybe Silas is right...maybe you should go forward with your story."

Jonathon narrowed his eyes and immediately shook his head. "We've been through this, Lucy," he said. "First of all, I'm not sure how Cold will respond. I'm not putting my family at risk. Secondly, do you really think the public is ready to listen to a couple of guys tell them that there is an island in the middle of the Bermuda Triangle inhabited by dinosaurs?"

Lucy smiled. "Well, you're not just *any* guys," she countered. "You're a respected paleontologist and Silas Treadwell is basically a worldwide celebrity thanks to his old show *Wild World*. You two have credibility. And besides, I've been to the island...I can contribute—oh, and then there's Annie."

The mention of Annie's name made him frown and he returned his gaze to the window. Annie Wedgeworth had been through two traumatic experiences on the island. The second one ended with her shooting her boyfriend and ultimately killing him to save Jonathon.

"You know Annie is not in a frame of mind to help with a book right now," he said sadly. "She's bounced around to so many different psychologists and psychiatrists I don't know if the poor woman will ever be right again."

Lucy took a deep breath. "Don't give up on her," she said. "She'll get through this…it's just going to take some time."

Unfortunately, Jonathon did not share Lucy's positivity, but he kept the thoughts to himself. "It doesn't matter," he grumbled. "It doesn't change the fact that I'm not ready to go public with this." He paused and glanced over his shoulder to watch Lily. "Like I said, I'm not endangering our family."

Lucy wanted to argue the issue further, but thought better of it. Truthfully, she could see both sides of the argument. She'd only met Mr. Cold once, and though he was cordial and seemed friendly, there was something very mysterious about him. Jonathon, on the other hand, had met with the man on numerous occasions and probably had a better grasp on who he actually was than she did. If he was worried about him coming after him for going public about the island, then who was she to tell him different.

Suddenly, the local newscast began to play on the radio and she turned it up slightly. The reporter began speaking about a massive storm building in the Atlantic Ocean. Hurricane Simon was approaching category five and both Lucy and Jonathon began thinking about a certain misty island that just happened to be right in the hurricane's path.

CHAPTER 4

The Island In The Mist

Charlotte Nelson, or Charlie as her friends called her, paced back and forth across the shiny laboratory floor. The walls of the room were covered with various metal cabinets and though the space in the middle was quite vast, something about the room made her feel claustrophobic. When she thought about it, she finally decided it must've had something to do with the lack of windows.

Well, one could say the same for just about this entire building, she thought.

"Dr. Nelson, are you alright?" a man's voice called out from the open doorway.

Charlie looked over and saw Dr. Matthew Walker leaning against the open door frame. He was wearing his lab coat and had his arms crossed as he stared at her. Charlie thought he was an attractive man with a head of thick brown hair, and a square jaw that reminded her of the Hollywood actors in the old black and white films she loved. Matthew was a doctor of veterinary medicine and he also had a degree in zoology with concentrations in neurobiology and animal behavior. In short, he was the man Mr. Cold had charged with putting together a program to train dinosaurs. Charlie, being the paleontologist who was already under contract with the government thanks to Cold, was hired on as his assistant.

"Hi, Matt," she said, strolling over to him. "I'm fine, just thinking about our impending doom."

Matt chuckled. "We're going to be fine," he said reassuringly. "When they built this facility, they knew that it would have to withstand the occasional hurricane."

Charlie stared into his eyes and wanted to believe him.

"But what if it doesn't?" she asked. "We're in a facility surrounded by dinosaurs and if the power goes out—"

"It won't," Matt said, and he reached over and grabbed her forearm. "But…if it did, there are backup generators. Everything will be fine, trust me."

Charlie chewed her lip and her eyes drifted away from his toward the floor.

"Look," Matt said. "You don't have to stay. Mr. Cold asked for volunteers, and you volunteered."

Charlie sighed. "I know," she said apologetically. "With my history at this place, I almost feel like I've got some responsibility here…to stay."

Matt smiled at her. His teeth were a brilliant white and perfect. "I don't want you to worry," he said, squeezing her forearm slightly. "You should leave until this blows over."

Charlie shook her head and looked back up at him. "No, I'm here to do a job and I'm going to do it. I don't know what I'm so scared of…this place is huge. As long as we've got power, I'm sure everything will be fine."

"Everything *will* be fine," Matt assured her again. "It's just you, me, George, and Glenn for the next three days, playing poker and watching *Andy Griffith Show* reruns until all of this is over."

Charlie smiled. "I'm so sick of that show," she groaned.

The recreation room in the facility was equipped with pinball machines, a ping pong table, pool table, a big screen television, and VHS player. The entire *Andy Griffith Show* series was available on VHS tapes and George Powell had made a habit of popping one in every evening at dinner time. It seemed that no matter what activities were going on in the rec room, the *Andy Griffith Show* had to always be on the television. It had become a running joke among the residents.

"I'm sure if we ask nicely, George will allow us to watch something different," Matt said hopefully.

Charlie shrugged and turned her attention to one of the monitors in the corner of the room. The monitor was one of many in the room, but this particular one was focused on the outdoor enclosure for some of the *Troodons* they'd been studying. The enclosure was more or less a gigantic cage that connected to a retractable door that led into the building. Once the *Troodons* entered through the doorway, they would be inside a large room with several cells that lined the wall. Each "cell" measured twenty feet by twenty feet and usually there was fresh meat in them to attract a *Troodon*. Once one of the dinosaurs stepped inside the cell, a door was lowered and the animal would become trapped. Once they were trapped, the training and other studies could begin.

Everything went well for quite a while, but it began to get harder and harder to get the intelligent dinosaurs to enter the cells as they quickly learned that upon their entry they would immediately become trapped. There was one *Troodon* in particular that seemed to be especially troublesome and stubborn. They'd named her Mother because she seemed to be the leader of the other *Troodons*. Charlie thought she acted almost like a mother to the others. It seemed as if she was behind the sudden difficulties in getting the *Troodons* into their cells. Charlie had noticed on more than one occasion that Mother seemed to almost be in some sort of conversation with the others. She seemed to be warning them.

Now as Charlie watched the monitor, she noticed all of the *Troodons* had quickly darted to one side of the enclosure. This alerted her and she quickly walked over to the monitor for a closer look.

"What's up?" Matt asked, noticing her concern.

Charlie squinted her eyes, looking closely. "Something is wrong," she said. "All of the *Troodons* just ran over to one side of the enclosure. It's almost as if—"

At that moment, she saw what had spooked them. In the dense jungle foliage, she noticed a dark presence moving menacingly nearby.

"What was *that*?" Matt asked as he noticed it too.

Charlie moved her face closer to the screen, almost to the point that her nose was touching it. She looked hard, desperately trying to make out the shape of the animal. It appeared to be quite massive and at first she feared that it was a *Tyrannosaurus rex*—but then she saw the distinguishing detail she was looking for. Along the dinosaur's back, there was a large structure that resembled that of a sail.

"Oh my God, is that the *Spinosaurus*?" she asked in disbelief.

Matt moved closer beside her. "I can't tell," he muttered. "Surely not. Why would it be this close to the facility?"

Charlie took a deep breath and shook her head. "I told them this was going to happen," she grumbled. "There is only one *Spinosaurus* on this entire island. It's been competing with the tyrannosaur population for quite a while for food and I feared sooner or later it would be driven to our end of the island."

Matt looked over at her. "Are you saying it's coming for the *Troodons*?"

Charlie crossed her arms and nodded, still staring at the screen. "I'm afraid so," she said.

Matt looked away from her and back to the screen. After he pondered the situation a moment, he marched over to a nearby phone that was attached to the wall. He punched in a few buttons and then began speaking.

"We've got a situation," he said very matter-of-factly. "Send Glenn Hardcastle to the *Troodon* containment level...I'll meet him there."

Matt slammed the phone back onto the receiver and marched out of the room. As he passed Charlie, he flashed a grin in an effort to assure her that he had the matter under control. Once he'd disappeared into the hallway, Charlie returned her attention back to the monitor. The *Spinosaurus* had now poked its head from out of the leafy vegetation and its eyes seemed to be focused directly on the eight *Troodons* huddled together on the opposite side of the enclosure.

Suddenly, Charlie had an overwhelming urge to take Matt's advice and leave the island until the hurricane passed through. She couldn't put her finger on it, but something deep inside her gut told her something very bad was on the horizon. The feeling was so strong it made her feel ill. She somehow shook the unsettling thoughts from her head and turned away from the monitor. She decided she needed a break. Maybe the *Andy Griffith Show* would be playing in the rec room.

***

Glenn Hardcastle had just stepped out of the shower when he'd received the call. It seemed that the only *Spinosaurus* on the island was getting much too comfortable around the compound and, to make matters worse, now it had taken great interest in the *Troodon* paddock. Hardcastle quickly pulled on his tan cargo pants and then went to work on his boots. As he pulled the laces tightly, he silently cursed Mr. Cornelius Cold.

Cold had asked for Hardcastle's input regarding the best way to construct buildings that would be "dinosaur proof." Hardcastle immediately informed him that there would be no such thing as a "dinosaur proof" building, but if he was really serious about keeping the workers safe, then more attention should be placed on the fencing.

Cold—or someone higher up the chain than him—had made the decision to make use of the compound that Eric Gill had built from the ground up. The "Triangle Building," as it had been named by the associates of Gill Enterprises, had been left exactly as it was. It was a multi-level building that consisted of twenty-five apartments. The hanger had also been left just as it had been under Eric Gill's reign. The office building had been left as well, but it had been added onto quite a bit. What was once a one-story 3,000 square foot structure, had now swelled into a five-story building with over 15,000 square feet of space. The entire top level had been constructed for the sole purpose of training dinosaurs. The fourth and third levels were made up of multiple laboratories. The second level was for the maintenance and operations crew, and the bottom level was made up of offices.

At the rear of the building, there was a large paddock used to contain the dinosaurs that were being studied. It was covered top to bottom with commercial-grade fencing and could be electrified if necessary. It was a safe place for the dinosaurs to be allowed outside for fresh air and to allow the scientists to prepare for whatever study it was they were going to do. From the third floor of the building, a one-hundred and fifty-foot skywalk attached to the Triangle Building to allow the employees easy access to the facility during any weather condition, day or night. Hardcastle had to admit that the improvements the federal government had made to the compound were very impressive—but then there was the matter of the fence.

The twenty-foot-high fence that surrounded the entire compound had always been troublesome. Shortly after Eric Gill had spent many thousands of dollars having it constructed, *Velociraptors*—the curious and deadly bipedal carnivores—immediately began trying to climb it. When Hardcastle had noticed this, he began to make a habit of monitoring the perimeter once every hour via a golf cart. It had gotten to where he was finding *Velociraptors* attempting to get inside at least twice a day.

After consulting the paleontologist on staff, he was advised that the next time he caught one of the raptors attempting to get inside, he should kill it and leave the body for the others to find. The paleontologist believed that the raptors were intelligent enough to come to the realization that whatever was beyond the fence was clearly more deadly than they when they found their dead counterpart. Fortunately, the theory seemed to work as the *Velociraptors* had not attempted to get inside the compound in any of the years since Hardcastle had shot and hung one of them from a large tree just beyond the rear fence.

Though he'd managed to control the raptor problem, the issue had exposed some clear design flaws with the fencing. The mesh that was used was too conducive for climbing and Hardcastle had advised Eric Gill on multiple occasions that it would be smart to change it. In addition to that, he believed it needed to be at least six feet higher with high-voltage electric fencing across the top. Finally, he thought it would be wise for there to be a secondary fence constructed outside of the main one, like those found around prisons. Of course, his advice fell on deaf ears and no changes were ever made and thus Hardcastle had continued his hourly rounds to check the fence.

He'd really hoped that Mr. Cold would be more receptive to his recommendations to make improvements but so far, that had not been the case. Cold had stubbornly declared that the buildings were where the attention and money needed to be spent.

And now we've got the Spinosaurus *knocking on the door*, Hardcastle thought with disgust.

He quickly buttoned his shirt and then snatched his hat off the tiny table where he ate his meals. As he headed out the door, he suddenly thought of Jonathon Williams. After the incident in New Orleans, Cold and Jonathon had a bit of a falling out. Despite Cold's insistence, Jonathon was adamant that he would not participate with any of the work being done on the island. Threats were made but Jonathon stood his ground and ultimately won the argument.

Hardcastle smiled when he thought of Jonathon. He'd tried to kill the man multiple times, but the paleontologist was one of the toughest adversaries he had ever faced. Jonathon had earned his respect and now he longed for his help on the island. As if facing a hurricane was not going to be tough enough, now he was going to have to deal with a hungry *Spinosaurus* too. He could certainly use the expertise, bravery, and raw toughness a guy like Jonathon had to get through the next several days. In his mind's eye, he pictured the man reclining in his nice comfortable living room with his beautiful wife and two-year-old daughter padding around the carpet.

Lucky prick, he thought.

CHAPTER 5

As soon as the elevator doors opened, Dr. Matthew Walker jogged toward the double glass doors that led out into the grounds of the compound. Once outside, the tail of his white lab coat flapped wildly in the wind. He peered to the sky and thought of Hurricane Simon. The category five storm was mere hours away from landfall and it seemed the strong gusts of wind were taunting him.

"You move fast, Doc," Hardcastle called out from behind him.

Matt whipped his head around and noticed that Hardcastle had just come through the same glass doors he'd just exited himself.

"I figured you would walk over from the Triangle Building and meet me out here," he said, placing his hands on his hips.

"Well, you thought wrong," Hardcastle answered. "I took the skywalk because I needed to retrieve this first." He held out a strange-looking contraption—a weapon that looked like a bazooka with a large bell at the end of the barrel similar to that of a tuba. Only there was no opening at the end of the "barrel," only a very large speaker.

"Here, you're gonna want to put these on," Hardcastle said, tossing Matt a pair of hearing protection earmuffs.

Matt caught the earmuffs and held them by a finger as he glanced down at the strange contraption Hardcastle was holding.

"Are you sure that's going to work?" he asked, clearly concerned.

Hardcastle looked down at his non-lethal weapon and then back up to Matt. "I don't know," he said with a grin. "It's the first time I've ever used it."

Matt sighed and shifted his feet, unable to hide his discomfort. "That *Spinosaurus* is one of the largest dinosaurs on the island, are you sure you want to take a chance with something that you've never even tested?"

Hardcastle threw the barrel over his shoulder and held the stock in his palm. "Come on, Doc, you worry too much," he said as he began to walk toward the rear of the building. "Besides, it works beautifully on bears…that much I do know."

Reluctantly, Matt followed him. When they drew near the paddock that contained the *Troodons*, Hardcastle slowed his progress dramatically and he motioned for Matt to slow down as well. Finally, he came to a complete stop.

35

"I don't see it," he whispered as he peered into the dense tropical vegetation just beyond the perimeter fence. He then glanced over toward the *Troodons* and noticed that they were still cowered on the side of the paddock furthest from the exterior fencing.

They know it's still out there, he thought.

He turned to Matt and said, "Okay, you stay here and get your earmuffs on. I'm going to go over for a closer look. I've got to get this thing pointed just right because I don't want the *Troodons* to get hit with friendly fire."

Matt screwed up his face and dropped his mouth open. "What are you talking about?" he asked. "What exactly does that thing do?"

Hardcastle had turned to walk away but stopped abruptly when Matt asked the question. He turned back toward him and said, "It's a sonic weapon—a prototype. Cold gave it to me," he said with a toothy grin. "This baby can emit sound waves a little over 200 decibels at full blast. That's enough to tear your internal organs apart if I point it in your direction, so whatever you do, keep your earmuffs on and stay behind me."

Hardcastle turned away and began creeping toward the fencing again but Matt grabbed his arm, stopping him.

"Wait," he hissed, trying to keep as quiet as possible. "Are you going to need that many decibels to incapacitate the *Spinosaurus*?"

Hardcastle sighed and appeared slightly annoyed. "I doubt it, Doc, but it's nice to know I've got that much…you know, just in case."

Matt continued to stare at him, shaking his head very slightly.

Hardcastle rolled his eyes. "If you must know, I'm going to start it out around 150 decibels and work my way up from there. I've got to be careful or I could kill it." He turned to walk away again.

"No, wait," Matt said, grabbing his arm yet again. "What if 150 isn't enough? How will it react?"

Hardcastle jerked his arm away. "I have no idea, Doc, but we're about to find out."

"Well, what if it reacts violently?" Matt asked nervously. "Are you prepared for that?"

Hardcastle clenched his teeth a moment, then said, "I'm gonna go do my job now, Doc. *Don't* grab my arm again!"

He turned away and quickly crept closer to the edge of the paddock. He took a quick moment to glance over his shoulder to make sure that Matt had put on the earmuffs as he'd been instructed. Fortunately, he had. Hardcastle had his own hearing protection, but he'd refrained from putting them on just yet. He needed his hearing for the moment to try and locate the *Spinosaurus*. An animal that large had enormous lungs too and when it breathed, it was relatively easy to hear.

As he crept closer and closer to the exterior fencing, he listened intently for any sound at all. Just when he'd about decided that the dinosaur had left, he heard what he was listening for. There was a relatively loud *whooshing* sound that began emanating from somewhere beyond the leafy green vegetation. Hardcastle stopped dead in his tracks and continued to listen. He estimated that the *Spinosaurus* was roughly thirty-five yards away and had seemingly lost interest in the *Troodons*—at least for the time being. And that was the problem. The dinosaur might lumber away for a little while, but it would be back. And unfortunately, the more comfortable it got, the more ambitious it was going to get. Sooner or later, it was going to try to tear into the fence and get to the easy prey in the paddock.

I gotta send a message right here and now, he thought as he carefully tossed his hat aside and placed the earmuffs over his head. He took three more steps forward, checked the decibel range on the sonic cannon, and then aimed the bell in the direction of the *Spinosaurus*. He pressed the "trigger" with conviction and a high-pitched tone immediately erupted from the barrel of the cannon. It was loud enough for his ears to faintly pick up the sound from within the confined safety of the earmuffs, but it was not nearly as intense as Hardcastle had anticipated. He was beginning to think the weapon had zero effect on the dinosaur when suddenly, he heard the muffled roar of the angry *Spinosaurus*. Then he felt the vibration begin beneath the soles of his boots. The enormous creature was moving and as the vibrations grew in intensity, he suddenly came to the realization that the dinosaur was stomping in his direction.

As soon as he understood what was happening, Hardcastle immediately turned his attention to the dial that adjusted the decibel level on the sonic cannon. He quickly turned it up to 175 and again pointed it in the direction of the *Spinosaurus*. As he did so, the monstrous creature poked its crocodilian-like head through the thick enveloping trees and opened its maw widely. The animal released another furious roar and it was the first time that Hardcastle had gotten such a good look at the *Spinosaurus's* rows of massive needle-like teeth.

Without further hesitation, he again put the cannon to use and blasted the *Spinosaurus* again. Amazingly, the animal continued to move forward and the extremely high-pitched sound waves only seemed to enrage it more. Hardcastle took a quick glance over his shoulder to check on the whereabouts of Matt. The doctor was nowhere to be found.

Figures, he thought and he made another quick adjustment to the dial, increasing the decibel level to 185. Again, he blasted the *Spinosaurus* with a barrage of intensely high-pitched sound waves. This time, the dinosaur stopped abruptly and released another furious roar. It seemed almost as if the *Spinosaurus* was trying to produce an even more deafening sound to counter the sonic cannon. Hardcastle held his ground and continued to keep the weapon trained on the looming threat thrashing and roaring just on the other side of the fence. Suddenly, something unexpected happened.

Without any warning at all, the *Spinosaurus* flailed its arm over the top of the barrier and then swept its claws downward, thus catching the coiled razor wire and the horizontal crossbar across the top of the fence. Hardcastle could only keep his finger planted on the trigger as he watched with growing fear as the horizontal bar slowly began to contort downward as the dinosaur continued to heave its strength and weight over the top of the fence. The barrier began to bend with more ease as it became more and more unstable. It was suddenly very clear that the *Spinosaurus* had forgotten all about the *Troodons* and now had its attention fully on Hardcastle. He contemplated releasing the trigger but didn't for fear that without it, there would be nothing left to slow down the animal's progress. Instead, he began to back away. In his mind's eye, he could see the nearest door that would provide entry into the building. He began to devise a plan and decided that if he could just get inside the building, he could then turn the sonic cannon to its highest decibel and blast the *Spinosaurus* with a high enough frequency to kill it. Now that the animal had breached the fencing, there would be no other choice.

It felt like an eternity before Hardcastle's back finally contacted the cool metal door that led back into the relative safety of the building. Miraculously, the fencing was still standing and somehow had kept, at least for now, the *Spinosaurus* from getting inside the compound. The animal was still enraged and seemed to genuinely be affected by the sonic weapon—just not in the way that Hardcastle had hoped. With one hand still manning the weapon, he slipped the other one behind him to open the door. He grabbed the handle and pushed his thumb downward on the latch—and to his horror, it was locked. Hardcastle gritted his teeth and tried his best not to panic. He began kicking the door with the heel of his boot, a frantic plea for help.

Surely, he thought, *the doc couldn't have gone far...*

As his leg began to tire, it was becoming quickly apparent that there was no one coming to open the door anytime soon. Hardcastle had just about made up his mind to release the trigger for the briefest of moments just to turn the dial to full blast. The *Spinosaurus* seemed to read his mind and released another deafening roar. It then lunged itself forward and the fence bent further inward.

It's going to get through, he thought. *I've literally got seconds to figure something out...*

The angry dinosaur's eyes widened and its crocodilian jaws snapped—it seemed to realize a meal was mere seconds away too. The fence began to creak a sickening wail as the dinosaur again used its weight to its advantage. Hardcastle could only look on and contemplate what he could've done differently in the moment to prevent the impending doom that was about to eat him alive. He wondered if he'd just gone ahead and made an adjustment on the sonic weapon, if that would've been enough to prevent it all. He took a deep breath and watched helplessly as the vertical fence posts began to fold over as if they were made of a metal no more significant than aluminum.

And then, he began to feel *it*.

The rumble under his feet was subtle and almost unnoticeable at first. In fact, when Hardcastle finally *did* notice it, he figured it was originating from the thrashing dinosaur trying with everything in its being to get to him. But then the rumbling began to increase, so much so that he decided an earthquake was occurring—and then a most welcome thing happened. The *Spinosaurus* seemed to become spooked by the strange occurrence and immediately ceased its assault on the fencing. Hardcastle looked on in grateful amazement as the dinosaur became rattled by the strange sensation beneath its large feet to the point of turning and running away into the jungle.

The earthquake went on for what Hardcastle estimated to be forty-five seconds before it ceased as abruptly as it began. With the *Spinosaurus* gone, he released the trigger on the sonic weapon, ripped the earmuffs from his head, and fell to his knees. His heart was beating so hard in his chest he could hear the thumping in his ears and for the first time in a long time, he felt utterly and completely scared. He stared at the torn and mangled fence that leaned awkwardly in toward him and wiped the sweat from his brow. The next forty-eight hours were going to get awfully interesting.

CHAPTER 6

"I could've died!" Hardcastle growled through clenched teeth as he shoved Matthew Walker against a locker.

They were in the employee break room on the third floor. After Glenn Hardcastle managed to cheat death, he immediately marched back indoors to search for Matt. In his mind, there was no blaming Matt for deserting him, but what he was angry about was the fact that he'd been inadvertently locked out of the building. At least it was inadvertent according to Matt.

"I had no idea that the door locked automatically from the inside!" he yelled in response. "I would've never locked you out intentionally!"

Hardcastle took a long look at him before taking a few steps away with his hands up. "Okay, Doc," he said. "So you just shut the door and ran straight up here like a coward? Is that what you're saying?"

Matt clenched his jaw. "I ran back in to get a weapon from the armory," he explained. "About the time I got to it, I felt the ground shaking. My first thought was that I was too late and the dinosaur was already crashing into the building."

Hardcastle took a deep breath, removed his hat, and scratched at his head. "That's a good story," he replied, unconvinced.

"It's the truth," Charlie said suddenly. She'd been leaning against the doorway listening to the two men bicker. "I was watching everything from the monitors in the lab. When I realized what was happening, I rushed downstairs to see if there was anything I could do to help. Matt was making his way to the armory when I got down to the second level. When the building began to shake, we both panicked and decided to head for the exit. By the time we got to the ground floor, you were coming in and it was over."

Hardcastle took another deep breath through his nose. He was clearly annoyed, but he seemed to be more accepting of Charlie's story. He liked and trusted her. He looked at her for a moment and then to Matt.

"Okay," he said finally. "I still think you're a coward, but if we're going to get through the next couple of days, we've got to get along."

Matt opened his mouth for a rebuttal but thought better of it. Instead, he let out an exasperated grunt and stormed out of the room.

Charlie's eyes followed him and once he was gone, she returned her attention to Hardcastle. "So, what are we going to do about the fence?"

Hardcastle returned his hat to the top of his head and rubbed at his eyes. He was tired and badly needed sleep. "How much time before the hurricane makes landfall?" he asked, stifling a yawn.

Charlie paused and glanced down at her watch. "The news says we've got approximately eight hours," she answered. "That puts it us right in the middle of the night."

Hardcastle sighed and shook his head. He had not been very concerned about the hurricane, but that was before the *Spinosaurus* had wrecked the fencing. He bit his lip and thought for a long moment trying to put some sort of plan of action together in his head. Unfortunately, exhaustion seemed to be affecting his thinking. With his shoulders slumped, he finally strolled over to the kitchen sink and began splashing cold water on his face.

"Well?" Charlie asked anxiously. "What are we going to do?"

Hardcastle turned the faucet off and raised his head to look at her. There was water dripping off his chin, but he didn't seem to notice.

"There isn't any time to do anything," he replied. "We've only got a few more hours of daylight left and considering it's just you, George, that coward partner of yours, and myself...well, unfortunately, we just don't have the manpower to make the necessary repairs."

It wasn't the answer Charlie wanted to hear.

"So you're telling me that not only do we have to ride out a category five hurricane," she began, her voice rising.

"It probably won't even be that when it makes landfall," Hardcastle interrupted.

Charlie rolled her eyes and continued. "So not only do we have to deal with the hurricane, we've also got to deal with the vulnerable position that damaged fence puts us in. A raptor will have no problem getting through that opening, do you realize that?"

Hardcastle took a deep breath and shot her a cold look. "Of course I know that," he growled loudly. "But just what would you have me do about it? If you've got an idea, I'm all ears!"

Charlie felt her blood pressure rise as she did not react well to people yelling at her. She opened her mouth to give him a real piece of her mind when suddenly she had an idea. Instead of yelling back at him, she smiled.

Hardcastle was unsure of how to respond. "What?" he asked, dumbfounded by her strange reaction.

"I think I have an idea," she replied, and she quickly strolled past him toward the exit. "Follow me, we don't have a lot of time."

***

"So do you think it'll hit the island?" Lucy asked as she and Jonathon watched the evening news report on the progression of Hurricane Simon.

"I don't know," he replied, rubbing the back of his neck. "The experts sure seem to think so…I hope not."

"Well, that island has been around at least for 65 million years," Lucy said with a nervous laugh. "Surely it has had its share of hurricanes over the years. I'm sure it'll be fine."

Jonathon did not reply; he just continued to stare at the television as a graphic appeared on screen showing the multiple projected paths the hurricane could take. The most likely one looked as if it would be a direct hit on the island. Lucy watched how intensely he was staring at the television and suddenly it became quite apparent to her what he was most concerned about. It wasn't the dinosaurs, although that was definitely a concern. What she felt concerned him most was the people that were working on the island. Lucy knew there were individuals that Jonathon had met on his last visit to the island that were persuaded to work there by Mr. Cold.

"Surely they evacuated," she told him softly, resting her hand on his forearm.

He looked over at her and smiled nervously. "I don't know," he said, shrugging. "Knowing Cold, that place is important enough for him to talk some of them into staying behind to look after things and ride out the storm."

Lucy shook her head dismissively. "Surely not," she said.

Jonathon raised his eyebrows slightly and continued to stare at the television.

"Well, even if they *do* stay—which they probably won't—but if they did, I'm sure there has got to be a safe building there to ride things out," she said, trying to reassure him.

Jonathon thought back to the buildings that Eric Gill had built. He thought that perhaps the Triangle building would be a safe place to get. The unique architectural design had to have some sort of purpose; maybe that was it. Jonathon pondered the compound a bit more and as he thought about it, what seemed to trouble him most was not the design of the buildings, but their close proximity to the beach. If the storm was intense enough—and a category five was as bad as it got—then a storm surge could be a real possibility. He remembered how devastating the storm surge had been on the Mississippi gulf coast during Hurricane

Camille back in the sixties. Camille had been a category five as well and he distinctly remembered hearing that the storm surge had peaked at twenty-four feet. Jonathon remembered visiting the gulf coast as a child and seeing a large post planted on the beach with a blue line painted on it to mark just how deep the water had gotten. It had been quite a bit over his head.

"Are you alright?" Lucy asked. She could clearly see he was deep in thought.

"Yeah, I'm alright," he replied, smiling at her. "There's no sense in worrying about it. All I can do is hope and pray they took the proper precautions."

"I'm sure they did," she replied. "*If* there is even anyone on the island."

Jonathon nodded, and then stood from the comfortable sofa. It was making him sleepy. He was about to head to the kitchen for a snack when he heard the weatherman continue to offer a doomsday description of Hurricane Simon. He made it sound awfully dangerous.

Surely there is no way Cold left them on that island, he thought.

As he strolled into the kitchen, he finally allowed himself to dismiss the possibility. *There's just no way...*

***

"So do you really think it was an earthquake?" Charlie asked as she led Hardcastle into the hangar.

"Don't know," he replied, shrugging. "I don't know what else it could've been. There isn't a dinosaur on the island that can shake the ground like that." He paused at the entrance to the hangar. "Alright, you got me out here, now what's this bright idea you've got?"

Charlie did not stop walking and did not look back. "This is my idea," she answered, waving her hand toward the large semi that was parked against the interior wall of the hanger.

The large truck and flatbed trailer immediately reminded him of the *Sarcosuchus* he and Eric Gill had tried—and ultimately succeeded in—removing from the island. In hindsight, he was almost ashamed of his behavior back then...almost. Money talked and he was glad to listen when it did.

"Okay, I'm listening," he said as he leaned against the large metal door.

"Do you think it'll still start? I haven't seen this thing run since...well, you remember," she said, her voice trailing off.

There was an awkward silence.

Hardcastle took a deep breath through his nose and allowed his eyes to drift toward the high metal ceiling. "Yeah, I remember," he replied flatly. After another long moment of silence, he added, "Look, I don't suppose we've ever talked a lot about all of that stuff."

Charlie raised her eyebrows and looked back at him. She then rested her back against the front grill of the semi and crossed her arms. "There's nothing to talk about," she replied. "That was over two years ago and Jonathon Williams seemed to think you were more on our side that we initially thought."

Hardcastle laughed. "He said that, did he?"

Charlie nodded.

Glenn Hardcastle rubbed the stubble on his jaw and after a couple of moments, he approached her. "Honey, whatever Jonathon told you about me was a complete lie. I was on my own side then just as I am now."

A slow smile crept across his face that reminded Charlie of the Cheshire cat from *Alice in Wonderland*. She shifted her weight and felt an uneasiness come over her that she could not explain. "I don't believe that," she said softly as he placed a hand on the hood of the truck several inches above her head.

"And why is that?" he asked, leaning over close to her face.

"Because," she replied, locking her eyes with his. "You're here now...on our side."

"I see," he replied just above a whisper. "And what exactly makes you think we're on the right side? I mean, after all, our white knight Jonathon is nowhere to be found on this island." He inched his face closer to hers.

Charlie narrowed her eyes and dodged his advance just in the nick of time. "So what I'm thinking," she said, returning her attention to the semi, "is we load a couple of the old Gill Enterprises jeeps on the back of the trailer and then we park it against the fence to reinforce the damage."

She walked away from Hardcastle and though he was annoyed by the way she'd avoided him, he did his best not to show it.

"This truck and those jeeps still have some value and use here," he said, rubbing the back of his neck.

She stopped and spun on her heel to face him. She brushed her blonde bangs out of her face and said, "I think our lives have more value than these vehicles," a flare of anger in her tone.

Hardcastle took a long look at the semi and then the jeeps. Whether he wanted to admit it or not, it was a pretty good idea and it was probably enough to hold the fence together until the hurricane blew over.

"Alright," he said finally. "I suppose it'll have to do until we get more manpower back on the island to make the appropriate repairs. If we strap the jeeps down, I figure the weight of them plus the trailer and truck *should* be enough to hold the *Spinosaurus* and any tyrannosaurs out."

"Good," Charlie replied. "Well, get to it then."

Hardcastle could only watch as she quickly scurried out of the hangar. He'd noticed that she'd become more and more uncomfortable when he was alone with her. He smiled as he sensed what was going on and then tried to force it out of his head. There was work to do and little time to get it done. A strong gust of wind suddenly blew through the compound and Hardcastle could see the tropical trees bend in protest outside the hangar. Hurricane Simon would be making his appearance in short time. Hardcastle adjusted his hat and then climbed aboard the large semi to see if it would start.

CHAPTER 7

10:23 p.m.

Hurricane Simon arrived and immediately made its presence known by ripping the entire roof off the hangar. Charlie, Hardcastle, Matt, and George did not witness the spectacular occurrence, but they all heard it. The sound was eerily like a crack of thunder, followed by a sickening wail of what undoubtedly was twisting metal. Upon hearing it, Hardcastle rushed toward an outside window to investigate just in time to see the remnants of the roof disappearing somewhere beyond the dense jungle canopy toward the jungle interior.

They were all hunkered down in an office on the first level. There had been a debate about where they should ride the storm out, but Matt had decided if something happened and they needed to make a quick escape, it would be best to be on the ground floor. Hardcastle disagreed and voiced his concerns about a possible storm surge that could fill the first floor with water. Despite his pleas, no one seemed to give his concerns a lot of consideration except for Charlie. In an attempt to mediate the growing tension between Matt and Hardcastle, she tried to take charge and made the decision that they should stay on the lower level unless water began to enter the building. Hardcastle appreciated what she was doing and didn't debate the matter any further.

"What about the *Troodons*?" Charlie asked just as the western wall of the hangar blew away.

"What about them?" Hardcastle asked. "They're in the paddock. If the paddock goes down, they're free and will no doubt disappear into the jungle."

Charlie frowned and placed her hands on her hips. "And all of the past two years of research we've been doing will be for nothing."

Matt walked alongside her and placed a hand on her shoulder. "No, I'm sure if they get loose, we'll be able to track them back down," he said. "I mean, it's not like there are a lot of places to hide here."

He had removed his lab coat and was now wearing a plaid shirt and slacks. His dark hair was combed in such a way that reminded Hardcastle of a Ken doll. Glenn had also noticed that the man's hands were manicured and appeared to be just as smooth as Charlie's. Matt Walker was not the sort of man he'd want to be caught in a foxhole with.

The wind suddenly howled loudly and they could hear the entire building vibrating.

"What do we do if the building goes down?" Charlie asked, unable to hide the fear in her voice.

"The building will hold," Hardcastle reassured her. "I was here for its construction and I can assure you that it was built right. On the other hand, the buildings that Eric Gill built for were constructed by men that cut plenty of corners to keep the cost down. It's not a surprise to me that the hangar went down."

Charlie nodded slowly and Glenn could see in her eyes that what he said comforted her a bit. George seemed to go with the flow and as usual, said little. He was clearly comfortable and unfazed by the furious wind outside. Matt seemed to become more antsy by the minute.

"I still think we should discuss what to do if this building goes down," he stammered. He was looking at the walls around him as he spoke.

Hardcastle rolled his eyes and huffed. "The building is *not* going to fall down," he grumbled.

The lights suddenly flickered. Charlie shifted uncomfortably in her chair.

"If the power goes down, me and George are ready," Hardcastle said, holding up a large flashlight. "Just relax; everything is going to be fine."

She smiled at him, but it was obviously forced. "I'm *trying* to relax," she said. "A nice glass of wine would really help the cause."

"Well if you'd have taken my suggestion about us staying on a higher floor, we'd be near the rec room where I know factually there is some wine," Hardcastle teased in response. "That wind out there isn't letting up...I'm telling you that within in the next hour, we're going to start dealing with water."

"Well, we'll cross that bridge when and if we come to it," Matt said. "I don't want to be on a higher floor if this building begins to come apart," he added. His eyes were still darting around in all directions. It was as if he was desperately searching for some sort of crack in the wall that would reinforce his theory.

"I see, so you'd rather be on the bottom floor when the building collapses," Hardcastle rebutted. "You'd be okay with being buried alive?"

Matt shot him a cold glare as another huge gust of wind pounded the building. The lights flickered again—more this time.

"I think I'm going to take a step outside to get a better feel for what this wind is doing," Hardcastle said as he approached the door. He grabbed a raincoat and put it on.

"Are you sure that's a good idea?" Matt asked, chasing after him.

"I'll only be a minute," Hardcastle replied without halting or looking back.

He quickly made his way to the double glass doors at the entrance of the building. The glass rattled with the wind as if it were warning him to stay inside. As he stepped into the windy, damp air, he immediately put a hand over his head to hold his hat in place. He noticed that the wind was becoming much more sustained and was getting stronger too. He estimated the winds were currently somewhere in the neighborhood of 80 miles per hour, which meant they weren't even close to seeing the worst of the storm yet. While he was still able to walk without getting blown away, he decided to check on the damaged fencing and the semi that he'd parked in front of it.

In the short time it took him to jog around to the rear of the building, he could already feel the wind speed increasing even more. He figured he only had a few minutes before walking around outside would be impossible. As he squinted, trying to get a good look at the mangled fencing, a large palm frond swept by him, narrowly missing his face. It served as a reminder that there would be other, larger debris that could potentially come from seemingly anywhere and knock him unconscious, or even potentially kill him. Satisfied that the fencing was still intact, though he wasn't sure for how long, Hardcastle turned to head back toward the entrance, the wind at his back.

As he drew near the building, he kept a hand on the brick wall, desperately searching for anything he could grip to keep him upright. Suddenly, he heard a strange sound echoing from behind him. He turned and realized it was coming from the *Troodon* paddock. He could just make out the five of them, with the large female in the center, staring at him from behind the fence. They seemed to be barking at him and he swore it looked and sounded as if they were trying to speak to him.

Were they pleading for help? he wondered. *Are they warning me about something?*

The sight of the *Troodons* glaring at him, along with the strange guttural noises they were making at him, was unnerving and he found himself moving even more quickly back toward the entrance. As he trudged along, he continued to hear the animals doing their best to *speak* to him, though he had absolutely no idea what they were trying to say.

Just as he grabbed the handle to reenter the building, another gust of wind, the strongest yet, rolled across the compound. Hardcastle watched in amazement as the air picked up an aluminum boat that had been turned upside down near the back gate. The boat was tossed high in the air—probably twenty feet—and it too disappeared somewhere beyond the canopy of the jungle just as the roof of the hangar had done. It was at that moment that the compound went completely dark. The power had finally gone out.

***

11:03 p.m.

The backup generators began humming mere seconds after the primary power source was lost. Hardcastle removed the wet raincoat and simply tossed it aside on the floor. He jogged back to the interior office where they'd decided to take refuge. When he stepped into the doorway, the first thing he noticed was that both Charlie and Matt had flashlights in hand, and they were both on.

"You need to cut those off," he barked at them. "We've got light for the time being, but if we lose it, we're going to need those flashlights."

Matt scowled at him and looked over to Charlie. She was looking at him as if she was waiting for him to tell her it was alright to cut the light off. When Hardcastle noticed it, he felt his blood pressure rise. The last person he felt that Charlie needed to be looking to for guidance was Matt Walker.

"He's right," Matt told her. "We need to save the batteries." He flicked his light off and she immediately followed his lead.

"What did it look like out there?" Charlie asked as she laid her light on a nearby desk.

"Windy," Hardcastle quipped. He casually pulled out the cushy chair from behind the desk and collapsed into it.

Matt narrowed his eyes and cleared his throat. "That's an $800 chair," he said. He could clearly see that Hardcastle's pants were soaking wet.

"Is that right?" he asked, and he kicked his muddy boots up on the desk for good measure. "It sure is comfortable."

Matt turned a deeper shade of red and opened his mouth to speak but thought better of it.

"Did you check on the fence?" Charlie asked, clearly sensing the growing tension between the two men. She wanted to diffuse it as quickly as possible.

Hardcastle nodded. "Yep, it's still standing," he said. He pulled his drenched hat off and began to wring it out over a nearby trash can. "I

49

saw something else too," he added, keeping his attention on his beloved hat.

"What?" George asked, suddenly joining the conversation. "What did you see?"

"The *Troodons*," he answered. "They were gathered at the side of the cage, looking at me."

George sat down on the edge of the desk as Charlie drew nearer.

"Did they do anything else?" she asked, figuring there had to be more to it than that. She ran a hand over her hair, caught it in the back, and then used her free hand to retrieve a rubber band from the desk. She put her hair in a ponytail and then yawned. She looked exhausted...they all did.

"Yeah, and I know this will sound crazy," Hardcastle replied, shifting in his chair. "But they seemed to be trying to get my attention. They were making some strange noises I've never heard them make before."

Charlie leaned closer and Matt did as well. "Noises?" she asked. "What did they sound like?"

Once he was satisfied the water was all gone, Hardcastle took a moment to reshape his hat back to its original form. "Well, it sounded like..." he paused and seemed to be choosing his words carefully.

"Sounded like what?" George urged.

Hardcastle took a deep breath and released a yawn of his own. He returned the hat to the top of his head and said, "Again, I know it sounds crazy but...I swear it sounded as if they were trying to speak to me."

Matt laughed and Hardcastle shot an icy stare at him but said nothing more.

Charlie blinked a couple of times and shook her head. "Wait, you're saying they were making noises that sounded like words?"

Hardcastle shook his head. "Nah, not exactly," he answered. "It's just that their mannerisms and the way they—"

He paused again as he noticed all three of them were staring hard at him.

"Look, I know how it sounds," he grumbled, getting up from the chair. He suddenly seemed angry. "I can't describe it...I could just tell they were trying to communicate with me. It's a feeling I had."

"A feeling?" Matt asked with a chuckle. "If I had a feeling that the animals were talking to me, I'd probably keep it to myself, Glenn."

"Look," Hardcastle growled as he took a step toward Matt. "Laugh it up if you want to, I really don't care. What I do care about is that this storm is still going to get plenty worse before it gets better. I'm going to insist yet again that we to a higher floor. From what I could tell outside, it's not a question of *if* water is going to start coming into the building, but *when*."

Matt rolled his eyes slightly, but said nothing. Hardcastle pretended not to notice because he felt he was on the verge of punching the doctor in the face.

"A storm surge from a category five hurricane will happen very quickly. When it begins to flood, it's going to happen a heck of a lot faster than I think any of you are expecting. We should go to higher ground right now," he added.

Charlie chewed her lip a moment, then said, "I think he's right."

Matt threw up a hand. "No," he said. "He is not. I told you that could be dangerous if the storm does something to the building."

Charlie continued to stare at Hardcastle and he stared right back.

"Matt, if you want to stay down here, you go ahead," she replied. "But I think that Glenn, George, and myself are going to go up to the third floor to ride this out in the rec room."

Matt looked at her and his expression was a mixture of bewilderment and hurt. He opened his mouth to speak, but instead, all he could muster was a sheepish grin. Charlie began to make her way toward the door to begin her trek to the rec room when she suddenly stopped and turned back to Hardcastle.

"If what you say is true, how much water do you think we could be dealing with?" she asked.

Hardcastle pondered the question a minute and said, "Hard to say. Could be anything from five feet to twenty-five feet."

Charlie's eyes widened. "That much?" she asked, clearly surprised by his answer.

He nodded.

"Well, then that settles it," she replied. "We can't leave the *Troodons* out there in that paddock. They could potentially drown."

The possibility had occurred to Hardcastle, but he'd kept it to himself.

"You're right," he agreed. "I think the best thing to do—the humane thing to do—would be to release them."

Matt suddenly stepped forward holding up both his hands. "No, no, wait," he stammered. "Now let's think about this. We've put a lot of time and effort into those dinosaurs," he said. "If we let them go, and we're unable to catch them again, we will have to start completely over again."

Hardcastle smiled at him. "Yeah, that sounds about right. Sucks for you," he said and he began to head toward the door.

51

"No, wait," Charlie said, grabbing his arm. "Matt's right, we've taught those animals so much. They can respond to all sorts of commands and you just told us a few minutes ago that they even seem to have their own language."

Hardcastle winced as he realized he'd said too much. He rubbed his eyes and asked, "So what do you suggest, Charlie?"

"We've got to move them to the lab on the fourth floor," she suggested. "They're used to being in there and will be comfortable in there."

Hardcastle considered the suggestion and took a deep breath through his nose as he thought. Ideally, if the animals had to be moved, in his opinion the cells on the ground level would be the best option. However, the issue with flooding would remain. In his opinion, moving the *Troodons* to the smaller cages in the fourth-floor laboratory *could* work except for one problem.

"The locks on those cages are controlled by electricity," he said. "If we lose power again, the locks *could* release."

"The key word there is *could*," Matt said. "What you're saying is, you are assuming they would release."

"I'd rather assume that they would release instead of assuming they don't," Hardcastle said through clenched teeth. "If you're wrong, we've got big, big problems. We could be trapped in this building with some dangerous dinosaurs."

"Both of you could be right," Charlie interrupted. "But it doesn't matter because those cages can be padlocked if need be. The electricity problem ultimately isn't that big of a problem."

"You're right," Matt said. "It's not, because first of all, the power isn't going to go out again. Secondly, if it did, the locks would not just magically release and let the dinosaurs out."

"You don't know that!" Hardcastle yelled as he slapped his forehead in disbelief.

"It doesn't matter!" Charlie screamed at them. "You're both acting like children at the worst possible time!"

The two men kept their mouths shut and did not argue the matter any further.

When Charlie was satisfied that they were done, she said, "Okay, so I think we can all agree that if we're going to do this, we need to do it now. The wind is going to get stronger and that paddock could go down. We need to do this now."

Hardcastle nodded and stormed out of the room. Clearly, he was still angry with Matt. George trailed after him, followed by Charlie. Matt leaned against the wall with his arms crossed for a long moment before he left the room. He was furious with Hardcastle and if he didn't take a moment to cool off, he knew things were going to get much worse. He thought about just staying right where he was and let them handle it. In fact, if it was not for his concern for Charlie, he was certain that was what he would do.

Finally, reluctantly, he shoved his hands in his pockets and trudged out of the room. He decided that Glenn Hardcastle wasn't as tough as his exterior appearance seemed to suggest. The only people he'd ever known that were as paranoid as he had all been cowards. Clearly, Hardcastle was no different. Somewhere deep inside, Matt secretly hoped that the backup generators *did* go out. Just so he could tell Hardcastle *I told you so*.

CHAPTER 8

Jonathon Williams had been unable to get any sleep throughout the entire night. His thoughts were elsewhere…more specifically at a secret island in the middle of the Bermuda Triangle. He could not stop wondering about whether or not there were any people on that island when the hurricane made landfall. Although logic told him there was no way that Cornelius Cold would leave people on an island full of dangerous dinosaurs in the middle of a hurricane, something deep in his gut kept telling him otherwise. He'd had feelings like that before, and usually they proved to be right.

During the night, Lily had been unable to sleep also. However, her insomnia was the product of a nasty head cold. Normally, it was Lucy that got up with the small child as it seemed Lily was in a stage where she much preferred to be in the arms of her mother over her father in times of sickness. This particular night, however, Jonathon scooped her up and took her to the recliner in the living room. There the two of them cuddled under an old patchwork quilt and watched live coverage of the hurricane. He saw pictures of the devastation that had already occurred across Puerto Rico and the projected path of the hurricane seemed to be northwesterly. As far as the United States went, it appeared that the Carolinas were going to take a direct hit.

The next morning, an orange ray of sunlight managed to pierce through the blinds that were set in the living room window. Much to Jonathon's dismay, the annoying light seemed to attack him just as he was about to doze off. Fortunately for Lily, she'd managed to get a couple of hours of sleep. The more upright position the recliner provided seemed to be what she needed to finally get a bit of rest. Jonathon had watched his daughter as she drifted off to sleep and he could not help but feel a slight bit of envy.

The television was still on and there were more live pictures—this time in daylight—of the tremendous damage that Hurricane Simon had inflicted on Puerto Rico again. So far, there were estimates of at least 32 casualties and that number was expected to rise. Jonathon allowed his mind to once again drift back to the mysterious island shrouded in mist right in the center of the Bermuda Triangle. If that storm hit it directly, and it was becoming more apparent to him that it did, the devastation could be severe enough to permanently change the island's geography.

On top of that, there would undoubtedly be many dead dinosaurs scattered from coast to coast.

Just as he was contemplating getting up and taking Lily back to her crib, Lucy strolled into the room. She was wearing a pink nightgown and still rubbing at her eyes. When she eventually looked down at him in the recliner, she paused to stretch and then smiled prettily when she saw Lily snoozing on his chest.

"Would you like for me to take her?" Lucy whispered.

Jonathon nodded. "Yeah, if you put her to bed, I'll get started on some breakfast," he replied.

"You will not," she countered as she gently took the baby. "You'll stay right there and rest and *I'll* make breakfast."

He watched her until she disappeared around the corner that led into the hallway. Once she was out of sight, Jonathon closed his eyes and again felt himself nearing sleep when once again another annoyance snatched him back away. The phone began ringing. He glanced over at the clock and silently wondered who on earth would be calling him at 7:45 a.m. on a Saturday. He was just about to force himself up out of the recliner when Lucy walked swiftly across the carpet in front of him.

"Stay there," she said, pointing at him. "I'll get the phone."

He listened as she picked up the phone and began a conversation. It started off friendly enough but quickly turned somewhat heated.

"Is it really necessary that you speak to him right this minute?" she asked, doing little to hide the anger in her tone.

After a pause, she appeared under the archway that led into the kitchen, the cordless phone pressed into her chest.

"It's your old friend," she said in a way that made it clear that whoever was on the line was anything but an actual friend. "Mr. Cold," she added when he looked at her with bewilderment.

Jonathon sighed and felt his jaw tighten. A bit of nausea hit him as his pulse began to race. He doubted it was a coincidence that Cold was calling him the morning after the hurricane had most likely swept across the island in the mist. Reluctantly, he motioned for her to hand him the phone.

"What have you done?" he asked as soon as he put the phone to his ear.

There was an awkward silence but he could hear breathing.

"I beg your pardon?" Cold asked. "What is it that you think I've done?"

"Cut the crap," Jonathon replied. "You left them on that island, didn't you?"

There was another pause, this one slightly longer than the first.

"There were a few volunteers that wanted to stay on the island and ride the storm out," he explained. He sounded almost apologetic.

Jonathon closed his eyes and shook his head in disbelief.

"And let me guess, they're in some kind of trouble now," he grumbled.

"The truth is, we're not really sure," he replied. "We have not been able to make any contact with them since a little after 10 p.m., Atlantic time. Obviously, I'm getting a little worried."

"Well, you should be," Jonathon snapped. "And don't give me that crap about them volunteering to stay there. If they volunteered to stay behind, it was because you made them feel like they didn't have a choice."

"Now that is simply untrue," Cold argued and for the first time there was a hint of anger in his voice. "The four people that remained behind did so on their own volition and had no contact with me about the matter."

Jonathon felt as if he'd sunk further into his chair, as if some invisible weight had just fallen firmly on his chest where Lily had been minutes earlier.

"So why are you calling me?" he asked.

"Well," Cold began. "Obviously, considering the dangers that exist on the island, I feel that it's imperative that we get over there and check on them as soon as possible," he said, and then he paused as if deep in thought. Then he said, "I won't lie to you, I'm fearing the worst. I'm not taking any chances on this initial visit. I want to send four mercenaries over there as soon as possible to check on them and get them out of there if need be."

"You still aren't answering my question," Jonathon said, rubbing at his temples. He could feel a headache coming on.

"I'm calling you because these men know nothing about the island," he said. "They will need a guide—a resource. They need you."

Jonathon chuckled. He was becoming quite irritated. "Why me?" he asked, begrudgingly. "There are others that know the island."

"Really?" Cold asked. "Like who?"

"Glenn Hardcastle," he answered quickly.

There was another long pause.

"Wait," Jonathon said, sensing what was causing the silence. "He's already there, isn't he?"

"Again," Cold continued. "Everyone that remained volunteered. It's very important that you understand that."

"Oh for crying out loud," Jonathon said through clenched teeth. "What about Silas Treadwell?"

"You can't be serious?" Cold said, sounding genuinely surprised. "Treadwell is not in the best of health these days. I think it would be unwise to send him."

Jonathon breathed deeply through his nose and as much as he hated to admit it, Cold was completely right about that. "What about Dr. Charlotte Nelson?" he asked. "She is more than capable and—"

"She is already there too," Cold interrupted.

The imaginary weight on Jonathon's chest got heavier. He opened his mouth to speak but for a long moment, he could not find the words. Finally, he said, "Who else is there?"

"George Powell, I think you've met him," he replied. "And Dr. Matthew Walker. I'm fairly certain you have *not* met him."

"Is he another paleontologist?"

"No," Cold replied. "He is a veterinarian and an animal behavioral specialist."

Jonathon gritted his teeth as the realization began to set in that he really was the only capable person of leading a search and rescue team to the island. His nausea continued to worsen and he genuinely felt as if he was about to throw up at any moment. "I swore I'd never return to that island," he said, sounding defeated.

"I realize that," Cold responded. "You must know that this phone call was not an easy one to make. The last time we spoke the conversation did not end on the best of terms. If there was someone else I trusted enough to call, you can be rest assured that I would have called them before you."

Jonathon knew what he needed to say, but he was trying to will himself to say it. He glanced back over to where Lucy was standing. She was still under the archway that led to the kitchen. He could see the concern on her face and knew the last thing she wanted to hear was that he had to go back to the island.

"Alright," he said softly. "Alright, I'll go."

He watched Lucy's eyes as they began to fill with tears. Clearly, she knew what he'd just agreed to do.

"Very good," Cold replied. He sounded relieved. "Can you get packed and ready to go by 10 p.m. tonight?"

"Sure," Jonathon replied. "You sending someone to pick me up?"

"A car will be there at 10 p.m. on the dot," Cold replied. "That'll give you the day to pack and spend a little extra time with your family. It'll give me the time needed to take care of the last-minute details."

"Alright, I'll be ready," Jonathon said.

"Thank you, Jonathon," Cold said. "I truly appreciate your willingness to help."

Suddenly, all Jonathon heard was dial tone. Lucy walked over to him, her shoulders slumped. She looked defeated. She climbed into the recliner with him and he wiped the tears from her face.

"I'm sorry. I promise you I'll be back as soon as possible," he whispered in her ear. "There are people I know that are trapped there. I couldn't live with myself if they end up dying because I didn't help out."

Lucy took a deep breath. "I understand," she said softly, and there was unmistakable anger in her voice too. "But that does not mean I have to like it."

CHAPTER 9

The car that Mr. Cold had promised arrived right on time. It was a black Cadillac and the driver was as quiet and mysterious as every other person that Jonathon had met that had any association with Cold. He kissed Lucy goodbye and promise he'd be back as soon as possible. The short walk from the front door of his home to the car was cold and dreary. Something about the environment around him was unsettling and he hoped it wasn't some sort of omen warning him of an impending door. He glanced over his shoulder one last time and waved to Lucy. He could see her eyes glistening, probably from tears but he couldn't be sure. He hoped not.

The driver piloted the car straight to Jackson-Evers International Airport and shortly after arriving, he drove the car through a gate near the south side of the property. From there, the car rumbled along some sort of short access road that led to a small hangar. Inside the hangar, a Lear jet was fueled and awaiting his arrival.

"You get out and get on board," the driver said gruffly as he put the vehicle in park. "I'll grab your belongings."

Jonathon opened the car door and set his sights on the steps that led into the interior of the luxurious looking aircraft. As he ascended, he spotted a familiar face waiting for him just inside the plane. It was Mr. Cold.

"Welcome aboard," he said with a wide smile. He held out his hand. Jonathon looked at it for a moment and then slowly took it.

"Let's let bygones be bygones, shall we?" Cold said. "Any differences you and I have had in the past can be left right here in Jackson as far as I'm concerned."

Jonathon shook his hand and gave him a half-smile as he moved into the plane. Once inside, he found a cushy leather seat near a window and tried to get comfortable. Cold sat in the seat across from him. He was wearing his usual black suit, but there was something different about him. At first, Jonathon was unable to figure it out, but after looking him over for a minute or two, he spotted it. Cold hadn't shaved. Every time he'd ever laid eyes on the man, his face had been as smooth as a baby's butt; however this time, it looked as rough as a coarse piece of sandpaper. And he looked tired…very tired.

Cold crossed his legs as he too tried to relax. He snapped his fingers and an attractive woman dressed in a pants suit moved swiftly to him.

"Allyson, would you mind bringing us a couple of glasses and a bottle of Scotch?" he asked her.

Cold and Allyson looked at each other a second too long and it seemed to Jonathon that maybe there was a romantic relationship between the two of them. When Cold turned his attention back to him he contemplated asking, but thought better of it.

"So I'm guessing we're heading to the island at first light?" Jonathon asked. He removed his hat and tossed it on the empty seat next to him.

Allyson returned and placed the two glasses on a tiny tray table next to Cold along with the Scotch. He wasted no time pouring them both a glass over ice cubes. He handed one over to Jonathon and he immediately took a sip. It was strong as he expected, but it was just what he needed to perk up a bit from the exhaustion he was feeling.

"That's exactly what the plan is," Cold replied, turning up his own glass to his lips.

"You've already got a boat ready and waiting for us?" Jonathon asked.

Cold shook his head and gently placed his now empty glass back on the table. He poured himself another. "Not a boat," he said. "A plane."

"A plane?" Jonathon asked, surprised. Suddenly, he remembered that Eric Gill, a pilot himself, had built a runway on the island next to the compound. "Are you sure the runway will be in a suitable condition to land?"

"No, of course I'm not," Cold replied. "If it's not, we'll have to make other arrangements. Don't worry about that part, I just want you to be focused to lead my men once on the ground."

"So I take it you're not joining us?" Jonathon asked, a little aggravated by the realization. It seemed Cold was always eager for others to do his dirty work—and it always had to be done his way.

Cold shook his head and downed his second glass. "No, but I'm putting you with men that I'd trust with my own life."

"And you want me to lead them?" Jonathon asked, a bit perplexed. "I thought I was there to help them navigate and guide them around the dinosaurs."

"You are, and that is why I want you to lead them. When you all arrive on the ground, these men will be under your command. The task is very simple: Get into the compound, locate the survivors, and get them out of there. Your knowledge of the island and the dangerous animals on it doesn't exist with anyone else. I trust you to make decisions that will not only assist my men in finding the survivors, but keeping you and them alive as well."

Jonathon shifted in his seat and popped his knuckles. He wasn't sure how comfortable he'd be ordering four mercenaries around.

"Cold, why didn't you get them off that island before the hurricane hit?" he asked suddenly. "Don't give me that crap about them all volunteering either. What have you got going on that island that is so important four people—three of which I know personally—would risk their lives to stay for?"

Cold stared at him a moment before finally turning his head and peering out the window. The plane was now rumbling down the runway. He reached down to put on his seatbelt and suggested that Jonathon did the same.

"We've been spending the past two years working with the *Troodons*," Cold said, raising his voice slightly to be heard clearly over the high-revving jet engines.

Jonathon felt a chill run up his spine and he immediately remembered what Silas had recently told him about his last encounter with *Troodons*.

"What do you mean, *working* with them?" he asked, leaning forward. "And I swear if you give me the spill again about trying to better humanity, I will probably jump out of this plane."

Cold sighed and rubbed a hand over his dark hair. "I suppose you still believe I'm trying to weaponize them?" he asked calmly.

"Are you going to tell me you're not?" Jonathon asked. He felt the plane lift from the runway. For a moment, he also felt butterflies in his stomach.

"Our boys in Desert Storm used dogs to assist them in the ground war," Cold replied. "The dogs are useful tools and in many cases, they save lives. Now if there is a creature on this planet that is even more intelligent than dogs—yet bigger and with more teeth—why would we not take advantage of that?"

Jonathon took a deep breath through his nose and began to laugh. If he weren't afraid of the consequences, he probably would've punched Cold out right then and there. "Okay, I need you to listen to me," he said, regaining his composure. "Putting dinosaurs on the ground in a war zone would be an extremely bad idea. These animals are not meant to coexist with man. It is true that the *Troodons* seemed to have higher than normal intelligence, but they will not allow you to turn them into soldiers. The first chance they get to escape, they will, and when they do, they will get hungry. When they get hungry, they will not only be a huge danger for human beings, but they could create a severely negative impact on the ecosystem."

Cold's eyebrows raised and he shook his head. "You and I will obviously never agree on this topic," he said. "But you should know that your counterpart Dr. Charlotte Nelson agrees that it can be done. Glenn Hardcastle agrees that it can be done as well."

"And one of the first things I'm gonna do when I get in front of them is try to convince them otherwise," Jonathon countered. "Glenn Hardcastle is there to collect a paycheck and nothing more. Charlie's participation in this pipe dream is a little more perplexing."

"You can try to persuade them if you wish," he replied. "But remember…they *volunteered* to stay there. I don't think changing their minds will be as simple as you think. They've invested a lot of time and effort—and have made great strides by the way."

Jonathon decided he'd argued the matter long enough. "I think I'm going to get some shut-eye," he said, reaching for his hat.

"That's a good idea," Cold agreed. "I'll wake you up when we land and you can sleep some more on the next plane ride to the island. Get all the rest you can because I need you to be sharp when you all arrive."

"Well on that, we finally agree," Jonathon said, leaning back into his seat. He put his hat on his head and pulled it down low over his eyes. Minutes later, he was fast asleep.

CHAPTER 10

Jonathon did not have to rely on Mr. Cold to wake him up. As soon as the plane touched the ground, the aircraft lurched when the tires contacted the asphalt and the slight jerk was enough to bring him out of his slumber. He immediately raised his arms to stretch and then slowly pushed his hat upward and out of his line of vision. It was still dark outside, but he could see the bright lights from the airport where they'd landed.

"Sleep well?" Cold asked. He was standing over him now and the first thing Jonathon noticed was that he was now clean shaven. His suit was different and he looked much more fresh than he had when he'd met him three and half hours ago.

"I've slept better," Jonathon replied, rising from his seat. He yawned and rubbed at his now sore neck.

The plane taxied into a private hangar and as Jonathon hurried toward the exit, he could not help but notice that Cold gave Allyson a peck on the cheek as he made his way to the steps. Once his luggage was retrieved, Cold and Jonathon were ushered into a Chevrolet Tahoe the color of midnight. Even the windows were tinted black.

"So what's our next stop?" Jonathon asked as he fastened his seatbelt.

"Can't tell you specifics," Cold replied. "Only that we're going to introduce you to the extraction team and we will have a briefing on the current situation on the island."

"I thought you weren't aware of what is occurring on the island," Jonathon said, his eyes narrowed.

"When I spoke to you yesterday morning, I didn't," Cold said. "Since then, we've sent a plane over to get a look at the damage."

Jonathon's interest peaked. "So what did you find?" he asked, turning his entire body toward Cold.

"We found pretty much what we expected to find," he replied. "There are a lot of trees down from one end of the island to the other."

"And the compound? How did it look?" Jonathon asked impatiently.

Cold's mouth became a straight line and there was a worried look in his eyes that Jonathon had not seen before. "The hurricane was still a category five when it made landfall," he explained. "We believed that at worst it would be a four by the time it reached the island…obviously, we were wrong."

Jonathon clenched his teeth as he felt his blood pressure rise. "Tell me," he growled.

Cold sighed and crossed his arms. "The hangar is gone," he said. "But for the most part, the other buildings are still standing, though they are damaged significantly. I think it's fair to say that they held up pretty well, just as we expected."

Jonathon felt a momentary relief wash over him, but it was short-lived. "I've got a feeling you just gave me the good news first."

Mr. Cold looked away and out the window. The sky was beginning to turn a beautiful shade of purple to the east where the sun was beginning to rise. "What we didn't count on was the storm surge," he said somberly.

Jonathon shook his head in disbelief. "You've got to be kidding me," he grumbled. "Of course a hurricane that size will most likely create a storm surge—and no further away than the compound was from the coast…my God, how bad did it get?"

"Pretty bad," Cold replied, turning his gaze back to Jonathon. "We estimate the water peaked at around twenty-five feet."

Jonathon looked down to the floor in disbelief. He immediately tried to remember how tall the Triangle Building was, and if he remembered correctly, it was tall enough to escape the water. "Do we know if they are alive?" he asked softly.

"We do not," Cold replied. "There was flooding still present throughout the compound, although we figure by the time you all arrive it will be gone for the most part. Fortunately, we made upgrades to the office building Eric Gill had constructed. It is now a five-story structure and has everything they need to stay comfortable until you get there."

Jonathon's eyes widened as he tried to picture a five-story office building sitting in the center of the compound.

"You will all have blueprints of the entire structure and it should be enough to help you navigate straight to where we believe they probably are," he added as he noticed Jonathon surprised expression.

Jonathon cleared his throat and shifted uncomfortably on the leather seat. He considered everything Cold had told him, but he felt something was still missing. "What are you not telling me?" he asked finally.

Cold seemed nervous—or maybe it was anxious. He again turned his gaze to the window where the sky was now turning a shade of orange.

"We see evidence that the fence was attacked by a very large dinosaur just before the hurricane," he said. "And other parts of the fencing were blown over during the storm. There is a paddock on the back of the structure where the *Troodons* were kept and it is now empty. We expected to find the animals dead inside it, from drowning."

"Are you telling me they broke out?" Jonathon asked.

Cold shook his head. "My spotters didn't see any evidence of that," he said. "What I fear is that they brought them into the interior cages."

"And this surprises you?" Jonathon asked. "I thought that was the whole point of them volunteering to stay there…to protect their work."

"Yes, but again, we didn't count on a 25-foot storm surge," Cold stammered. "My fear is that the backup generators did not hold up, which means the facility has no electricity."

Jonathon rubbed the stubble on his chin and stared at him, unsure of where he was going with this.

"The locks for the indoor cages are electronic," Cold explained. "There is a way to lock them manually of course, but in the middle of a hurricane, I just have my concerns that possibly that little detail could've been missed."

Jonathon took a deep breath as he felt his heart rate increase. Suddenly, it was becoming clear why there was a sense of urgency to get over to the island. "So you're telling me that you fear the compound is vulnerable to dinosaurs on the outside because of the broken fencing?" he asked.

Cold nodded.

"And you're concerned that they're vulnerable inside because you feel they brought the *Troodons* inside and locked them into cages that basically have a design flaw that can allow them to get out when the power fails?"

"That is correct," Cold said just above a whisper. "There are a lot of unknowns and I feel that the sooner we get you to the island, the better their odds are for survival."

***

Once they were off the plane, another black sport utility vehicle awaited them.

"Do you guys get some sort of fleet discount for these things?" Jonathon asked sarcastically.

"Something like that," Cold replied, opening the rear door for him.

Jonathon climbed in and was surprised to see that the driver for this vehicle was the same man that had picked him up in Jackson.

Did he take the same plane?

Strangely, Jonathon suddenly realized he had not even bothered to ask exactly where they were. He guessed Florida, but the airport looked unfamiliar. Then again, it had been dark when they were taxiing down the runway. The sun began to rise and he noticed the environment around him slowly come alive with color.

"Cold, where exactly are we at?" he asked, as the man climbed into the vehicle with him.

"Miami International Airport," he answered, closing the door.

"And may I ask where you are taking me now?" Jonathon said, looking out the window.

Cold looked out his own window and chuckled slightly. "I'm taking you to meet the team that is awaiting your arrival at the next plane," he replied nonchalantly.

Jonathon wanted to ask more questions but his stomach suddenly got his attention by growling loudly. Mr. Cold whipped his head around from the window and smiled widely at him.

"Don't worry," he said, glancing down at Jonathon's stomach. "Breakfast is awaiting your arrival too."

In less than ten minutes, the vehicle pulled into yet another hangar with a group of about fifteen to twenty people surrounding another airplane. This particular plane was a prop and it didn't look anywhere close to as lavish as the one he'd just arrived in.

"Here we are," Cold said, snatching the door handle as soon as the vehicle lurched to a stop.

Jonathon eyed the group that seemed to be trying desperately to get a good look at him through the car's glass. As he peered back at them, he was comforted in knowing they couldn't see him at all through the dark-tinted windows.

They can see me when I'm ready for them to see me, he thought. He watched as Cold began shaking hands with three men that looked as if they'd give Arnold Schwarzenegger a run for his money in an arm wrestling competition. After he'd shaken all their hands, he looked over his shoulder with a puzzled expression. Jonathon could tell he was wondering why he had not gotten out of the car yet. He took a deep breath and decided it was time to make his grand entrance.

"There is the man of the hour," Cold said, and he clapped somewhat theatrically. It made Jonathon incredibly uncomfortable.

One of the big men flashed a wide grin of crooked teeth. Though his mouth was ugly, his personality certainly was not.

"Man, is it an honor to meet you," he said, shoving a big hand out to shake Jonathon's.

"The pleasure is all mine," Jonathon replied, trying his best not to show his new friend the pain he was feeling as his hand suddenly felt like it had been shut in a vice.

"My name is Cliff Gordon. I'm a former infantryman with the U.S. Army," the man said. He had a southern accent, but it clearly wasn't from anywhere near Mississippi.

"Nice to meet you. I'm assuming you'll be joining me on the island?" he said in reply.

The big man nodded. He was entirely bald and there was sweat already beginning to bead up on his forehead. "Yeah, I've heard a lot of stories about some pretty amazing things you've done on the island," Cliff replied. "I can't believe Mr. Cold talked you into coming back."

Jonathon raised an eyebrow. "Well, that makes two of us, Cliff."

"Cliff Gordon is the brawn of the operation," Cold said, stepping between the two of them. He glanced to his right and pointed at another man that Jonathon guessed stood about six feet five inches. He had a blond crewcut and mustache. There was a cigar hanging out of his mouth.

"That is Mr. Victor O'Connell," he said. "Former Navy Seal, and a darn good one from what I've heard."

"You heard right," Victor replied, removing the cigar from his mouth. He spat on the ground. "You're looking at the finest soldier on your team, Mr. Williams," he added.

Jonathon smiled as he looked him over. The man looked to be in his mid-thirties and everything from the way he talked with his Mid-Western accent to the way he moved oozed cockiness. There was something about him that made Jonathon like him immediately.

"Is that right?" he asked.

Victor nodded and returned the cigar to his mouth.

Jonathon crossed his arms and looked back to Mr. Cold. "So if Cliff is the brawn, I'm assuming Victor is the brains?" he asked.

Cold coughed. It sounded as if he were trying to stifle a laugh. "No, certainly not," he said. "He's just more brawn."

Jonathon looked back to Victor and immediately noticed the big man's eyes narrow. He clearly wasn't amused with Cold.

That makes two of them I like, thought Jonathon.

A third man arrived, similar in size to Victor. His hair was also styled in a crewcut and the gray color spoke volumes about his age. He was even dressed like Victor. He wore an army green tank top and camouflage cargo pants. Both men reminded Jonathon of G.I. Joe.

"Hank Bailey," the man said, holding out his hand.

Jonathon took it and felt an ominous squeeze.

"Quite a grip you got there," he said, and he pulled his hand away. It hurt, but he tried not to show it.

Hank held his hand just a second longer and stared at him, stone-faced. When he finally released it, he allowed a slight smile to creep across his lips. The man said nothing more and he turned and made his way toward the plane.

"Don't mind him," a feminine voice called out from behind him. "Just think of Hank as the strong but silent type."

He turned to see who was speaking and found a woman standing there. She was wearing a black tank top and green cargo pants. Her blonde hair was pulled up into a ponytail. Jonathon was unable to see her eyes due to the fact they were hidden behind mirrored Aviator sunglasses. The woman was clearly fit and muscular, but none of that took away from her femininity.

"Jonathon Williams, I presume," she said, snatching the Aviators from her face. Her eyes were green.

"That's me," Jonathon said, shaking her hand.

"My name is Harley Cash. I'm a former assassin for the Central Intelligence Agency," she said.

Jonathon's eyes widened at the revelation.

"Cold and I go way back," she continued. "He put this team together and twisted my arm into commanding it."

Jonathon clenched his jaw and scratched the back of his neck. He looked to Cold. "I thought you said I would be in charge."

Harley looked at Cold and cocked her head to the side. "I thought you explained all this," she said.

Cold held up a hand. "I did," he said quickly. "Jonathon, I guess I should've been more detailed with my explanation. You are in charge, just as I said…but the men report to Harley. Harley reports to you."

"Ah," Jonathon said, feeling the tension ease out of him. He liked that arrangement much better. "Well, Ms. Cash, I'm looking forward to working with you," he said.

"The feeling is mutual," she said as she returned the sunglasses to her face. "I just hope our work will be brief. The goal is obviously to get in and get out as quickly as possible."

"I wouldn't have it any other way," Jonathon replied. "I think we're going to get along just fine."

"Great," she said gleefully and then looked toward the plane. "Breakfast is waiting on board." She made a gesture with her hand and said, "After you, boss."

Jonathon smiled and climbed aboard.

CHAPTER 11

Almost 36 hours earlier...

What was seemingly minutes before the water began flowing in under the first story doors, Charlie, Hardcastle, Matt, and George managed to work swiftly and transported all five *Troodons* to their respective cells on the fifth floor without incident. Once they felt the animals were secure, the four of them played poker for what Charlie guessed had to have been at least an hour before Hardcastle decided to go downstairs and check to see where the water level was at. She knew immediately it must've been bad by the expression on his face when he returned.

"Water is creeping up the stairs," he said grimly. "I can't even get to the second floor."

"You've got to be kidding," Matt said in disbelief.

Charlie would not have been surprised if Glenn Hardcastle took the opportunity to take a swipe at Matt for not wanting to take his advice to move to higher ground, but it seemed the situation was dire enough that he would be unable to get any joy from doing so.

"I'm not kidding," he replied. He walked over to the kitchen sink and splashed water over his face. He was clearly suffering from extreme exhaustion.

"Should we move to a higher floor?" Charlie asked, trying not to sound panicked. Unfortunately, Hardcastle's tone and body language was doing little to keep her calm.

"No," Hardcastle replied. "At least not yet. I doubt that the water will get much higher than that. I'll check it again in another half an hour and then we'll know."

His assessment calmed her—at least a little. After all, he'd been right about the storm surge, surely he knew what he was talking about regarding its recession as well.

"I think the best thing any of us can do right now is to get some sleep," Matt said. He grabbed a coat that was hanging on a nearby coat rack, rolled it up into a makeshift pillow, and then promptly laid across the rug in front of the television to take a nap.

"Actually, that's probably a good idea," she said, yawning. "Why don't we take shifts until we all get a little bit of sleep."

Hardcastle nodded, agreeing with the suggestion. His eyelids were heavy, but he knew it would be up to him to take the first shift.

"Get some sleep," George Powell said.

Hardcastle glanced to his right and saw George sitting in an old wooden chair. He was leaning toward him with his elbows resting on his knees, hands clasped together. He looked tired, but it was obvious that George wasn't quite as tired as Glenn was.

"Are you sure?" Hardcastle asked.

George nodded. "I am sure," he replied. "I've been drinking coffee constantly while you all have bickered about what to do. I'm wide awake."

Hardcastle sighed. "Alright," he said with a smile. "You've convinced me. You take the first shift, I'll take the second."

He glanced at his watch.

"You need to check the stairwell in half an hour," he reminded George. "And wake me up in an hour and a half."

George nodded. "Get some sleep," he said. "I'll wake you up if something goes wrong."

Due to extreme exhaustion, Charlie quickly fell asleep once she collapsed onto the sofa. She'd already heard Matt snoring and the last thing she'd seen was Hardcastle settling in for a nap in the recliner on the opposite side of the room. Something about the thought of floodwater being beneath them, and dinosaurs being above them was quite unsettling as she drifted off to sleep.

***

Screaming.

The screaming was horrific, bloodcurdling even, and it was very obviously originating from George Powell.

"What the hell?" Matt muttered as he jerked awake.

Charlie rolled off the sofa. She'd been having a nightmare and at first thought the screaming had been in her dream. For a few moments, she thought she was still asleep. Once she realized she was indeed awake, the first thing she noticed was that the power was out.

Glenn Hardcastle seemed to have been on the very edge of consciousness as he jumped from the recliner and retrieved the rifle that had been leaning against the wall next to his chair. Fully awake and very sharp, he immediately sprang into action quickly, and with his rifle in hand, he stormed into the hallway just in time to see the *Troodons* ripping into George Powell's torso. George screamed in agony and clawed at the back of the vicious animal's head and neck as it tore into him. Though it was painfully obvious that George was a goner, fury compelled Hardcastle to fire a shot at the *Troodon* nearest him. The bullet tore through the animal's thigh and the report from the rifle was all it took to send the savage creatures scattering. Glenn could only look on as three of the dinosaurs—one of them now wounded—raced up the stairwell to the fourth floor while the other two ran down toward the second floor. It appeared that the water had receded quite a bit, but at a glance, it still appeared to be ankle deep. Hardcastle could easily hear the fleeing dinosaurs splashing through the water as they made their escape. He considered pursuing, but thought it would not be wise to do so without thinking it through first.

He momentarily returned his attention to George. The man was motionless and his abdomen had become a sickening hollow cavity. His mouth was frozen open in terror. The sight made him shiver and he wanted to get away from it. He willed himself to move back toward the recreation room. The *Troodons* would be back, he was sure of that.

"What is going on?" Matt asked as Hardcastle reappeared in the doorway.

Hardcastle momentarily ignored him as he quickly shut the door behind him. He looked around the room, glanced over at the couch, and then proceeded to move it in front of the door.

"He's dead, isn't he?" Charlie asked.

Glenn Hardcastle removed his hat, raked his fingers through his hair, and then leaned against the nearest wall. He was facing it, arms outstretched, palms supporting him.

"Is George dead?" Matt asked softly.

Hardcastle clenched his jaw and nodded his head slowly.

"Oh my God," Charlie said. Her eyes welled up and before she knew it, tears were streaming down her face. "Poor George...this can't be happening."

"Was it the *Troodons*?" Matt asked.

"Yeah, it was the *Troodons*," Hardcastle replied coldly. He suddenly stood up straight and marched up to Matt, grabbing him by the collar of this shirt. "Did you use the manual locks like I told you?"

Charlie looked on as the two men locked eyes with each other, their faces only inches apart. The just stared at each other for a long minute before Matt looked away.

"This isn't my fault," he mumbled.

Hardcastle immediately grabbed Matt's chin and forcefully turned his face back toward his.

"Did you use the manual locks?" he repeated through clenched teeth.

Matt took a deep breath and Charlie thought she saw his lip tremble. "No," he muttered. "I didn't because I told you it's not—"

Hardcastle cut him off by throwing a fist into his jaw. Matt immediately collapsed to the floor.

"Stop it!" Charlie screamed as she ran between them. She pushed Glenn backward. "This isn't going to help anything!"

Hardcastle scowled at her. "If that garbage there in the floor had listened to me, George Powell would be alive right now," he growled. "I should kill him right now."

Matt got on his hands and knees and then took a moment to rub his jaw before looking up to Hardcastle. There were tears in his eyes.

"I'm sorry," he said as he began to sob. "It's my fault that he's dead."

Charlie turned her attention from Hardcastle to Matt. "Get off the floor and shake it off! There is nothing you can do about it, and we need you now." Charlie again faced Hardcastle. "We need him!" she screamed. "Our chances are a lot better with him than without him!"

Hardcastle glared at her with an icy stare. "Our chances would've been much better with George here too," he said. He then looked to Matt and said, "Get up and stop with the crying," he grumbled. "We'll deal with your stupidity later."

Now comfortable that they were not going to kill each other, Charlie began to pace the room, her arms crossed. She was clearly deep in thought and seemed angry. "So what do we do now?" she asked, sounding determined.

"Until the water recedes some more, there isn't a whole lot we *can* do," Hardcastle said, sounding defeated. "I'm not thrilled about it any more than you are, but the only thing that makes sense right now is for us to stay put."

Charlie took a deep breath and leaned against the wall. She ran both hands over her blonde hair. "How long before Cold sends help?"

Hardcastle shrugged. "Probably already working on it," he replied. "Help could already be on the way for all we know." He marched to the kitchen counter and began fumbling around with the coffee pot when he suddenly remembered there was no power. Unable to contain his anger any longer, he threw the empty coffee pot against the wall. Shattered glass went in all directions.

Matt was still seated on the floor and Hardcastle's outburst made him jump abruptly. "Was that really necessary?" he yelled. His face was still slick from crying and he was clearly just as angry with the situation.

Hardcastle whirled a disgusted look in his direction. "No," he grumbled. "But it sure made me feel better."

Matt opened his mouth to respond but at that moment, the ground under their feet began to vibrate.

"Not again," Charlie complained as she grabbed a nearby chair for support.

The earth began to rumble with even more intensity than the first time. They could all feel the building shifting and swaying slightly all around them.

"This thing is going to collapse!" Matt yelled. "I told you it was dangerous to come up here!"

Hardcastle shot him a cold glare and Charlie could tell he would've loved nothing more than to pummel him. Unfortunately, however, for a moment it seemed that Matt was right. The building *did* feel as though it was about to collapse. Charlie looked on in total fear as the sheetrock on the walls and ceiling cracked apart. White dust rained from above her head and she could hear Matt jabbering away, though she couldn't understand what he was saying. Whatever it was, he spoke fast and his tone was laced with perhaps more fear than even she was experiencing.

And suddenly, just as quickly as it began, the rumbling and shaking stopped.

Glenn Hardcastle took a deep breath and removed his hat. He beat it against his pants leg in effort to remove the thin coating of sheetrock dust. Once he returned the hat to his head, he marched straight toward Matt. He was still seated on the floor and he was unable to hide the concern in his eyes as Hardcastle approached.

"Get away from me!" he yelled. "Don't come any closer!"

Hardcastle stopped within six feet of him and knelt to one knee. "Okay, you keep saying we need to get out of here," he began. "Well, you've got my attention. When this water recedes, I know where we can go but for us to do that, you and I have got to be on the same page."

Matt wiped sweat away from his brow with his shirt sleeve and exhaled slowly as he came to the realization that Hardcastle was not going to hurt him. "I'm listening," he muttered softly.

Hardcastle wiped his mouth with the palm of his hand and looked toward the exit, still barricaded by the couch. He thought he'd heard something.

"There is an underground bunker about a mile from here," he said, dismissing the phantom noise he'd heard. "If the three of us can get there, there isn't anything on this island that can get to us until the cavalry arrives."

Matt's eyes lit up. "So, if we can just get to a jeep—"

"Forget about the jeeps," Hardcastle interrupted. "Remember, most of the compound has been under over twenty feet of water...and it *still* isn't completely gone. I seriously doubt we'll be able to get any vehicle around here running. We'll have to do it on foot."

Charlie began laughing maniacally. "You're kidding, right?" she asked, trying to catch her breath.

Hardcastle chewed his lip as he looked over at her. "I'm afraid not," he said. "At the rate this water is receding, by tomorrow morning, it should be all but gone."

"Well, that's a great plan, Glenn," Matt grumbled, his words oozing sarcasm. "But what about—oh, I don't know…the dinosaurs?"

Hardcastle closed his eyes tightly and bit his lip to keep himself from saying something he'd regret. As much as he couldn't stand him right now, the fact still remained that he needed Matt's help.

"The safest time to try something like this is the early morning hours," he replied. "Most of the meat-eaters are settling in to sleep after a night of hunting."

"It's still dangerous," Charlie chimed in.

"It's suicide," Matt agreed.

Hardcastle crossed his arms and leaned against the side of the refrigerator. "It's the only chance I think we have," he replied. "We can only stay here so long before the *Troodons* figure out a way to get us. If you two have a better idea, I'd like to hear it."

"Actually, I do," Matt said after he pondered the suggestion for a moment.

Hardcastle raised his eyebrows and pushed his hat back. "Well, let's hear it, Doc," he said.

"I know the bunker you're talking about," he replied. "It's the closest one to the compound—maybe a couple of miles away."

"That's correct," Hardcastle said. "It's just under a mile and a half away."

"And it's fitted with an underground tunnel that connects it to the compound," he added.

Hardcastle sighed and shook his head. "I know all about that tunnel," he replied. "Eric had that thing built when he built the area that is now the ground floor of this building. And I hate to burst your bubble, but without power, the only way into that tunnel is from the bunker. The door is padlocked from the inside."

Charlie paced the floor. "And how exactly do you know that?" she asked, sounding quite annoyed.

"I know because I'm the one that installed the lock," Hardcastle answered.

Matt and Charlie stared at him, confused.

Hardcastle shoved his hands in his pockets and leaned harder on the refrigerator. "That tunnel is not structurally safe anymore. I started noticing stress cracks in several places about a year after it was built. Eric got a little too economical on it and didn't use the commercial grade concrete that is needed to support the weight of eight feet of soil," he explained. "There is a lock on this end of the tunnel too. It's no longer safe for anyone to go into it. And that was before the earthquakes started...I doubt it's even clear anymore."

"But *if* it is clear..." Charlie said.

"It's our ticket to safety," Matt finished.

"That's a mighty big *if*," Hardcastle cautioned.

Matt pondered the situation for a solid minute before suggesting, "What if we make our way through the tunnel from this end, and when we arrive at the door for the bunker, we somehow break the door down."

Suddenly, it was Hardcastle's turn for maniacal laughter. "You've got to be joking," he said. "That door is six inches of pure steel, and I didn't go cheap on the lock for it either."

"And it would be dangerous for us if we got stuck on the far end of a one-mile tunnel when an earthquake could start up again at any moment," Charlie added.

"Right," Hardcastle said, pointing at her.

"I think the argument could be made that it's equally dangerous for us to go trouncing through the jungle on foot to get into the bunker," Matt argued. "With the power out, how do we even know we can get into it?"

"I'd have thought by now you'd have finally accepted the fact that the power failure has caused all of the locks to release," Hardcastle sneered. "If you need a reminder, go look at all the blood in the hallway."

Matt looked away and said nothing. Charlie could feel the tension building again.

"Okay, what about this," she began. "Only one of us goes to the bunker. That person unlocks the door and then makes their way back through the tunnel toward the compound to retrieve the other two."

Hardcastle rubbed his chin as he pondered the idea. "That's still way more time for one person to be in that tunnel than I'm comfortable with," he said. "And let's say someone makes it and enters the tunnel only to find that halfway back it's collapsed and impassable?"

Charlie frowned. "I didn't think about that," she said.

"The radios," Matt said. "We've got the two-way radios."

Hardcastle perked up and opened one of the cabinet doors on the wall. After a minute of searching, he found what he was looking for.

"Right. Whoever the lucky person is that makes the trip to the bunker takes a two-way radio with them," he said as he turned the knobs on the devices to make sure they were working. "If they find the tunnel is not operational, they can radio the other two and they will have to pony up and make the trip through the jungle too."

Charlie smiled. "I think that's it...that's our plan," she said gleefully.

The three of them celebrated briefly when suddenly reality brought them crashing back down.

"So, who's going to be the lucky one to make the trip?" Matt asked. They all looked at each other for a long minute.

"We draw straws," Charlie suggested.

"I'll draw," Matt said, and there was a slight tremble in his voice.

"No one is drawing straws," Hardcastle said. "We all know that it's got to be me. You both knew it when we were drawing this crazy plan up...don't play dumb, it's insulting."

"No," Charlie replied firmly. "We draw straws. It's the only fair way to do this."

Hardcastle laughed. "Yeah, have you forgotten that there are five *Troodons* roaming around outside that door? Whoever is going may have to deal with them. You both know there is no one else trained to deal with this situation better than me."

Matt looked at Charlie. "He's right," he said, a little too quickly.

Charlie took a deep breath. It was getting hotter in the building by the minute and she could feel beads of sweat sliding downward between her shoulder blades. The anxiety she was feeling wasn't helping the matter either.

"Are you absolutely sure?" she asked.

Hardcastle nodded slowly. "And so are you," he added with a smile.

He turned away and began to rummage through the kitchen drawers. He plundered until he found the largest knife available. He ran his thumb over the blade gently. It was extremely sharp. It wasn't much, but it was a weapon.

"You think you can kill them with that?" Matt asked, pointing toward the knife.

"No," Hardcastle replied. "I think I can kill them with this," he said, pulling the gun from his waistband. "But when I run out of bullets, I'll need backup."

Charlie looked to the knife and back up into Hardcastle's eyes. "I don't know about this," she said, unable to contain her worry.

"It's the only option we've got," Hardcastle replied as he moved to the door. He paused and removed a ring of keys from his pocket. He picked through the keys until he found the one he was looking for, removed it, and handed it to Charlie. "That's the key you'll need to remove the padlock on this end," he said. "Whatever you do, don't lose it!"

"Don't worry," she replied, dropping the small gold key into her pocket.

Hardcastle paced the floor for a few minutes in thought, when suddenly an idea popped into his head. He manhandled the couch out of the way and slowly cracked the door open so that he could see into the hall. One direction looked clear, but he was unable to see the other way.

"Use the knife," Charlie suggested.

Hardcastle glanced back at her, at first unsure of what she meant. Suddenly, it hit him. He pulled the knife from his belt, slowly pushed it into the hallway, and then used it as a mirror to see if there was any danger waiting on him outside his field of vision. Satisfied the coast was clear, he began to exit the room.

"Push the couch back over the door," he called back to them.

"What are you doing?" Charlie asked. "You said the water below wouldn't be gone until in the morning!"

Hardcastle glanced over his shoulder at her. "Right," he said. "Which is why I'm taking the skywalk over to the Triangle Building. That building was constructed on higher ground. I'm hoping that there is some dry land on the other side of it—or at least that it'll be shallow enough for me to wade through it until I get to dry land. And besides, maybe the *Troodons* will follow me and leave this building too. Wish me luck."

"I'm still not sure about this," Charlie replied. Suddenly, it occurred to her that she should give him an extra warning about the large female *Troodon*...the one they called Mother, but it was too late.

Glenn Hardcastle was gone.

CHAPTER 12

As it turned out, breakfast basically consisted of a couple of McDonald's sausage biscuits. It was somewhat disappointing, but Jonathon was hungry enough he simply didn't care. Once he'd completed his second biscuit, he dabbed the grease away from his lips with a napkin and looked over at Cornelius Cold seated next to him.

"I'm still not clear on why you're coming along," he said. He had to raise his voice slightly so that he could be heard over the noisy plane engines.

Mr. Cold took a sip of orange juice through a straw. "I'm not going to be getting off the plane," he explained. "However, I would like to get a view of the damage done to the compound and the island in general. We'll have to start making preparations to make repairs."

Jonathon nodded and then took a drink from his own bottle of orange juice. Harley was seated in a seat in front of and facing him. She was munching on a second biscuit of her own and still wearing the mirrored Aviator sunglasses. It was impossible to tell what she was looking at.

"So, you've been working with Cold for a while now?" Jonathon asked her.

She nodded. "About ten years," she said. "The past two years we've worked together very closely all over the world."

Jonathon raised his eyebrows and looked over at Cold. "Is that right?" he said. "And just what exactly do you guys do all over the world?"

"If we told you that, we'd have to kill you," Harley replied with a wide smile.

Cold allowed a slight chuckle and leaned closer so that Jonathon could hear him. "I know you're aware of the operation Eric Gill was running off the island," he began. "After reviewing all the paperwork and files in his office, we figured out he'd sold seventeen dinosaurs to different black market buyers all over the world. Harley and I have worked closely to get them all back."

Jonathon felt his interest peak. He looked back to Harley. "So, you've got experience with these animals then?"

"If you consider 'experience' as moving a dinosaur from one cage to another, then yeah, I've got a lot of that," she replied, still smiling.

Jonathon nodded and peered out the window. He hadn't thought of it that way, but he supposed getting the animals and transporting them somewhere else was probably a fairly easy process.

"It's the people we have had to worry about," Cold said, as if reading his thoughts. "The people that we had to go and take these animals from spent a great deal of money for them and were not too happy about us taking them away."

"Any of them get violent about it?" Jonathon asked.

Harley's smile instantly disappeared. "Oh yes, a couple of them did…they lost their lives over it."

Jonathon felt himself involuntarily swallow hard. He knew that Harley said she'd been an assassin, but she didn't really look like the portrait of a trained killer. As he pondered that thought, the plane hit a bit of turbulence and it was enough to cause him to bang his head against the window.

Harley chuckled. "Do you like flying?" she asked.

Jonathon rubbed his head and glanced over at her. "I used to," he grumbled. "I think I'm starting to hate it though."

"Ha, well have you ever sky-dived?" she asked, and something about the way she said it reminded him of the excitement a small child gets when they learn to do something new.

He shook his head. "Nah, I'm fine with staying inside of the perfectly good airplane," he said with a smile.

Harley began to laugh and she looked over to Mr. Cold only to see him immediately look away in an effort to avoid eye contact. Suddenly, a very bad feeling began to come over Jonathon. He looked back to Harley with his eyes narrowed.

"Don't tell me we're going to jump out of this airplane today," he said very matter-of-factly.

Harley immediately stopped laughing and returned her sunglasses to her face. "Okay, I won't tell you anything," she replied. "I'll just drag your ass out with me."

She then got up from her seat and made her way toward the cockpit. Jonathon felt his anxiety level begin to rise significantly. He looked over to the seats on the opposite side of the plane and saw Victor looking at him, a wide smile on his face. Cliff was looking at him too, although his expression was slightly more sympathetic. Hank Bailey was asleep and seemed to be oblivious to the rest of the world. Jonathon could see that his mouth was agape and he was drooling. Mr. Cold was still looking away.

"Look at me," Jonathon said to him through clenched teeth.

Cold slowly turned his head forward, but he stopped short of looking at him. "I was afraid if I told you that you would refuse to come along," he said.

"Well, you would've been correct," Jonathon snapped. "Why can't we just land on the airstrip?"

"Think about it, Jonathon," Cold replied, finally looking at him. He seemed annoyed by the question. "A category five hurricane just pummeled the island. I assure you the airstrip is in no condition for us to safely land."

"I'm not jumping out of this airplane," Jonathon said adamantly. He was furious and made no attempt to hide it.

Harley Cash returned from the cockpit with a harness in her hand. "You *are* going to jump out of this airplane," she said, leaning toward Jonathon. "But you're not doing it alone. You'll tandem with me."

She held out the harness to him. He looked at it and felt a wave of nausea come over him. "You're sure that thing will hold me?" he asked.

"I guarantee that it will," she replied. "Trust me, I've done this countless times. You will be fine."

Jonathon stared at it a few seconds longer before finally taking the harness.

Harley smiled. "Put it on, and let me know when you've got it on so I can look you over. We're jumping in five minutes."

Jonathon nodded, unable to speak. He wasn't sure if it was due to excitement or sheer fear. He then looked around and noticed Cliff and Victor were putting on their parachutes. Mr. Cold had gotten up and was leaning over Hank's seat, whispering something into his ear—he was apparently awake now. Jonathon wondered what they could be speaking about in such secrecy but his mind was too occupied with thoughts of freefalling to his death to be overly concerned about it.

Harley had just finished putting on her own parachute when she returned to check on Jonathon's progress.

"How high are we right now?" he asked as she handed him a pair of goggles.

She smiled widely. "I'm not saying anything to contribute to your distress," she said as she pulled her own goggles over her face. She looked around and motioned for the rest of the team to draw closer. Once the other men had huddled around her, she said, "Okay, Jonathon and I will go first, followed by Hank, Cliff, and finally Victor. We all meet at the rendezvous point as soon as possible. Remember that time is of the essence. The longer we have to wait on everyone to arrive, the more vulnerable we become."

"We got it, Cash," Hank said as he shoved a handgun into a holster around his thigh. "Let's get on with this."

Harley glared at him for a fraction of a second, but it was long enough for Jonathon to catch it. There was a hint of annoyance in her eyes. "Visibility is going to be bad until we get through the thick mist that envelopes the island," she continued. "That makes hitting our mark a little challenging. Once you're through the mist, there will be approximately 1200 more feet to go before we reach the ground. Obviously, there is no way to predict what could be waiting on you when you're through."

Jonathon swallowed hard as he thought about the hungry tyrannosaurs he'd encountered on the island in his prior visits. The worst-case scenarios he could think of were plentiful and he suddenly found himself trying to remember how Mr. Cold had talked him into returning to the island again. With great reluctance, he removed his fedora and shoved it into his duffel bag. Losing it would undoubtedly make this trip worse than it already was.

"Any questions?" Harley asked. All of the men shook their heads in unison.

"We will do a low pass to check on you before we leave the area," Cold said.

Harley looked at him, somewhat surprised. "Are you sure that's a good idea?" she asked. "I can radio you if there is a problem."

Cold waved her off. "I want to be sure that you all are alright while we're still nearby and can offer assistance if needed," he said. "One quick pass below the mist and we will get out of here."

"Alright," Harley replied. "But make sure you circle for about ten minutes to give us time to get out of the way. I'd hate for you to come through the mist only to immediately get tangled up in someone's parachute."

Cold gave her a thumbs up and then looked to the rest of the team. "Good luck to all of you," he said. "Find our folks and get them to safety." He then took a seat and fastened his seat belt.

Harley looked to Victor and gave him a slight nod. He responded by taking a position next to the side door and then promptly worked the latch until it opened. A gust of wind tore through the interior fuselage of the plane and with it, Jonathon's anxiety level increased significantly. Harley moved behind him and began tugging on the harness to make sure it was tight and ready for her to connect. When satisfied, she leaned over and said, "Well, this is it, are you ready?"

"You know I'm not," Jonathon replied as he glanced toward the door.

She laughed. "I thought you'd say something like that," she replied. "Nevertheless, we are going now. Just relax and try to enjoy it."

Before Jonathon was even able to contemplate the matter further, Harley had managed to steer him toward the door. The two of them stood there for what seemed like an eternity and it gave Jonathon plenty of time to survey to earth below him. For the most part, all he could see was blue water, but after a few moments, he noticed a familiar splotch of white to break up the monotony. It appeared to be a cloud hovering on top of the water, but he knew full well that it was the island shrouded in mist that he'd become all too acquainted with. He looked over his shoulder to Harley but she didn't look at him. Her concentration was set directly on the misty island below. She leaned forward multiple times to get a look at the ground and then suddenly, without a word, she firmly shoved him out of the airplane. Suddenly, the world as he once knew it was spinning.

He didn't know if he was physically spinning, but between the nausea and overwhelming rush of adrenaline, it was hard for him to tell. The wind rushing past made it impossible to hear anything or talk to Harley. He closed his eyes for a few seconds, but the curiosity of the experience was too overwhelming. Slowly, he cracked his eyes open and decided to do as Harley had instructed, relax and try to enjoy it. The freefall didn't last as long as he thought it would, but it was plenty of time for them to close in considerably on the misty ceiling over the island. Then, with seemingly no warning at all, the chute deployed and their acceleration was slowed dramatically.

Jonathon sighed with relief. "Well, that wasn't so bad," he said, trying to get his heart rate back to a reasonable pace.

"Isn't it fun?" Harley asked while stifling laughter. "You should try it sometime over the mainland, it's much more beautiful. This is just plain boring," she added, exasperated.

Jonathon surveyed the environment below him and immediately understood what she meant. Still, as far as the eye could see there was only water—and then there was the island. As they descended closer, for the first time ever, Jonathon was able to get a good grasp regarding the island's size. It was far bigger than he initially thought, and as much as he'd trekked across it, it suddenly became obvious to him that there was a lot of that island he'd never seen. There was no telling how many additional species of dinosaurs existed there that he hadn't even encountered yet. The shape of the island roughly resembled that of an elephant, and although he was still unable to see the ground, Jonathon could tell that the mist seemed to cling tightly to the outline of the island.

"How thick do you think it'll be?" Harley asked him just as they began to penetrate the white fog.

Jonathon shook his head. "Up here, I have no idea," he replied. "I know that when I've gone through it on the water, it was probably close to a quarter of a mile.

"Wow," she said, surprised. "That's pretty thick."

Seconds later, they were fully immersed in the dense mist. Jonathon could feel the moisture beading up on his face and suddenly his visibility turned to zero.

"We're completely blind," Harley whispered, and he could hear the unmistakable hint of uncertainty in her voice. She was slightly scared, unable to hide it.

"It's always thick like this…it won't last too long," Jonathon said, trying his best to reassure her.

The moisture in the dense air was so thick, the clothes both of them were wearing was quickly becoming soaking wet. Harley felt the weight of the water on her shirt and hated the clinging sensation…it made her feel claustrophobic, a phobia she'd battled since childhood.

"Jonathon, do you have any phobias?" she asked suddenly.

Jonathon chuckled nervously. "Yeah, heights," he replied.

"I don't buy that," she answered. "If you were truly afraid of heights, you'd have passed out by now."

"Well, we're not on the ground yet," he quipped. "I'm probably in shock."

"I'm proud of how you handled it," Harley said, obviously trying her best to encourage him. She paused, then said, "I suffer from claustrophobia."

"Yeah?"

"Yeah," she replied. "And this dense fog is making it rear its ugly head."

"Well, try not to think about it," Jonathon said. "Trust me, what you're experiencing right now will pale in comparison to some of what you'll see once we're on the ground."

At that moment, there was a shrill, piercing shriek from somewhere behind them hidden away beyond the fog.

"What was that?" Harley said quickly, looking around her shoulder. It was impossible to see anything. The loud shrill happened again, this time sounding closer.

"Harley, I think I spoke prematurely when I said the real worry begins once we're on the ground," he stammered, looking in all directions. "Is there a way to move a little faster?"

"Aside from cutting the chute loose, no," she replied, sounding a bit panicked. "What is it?"

"Sounds like some kind of pterosaur," Jonathon answered.

"Have you ever dealt with them before?" she asked.

Jonathon thought back to his first trip to the island, now nearly ten years later. "Yeah," he said, trying to keep his voice steady. "We're in a lot of danger right now."

Harley shivered. "That's not what I wanted to hear." There was another shriek, quieter this time, yet there was still no doubt that the pterosaur was even closer.

"What do we do?" Harley asked, now terrified.

"There's nothing we can do but be ready," Jonathon replied, sounding defeated. He tried to reach for the knife on his belt, but his harness was making it difficult. "Do you have any weapons?" he asked, trying to look back at Harley.

She shook her head. "Yeah, I've got plenty of firepower in my bag, but that's not doing us any good, is it?"

Jonathon was situated in a slightly lower position than Harley and he had a better reach for the bag that dangled from her waist. "I'm going to try and get into it," he said, and he immediately began fumbling for the zipper.

At that moment, the large pterosaur that had been hunting them suddenly swooped violently into the parachute. The large animal released its shrill call and Jonathon then realized his attempt to get his hands on some sort of a weapon was too late. He heard Harley scream and then became aware he was screaming as well. He looked up just in time to see the pterosaur tearing through the fabric, thus making their parachute useless. Suddenly, it became quite apparent that the pace of their descent increased significantly. The pterosaur had become entangled in the parachute and Jonathon could see the beast's large talons crashing down over him. It was the last thing he saw before he lost consciousness.

CHAPTER 13

Glenn Hardcastle padded across the tile flooring as quietly as he possibly could. The handgun he was carrying comforted him, but it wasn't nearly enough to stop most of the dinosaurs on the island. He wondered how useful it would be against the *Troodons*. The animals were extremely intelligent, and since he'd already shot one of them, he hoped it would be enough to keep them away. If he could just make it to the Triangle Building, he believed he'd have a brief respite before the real danger began. That was assuming of course that no dinosaurs had found a way in.

As he turned the corner that would lead him to the skyway, he stopped abruptly at the sight before him. The double doors that led to the skywalk were torn loose from their hinges. Clearly, something had broken through them.

"Well, isn't this just great," Hardcastle muttered under his breath. "So much for the Triangle Building being free and clear."

He gripped the gun tightly and moved slowly past the mangled doors. The afternoon light shone through the row of full view windows that covered the expanse of both sides of the skywalk. As he moved onto the walkway, he then noticed that the doors on the opposite end were torn open as well. The *Troodons* had apparently made their way into the Triangle Building. Whether or not they were still in there was another matter he'd have to confront in the very near future. He continued to walk lightly across the carpeted floor, still doing his best to make as little noise as possible. As he reached the midway point of the skywalk, he caught movement outside from the corner of his eye. He turned to peer through the window just in time to see the *Spinosaurus* lumbering toward the rear of the office building. The vicious beast had apparently finally gained entrance into the compound. It was undoubtedly heading back toward the *Troodon* paddock where it had shown great interest only a couple of days before. Hardcastle froze and crouched down low in what he knew was a futile attempt to remain unseen. The reality was that if the massive dinosaur turned around, there would be nothing hiding him from plain view. Fortunately, the *Spinosaurus's* attention seemed to be on something behind the building and seconds later, it was out of sight.

Hardcastle exhaled a sigh of relief and wiped the sweat away from his brow. Slowly, he regained his footing and just as he took his first step forward, he noticed a fearsome sight watching him from just beyond the mangled doors that led into the Triangle Building. It was a *Troodon* and it was standing deadly still, just watching him. Hardcastle immediately recognized it as one of the five that had escaped from the fifth floor. He took a step back and the animal cocked its head to the side as it watched him.

"Easy," he whispered, holding up a hand. He took another step back.

The *Troodon* took two steps forward and hissed at him.

"I hear you, I'm leaving now," Hardcastle grumbled. He moved his finger to the trigger of the gun he was holding and took another step backward.

This time, much to his dismay, the *Troodon* opened its jaws and barked its strange guttural call that he'd become too accustomed to. He knew from experience that the animal was calling for help and soon there would be more *Troodons* to contend with. He picked up his pace and backed away more quickly. As he did so, he kept the gun pointed at the *Troodon*. Strangely, the animal remained just inside the doorway of the Triangle Building. Just as Hardcastle had almost made his way back into the office building, he heard a sound that made his heart drop. He whipped his head around and discovered that two more *Troodons* had snuck up behind him. One of them was injured, bleeding from one of its legs. The other larger one was the leader...the one called Mother. She eyed him coldly.

He turned his gun toward the new arrivals and, as he expected, the dinosaurs remembered what the weapon was capable of doing to them. Particularly, the injured dinosaur, the one that had been shot, wailed with fury at the sight of the gun.

"Yeah, you remember what this does, don't you?" Hardcastle said, doing his best to remain calm. He quickly glanced back toward the other end of the skywalk and could see that the other *Troodon* was still standing there, just watching.

What is he waiting on? he wondered.

Suddenly, Mother began barking furiously. The sounds were eerie and sounded very much like she was speaking in an unknown language. Whatever it was that she'd "said," it wasn't good because the other two *Troodons* immediately began moving toward him. Hardcastle moved back toward the center of the skywalk and waved the gun from one *Troodon* and back to the other, unsure which direction he should try and blast his way through. He had little time to contemplate the decision and just as he'd about decided to open fire in the direction of the *Troodon* that had come from the Triangle Building, something very unexpected happened.

The *Spinosaurus* that had only moments before disappeared behind the office building was back, having apparently heard the barking *Troodons*. The massive dinosaur announced its presence with a deafening roar, and before Hardcastle or the *Troodons* had an opportunity to react, the animal crashed its head into the large glass windows. Hardcastle rolled out of the way just in time as the *Spinosaurus's* jaws snapped viciously at him. The *Troodons*, seemingly seeing the situation as an opportunity, immediately darted toward the *Spinosaurus's* vulnerable head. In unison, the three smaller dinosaurs began clawing, biting, and ripping at the larger dinosaur's flesh. Hardcastle closed his eyes tightly as the *Spinosaurus* roared loudly again, though he couldn't tell if it was due to the animal being in pain, or if it was just pure rage. Whatever the reason, the dinosaur immediately tried to pull its head away from the danger, but suddenly came to the realization that it had become stuck.

Hardcastle quickly got on his feet and decided the moment was perfect for him to make his escape. As he took off running, he felt the skywalk began to twist and vibrate under his feet. When he was mere feet away from the entrance to the Triangle Building, the skyway was suddenly jolted violently enough to knock him off his feet. He glanced over his shoulder and saw that the *Spinosaurus* was thrashing its head from side to side in a desperate attempt to free itself. The *Troodons* had already done significant damage to the animal's head and it became very apparent to Hardcastle that the dinosaur had already lost an eye.

The reptilian skin covering the *Spinosaurus's* head was ripped and torn substantially from the attack it was being forced to endure. Hardcastle tried to regain his footing, but before he could do so, he heard the unmistakable sound of bending metal followed by the wailing cries of one of the *Troodons*. He looked again just in time to see one of the *Troodons*—the one he'd shot—as it was being crushed in the *Spinosaurus's* jaws. The massive dinosaur had finally wrenched itself free of the window, but in doing so, the structural integrity of the skywalk had become compromised and it began to collapse. Suddenly, the skywalk broke apart in the middle and—with no support—both sides swung downward. Fortunately, the ends attached to the buildings were fastened well and Hardcastle was pleased to see that, though the structure bent significantly, it still held. The *Troodons* on the opposite end of the skywalk managed to scramble away back into the office building.

Unfortunately, gravity was not on his side, and he suddenly felt himself sliding downward toward the open end of the skywalk. If that wasn't bad enough, he also came to the realization that the *Spinosaurus* had spotted him with its remaining good eye. The vicious beast forced its long snout through the open end of the broken skywalk and began snapping furiously at Hardcastle. He'd managed to grab one of the aluminum grids over the window with his free hand. It kept him from sliding downward into the *Spinosaurus's* jaws, but it did nothing to aid him in an escape. The fact of the matter was, he was currently stuck and moving upward wasn't going to be possible until the *Spinosaurus* left him alone. He found himself longing to have the sonic weapon that had worked so well on the creature the last time he encountered it.

As he clung tightly to the window grid, his mind drifted back to the last time he'd seen Jonathon Williams. His current situation felt eerily similar, except this time it was he was that was on the verge of being eaten alive, not Jonathon. As his arm began to ache, he looked down at the gun still tightly in his grasp. He really didn't want to empty the magazine, but in his current predicament, he didn't really see another option. With reluctance, he pointed the barrel toward the angry *Spinosaurus* and waited for the right moment. The dinosaur kept snapping its jaws quickly and it stubbornly refused to give Hardcastle the look that he was wanting. Now angry, Hardcastle decided to take matters into his own hands. He pulled the trigger and promptly fired a shot into the fleshy part of the *Spinosaurus's* nose. The animal opened its maw and released a deafening roar. With the animal's mouth now wide open, Hardcastle began pulling the trigger repeatedly, unleashing a barrage of small caliber firepower into the throat of the furious dinosaur. He could feel the heat that expelled from the dinosaur's large lungs, and the putrid smell that came with it instantly made him nauseous. The scent of the *Spinosaurus's* breath was a combination of death and decay on a level that he'd never experienced.

At first, the bullets seemed to do nothing but make the dinosaur angrier than it already was. Just as Hardcastle was beginning to contemplate what his next course of action should be, the *Spinosaurus* slowly began to pull its head out of the skywalk. He then watched as the wounded animal clumsily lumbered out of the compound and into the jungle foliage, leaving a massive wake in the water behind it as it walked. It was clearly affected by the bullets he'd just dispensed into its throat and Hardcastle wondered if it was retreating to die. There was a time he'd have felt a bit of remorse about that possibility. Today, however, he hoped he'd be so lucky.

Hardcastle considered tossing the firearm into the floodwaters below. Since the magazine was now empty, and he didn't know where he'd get more ammunition, he couldn't think of a good reason to hang onto it. However, if he *did* happen to come across some ammo, he'd feel mighty silly if he disposed of it. He decided to stuff it in the back of his waistband and go to work on getting climbing out of the skywalk. Hardcastle looked upward and decided his best course of action would be to use the window grids to pull himself up with one hand, while digging his other hand into the carpet. Fortunately, the boots he was wearing had a lot of tread so he felt good about getting some help from his feet. With great care, he reached up for the grid on the next window while simultaneously digging the toe of his boot into the carpet and pushing upward. The plan seemed to work perfectly until Hardcastle reached the last window. As soon as he grabbed the grid, it broke free and he tumbled end over end into the murky water below.

CHAPTER 14

"Wake up!" Harley shouted.

She slapped Jonathon hard across the face and he immediately sat straight up. For a few moments, he felt the most disoriented feeling he'd ever experienced in his entire life. He looked around in all directions and quickly realized he was on a beach. At first, he considered the strong possibility that he was dreaming, but then he noticed the mist surrounding the island and reality came crashing back.

"Are you alright?" Harley asked. Her mirrored sunglasses were long gone and there was blood smeared across her face. It was even in her hair.

"I'm fine," Jonathon replied, but as he spoke, he felt a burning sensation originating from his cheek. He reached up and felt a deep gash in his face. When he looked at his fingers, they were covered in blood. "Oh my God," he muttered with a gasp. Suddenly, he remembered the pterosaur.

"It looks bad," Harley said. She was squinting and looking closely at the wound. "It's definitely going to need stitches. Your face will never look the same," she said with a mischievous smirk.

As bad as his face felt, he was glad to see Harley smirking. It told him that she didn't think his injury was anything to be *too* concerned about for the time being.

"What happened to the pterosaur?" Jonathon asked. "And how in the world are we not dead? The last thing I remember was our chute getting torn apart and we were freefalling again."

Harley was now standing over him. She was redoing her ponytail as her hair had become quite disheveled from the ordeal they'd just endured.

"Well," she began. "For starters, that dino-bird that attacked us became tangled up in the chute and it never got free. It's currently somewhere out there," she said, gesturing toward the sea. "We landed just in time for me to see it sink beneath the waves. It'll probably wash up here later."

Jonathon looked out to the rolling waves and squinted his eyes. He scanned the waters but saw no sign of a dead pterosaur or a parachute.

"Okay, that makes sense," he said, returning his attention to her. "Now, how are we not joining that thing in the afterlife right now?"

Harley smiled, seemingly taking it as a good sign that Jonathon still had a sense of humor. "Well, *that thing* fell on top of us, its claws cut into my scalp, but it got your face a lot worse. You took a hard-enough hit that I guess it knocked you unconscious. It was about that time that I went for the reserve chute and when it deployed, we immediately decelerated, but the bird kept on falling." She slapped her hands together to illustrate the pterosaur's impact with the water.

"Wow," he responded, trying to picture it all in his mind's eye. "In that case, I'm glad I got knocked out. Where are the others?"

Harley jerked the radio off her belt. "I was just about to check on that," she said, holding the gadget up to her mouth. "Guys, we had a little complication that put us off target, but we are safe on the ground. I need everyone to check in right now, over."

After a brief silence, the radio crackled to life. "This is Victor, I've got Cliff with me and we're on target, over..."

Harley smiled and seemed happy to hear his voice. "Keep your current position, we will make our way to you. Hank, you out there? Over..."

The radio remained silent, and at that moment, they could hear the distant rumbling of the prop plane they'd just jumped out of. Cold was apparently making his flyby to check to see if they were all on target. She and Jonathon scanned the sky in all directions for a visual of the plane but finally decided that the trees must have been blocking their view from their current position. Harley was just about to try and radio Hank again when suddenly the pitch of the plane's engines changed dramatically. Though they were still unable to see it, the plane was almost certainly in trouble.

"Victor, what's going on with the plane?" Harley asked, the pitch of her voice rising with excitement.

"They've hit something!" Victor screamed in reply. "Or something hit it! They're going down! They're crashing!"

Jonathon had not known Victor for very long, but he could tell that whatever he was seeing had made him very distraught. He and Harley stood on the beach, still staring at the blank sky. The emotions they felt were a combination of fear and helplessness. They could only stand and listen as the plane plummeted to the earth. Seconds later, there was a loud crash followed shortly by a plume of black smoke.

"We've got to get to them!" Harley shouted, and she immediately began running.

"Wait!" Jonathon said, grabbing her arm.

She whirled around and looked at him, wild-eyed. "Wait for *what*?" she asked, dumbfounded. "They're in trouble…they could be seriously injured!"

"Or they could be dead!" Jonathon shouted back.

The statement seemed to strike Harley like a slap to the face. "You don't know that," she replied, disgusted. "If there is any chance of saving them, we've got to move…now!"

Jonathon held his hands up in an apologetic manner. "Look, it's not that I don't *want* to go rushing over there and help them," he explained. "But you've got to remember that there are some pretty mean monsters on this island that will immediately start moving toward that crash site." He took his hand and cupped it over his eyes as he gazed at the horizon over the tree line. "Based on where that smoke is billowing, I'm pretty sure that they crashed somewhere near the tyrannosaur's territory. There are several and we won't stand a chance against them!"

Harley clenched her jaw and gritted her teeth. Jonathon could see that she was beginning to see his point, but she was reluctant to admit it.

"So, you're suggesting we just let them die?" she asked bitterly.

"At the compound, there are armored jeeps that we can use to try and take a shot at rescuing them—if they are indeed alive," he said. "Not to mention, you've got two other men over there that are armed and can help with the effort—and trust me, we'll need all the help we can get."

Harley pursed her lips and thought for a moment. Finally, she spoke into the radio. "Victor, do you have a visual on the crash site?"

Static…then, "No, I see thick smoke but I can't see anything," he replied. "Harley, if they are still in that plane, they're cooked."

Harley winced at his choice of words. "Well, if they're not in the plane, they're extremely vulnerable," she said. "Do you have a visual on the compound?"

"Yes," he replied. "There is still quite a bit of flood water here, but based on the waterline I'm seeing on the nearby trees, it's receding very fast."

Harley looked at Jonathon as she spoke to Victor again. "Do you see any vehicles on the property? Were they submerged in water?"

"Oh, hell yeah," he answered. "I see a couple of armored trucks but there is no doubt they were underwater twenty-four hours ago."

Harley dropped the radio from her mouth and sighed. "So there goes your armored rescue idea," she said, glancing at Jonathon.

He took a deep breath and rubbed at the stubble on his chin. "Alright," he said, sounding defeated. "So, let's get to the compound and we'll formulate a plan there. Don't forget the reason we're here. We need to check and see if there are survivors in the compound."

"And I've got a man missing," Harley added. "Hank is out there somewhere and we've got to find him too."

She brought the radio up to her mouth again. "Victor, since you and Cliff are already there, why don't you go ahead and check the compound for survivors. We will be there shortly."

"10-4," Victor replied. "Watch out for the nasty dinos...we've spotted a couple of little ones," he added. "I think they're harmless though."

Jonathon motioned for Harley to toss him the radio. He caught it, then said. "Hey, Victor, it's Jonathon; don't engage any dinosaurs you see unless you're attacked," he warned. "Even the smaller ones that do not look dangerous could potentially attack you if they feel threatened. There are some smaller carnivores that won't hesitate to make a meal out of you."

There was a brief pause, and then, "Well thanks, Doctor...I didn't know you cared," he replied. "We'll refrain from petting the animals."

Jonathon tossed the radio back. Harley immediately held it to her mouth and said, "Hank, if you're out there and you can hear me, try and make it to the compound if you can."

She dropped the radio by her side and waited for a long moment in hopes that she'd get some sort of reply.

"Alright, let's get moving," Jonathon said finally, trying to keep her focused. He retrieved his hat from his bag and pulled it onto his head. "I think the safest thing for us to do is to stick to the beach until we no longer have a choice but to cut across through the jungle."

Harley put the strap of her assault rifle over her shoulder and nodded. "Alright," she said. "As Cold said, you are in charge."

Jonathon stared at her for a moment as she held the large assault rifle in a manner that suggested it was as natural to her as riding a bike. Her bare arms and shoulders were glistening from sweat and blood, but he could still see the muscle tone. Now that they were on the ground and things had gone wrong, he could clearly see that she was in her element. It comforted him. He knew the truth and refused to kid himself on the matter. If things got bad, Harley Cash would be the one in charge, and he was just fine with that.

***

Hank Bailey listened to Harley's pleas for him to answer, but despite her worried tone, he felt no remorse when he refused to answer. He'd landed quite safely, but she—and the others—did not need to know that. This was all part of the plan, and the sooner that they accepted he

93

was dead, the better. Hank had managed to land in the valley, and as soon as his feet hit the ground, his real mission began. He pulled the portable GPS unit from his duffel bag and took note of the distance from his present location to the cave. Had things gone perfectly, he'd have landed much closer. Unfortunately, however, as he descended he noticed a large herd of *Styracosaurus* lumbering toward the western side of the valley. This was one of the dinosaurs he'd been warned about. He knew that, although they were herbivores, the gentle giants could become quite vicious if they felt threatened. He took a brief moment to watch them with great amazement. The animal reminded him a lot of a *Triceratops*, but the frill that rose from the back of its head appeared to be much larger, mostly thanks to the spiked horns that jutted upward like a majestic crown. The dinosaur was a deep gray, the color of stone, and he imagined the creature was probably as solid as stone too.

With his rifle at the ready, Hank began trekking north toward the nearby jungle. He felt it was best—and safest—to move along the wood line and make use of the shadows to conceal his presence. He moved swiftly, and just as he'd reached the jungle canopy, he heard the sound of Cold's distressed plane as it fell out of the sky. Hank could only stare, with his mouth gaped open, as the plane streaked by and slammed hard into the valley on the opposite side from where he was situated. Soil shot into the air and it looked as if an asteroid had just crashed into the island. Seconds later, smoke began, followed by fire.

Hank sighed and bit his lip. He felt his pulse begin to race as suddenly he began to feel the full weight of his current predicament. The only person—to his knowledge—that knew of the actual reason he was on the island, was Mr. Cold. Now, for all he knew, Cold was dead. Hank slapped a mosquito off the back of his neck and quickly decided that he had a new mission. If Cold was alive, he had to get to him—and fast.

CHAPTER 15

It had been a large pterosaur that had taken them down. Actually, it had been more than one, but things had happened so fast, Cold would never know exactly how many. He'd been staring out the window, watching intently for confirmation that his team had landed at their intended target. Suddenly, he heard the pilot scream, and he looked ahead just in time to see a swarm of pterosaurs flying in their path. There was no time to react.

Cold had never been involved in a plane crash before, and though he was a man known for his lack of fear, for the first time in a long time, he felt nothing but. He held onto the armrest with so much intensity that he would not have been surprised if he would have broken it. The cabin was flooded with the sickening sound of alarms and the wail of the screaming prop engines. Cold closed his eyes as he felt the plane begin to roll over as it made its terrifying quick descent. He heard the pilot call out to God and then there was a violent crash. Cold felt all of the wind leave his body and then the world went silent and dark.

He awoke gasping, but the world was still dark. It didn't take long for Cold to realize that the world was still dark because the fuselage had quickly filled with black smoke. He felt as if there was a great weight on his chest and he tried with extreme desperation to catch his breath. Of course, with the atmosphere around him comprised of nothing but smoke, it quickly occurred to him that even if he *could* catch a breath, he'd still be in dire trouble. Cold was unsure of how long he'd been unconscious. Ironically, the sheer fact that he'd been unable to get a breath was probably a contributing factor to his still being alive.

With great urgency, he clawed and ripped at his seat restraint until he was free. On his hands and knees—and still involuntarily gasping for air—Cold crawled and rolled his way in the direction of the only hint of light he'd managed to see. Fortunately, the fuselage had been nearly ripped in two and Cold managed to find an opening large enough for him to clamber out. Once outside, he crawled and dragged himself through the muddy earth. He could feel the heat intensifying behind him as the plane became engulfed in flames. Again, he tried with utter desperation to take a gulp of fresh air and finally—mercifully—his lungs got the relief they needed. As he lay on his back, for the first time, he began to relax. It seemed he was going to cheat death, and though he knew there were dangerous dinosaurs all around him, he knew the others would come for him.

Cold slowly pulled himself off his back and onto his knees. He quickly removed his sport coat and tossed it aside. It was then that he noticed that one of his ordinarily white shirt sleeves had turned red. His adrenaline had undoubtedly temporarily shielded him from the pain that he immediately began to experience when he noticed the jagged piece of metal protruding from his forearm. He grimaced as he pulled the sleeve back and then went to work on removing the foreign object from his flesh. One tug forced him to scream and as he spat a curse word in disgust, he quickly reminded himself that he needed to keep quiet. The piece of metal did not budge, and though he was wounded, his current predicament would get far worse if a nasty carnivore heard him wailing in pain.

There was a moan to his right and Cold instantly noticed the pilot lying on his back, roughly thirty yards in front of the wreckage. There was a large puddle of water near him and Cold considered how fortunate the man was to not have landed there as he could've easily drowned.

Had he somehow been thrown from the plane? he wondered.

Cold got on his feet and jogged over to the injured pilot. Once by his side, he again dropped to his knees and scanned over his body for injuries. The man had a great deal of blood coming from somewhere at the back of his head. Cold knew head injuries always produced a great deal of blood and were often not as bad as they looked. He assumed the man at the very least had a concussion, but of course, the possibility of a fractured skull was real as well. The pilot was wearing a short-sleeved polo shirt and the next thing Cold noticed was that his wrist was severely swollen.

Probably broken, he thought.

As his eyes moved further down the pilot's body, he came across the worst injury of all. The man was suffering from a compound fracture so severe that his leg was nearly completely severed. There was no doubt that his tibia and fibula were both completely broken as both were visible. The only thing that seemed to be holding his leg together at all was a bit of skin and muscle. Cold winced as he looked over the gruesome injury but made sure his voice remained calm.

"You're going to be fine," Cold told him softly, although he himself didn't believe it. "Just remain calm…help is on the way."

Mr. Cold looked around as he spoke in hopes that he would indeed see a familiar face approaching. When he saw none, again his thoughts returned to the dinosaur inhabitants of the island. The fire and smoke would almost certainly draw unwanted attention from the larger animals.

As he looked back toward the pilot, he experienced a revelation that made a chill run up his spine. The large puddle that the pilot had narrowly avoided landing in was actually a large three-toed print filled with water.

Tyrannosaur, he thought.

This was obviously an unwelcome sight but it gave him a clear indication of where he was on the island. Tyrannosaurs were very territorial and the ones that inhabited the island had always claimed the west-central portion of land. Clearly, he could not stay here…but leaving the pilot was not an option either. He briefly considered trying to throw the man over his shoulder and carry him away, but the burning pain in his right forearm reminded him that he was injured as well. There were guns in the plane, but as he peered over at the blazing inferno he'd just escaped, he knew he would remain unarmed. Suddenly, a deep, gruff voice called out to him from behind.

"Boss, are you alright?" Hank asked, his eyes wide with amazement. He peered at the fire-engulfed plane and then back to Mr. Cold.

Cold for his part felt an immediate sensation of relief wash over him.

"Hank," he said, his voice raspy. "Am I ever glad to see you. We can't stay here, there are—"

His words were cut off as an angry roar erupted from somewhere behind the dense foliage of the jungle. The sound was loud enough to make the injured pilot's eyes open wide.

"What was that?" he asked, panicked. He coughed and Cold noticed blood appearing at the corners of his mouth. The man then tried to sit up but quickly realized his body would not be able to cooperate.

"Stay still," Cold ordered him, his eyes scanning the jungle for any signs of movement. He saw nothing, but did feel a vibration under his knees.

"Did you feel that?" Hank asked, pointing his gun toward the jungle vegetation.

"I did," Cold replied, and as he felt it again, he noticed the water in the large puddle next to him ripple in response.

"We've got to move," Hank said, sounding amazingly calm. "Obviously, that's a rex and we do not need to be here when it arrives."

"I agree," Cold replied, and he gestured for Hank to come and assist him with the pilot.

The mercenary glanced at the pitiful pilot and clenched his jaw. It was obvious to him that the pilot had lost a tremendous amount of blood and his chances of survival were slim to none. Mr. Cold was an intelligent man that had plenty of combat experience and had seen injuries like this in the past. Hank wondered why he was even contemplating moving a man with injuries this grave as it would only slow them down and further endanger their own lives. The only thing he could think of was that possibly Mr. Cold was suffering from mild shock. He wasn't thinking clearly. The ground vibrated again.

"Sir, we have to leave him," Hank said, his tone flat.

Mr. Cold looked up at him, wide-eyed and surprised. "What?" he asked.

"We have to leave him," he replied. "He is not going to make it and he will only slow us down."

The pilot again tried to rise and his eyes were now fully open. "No," he cried out fearfully. "Do not leave me here, *please*," he pled, and he grabbed Cold's arm tightly.

Cold looked down at the man and could see the terror in his eyes. He could also see the growing puddle of blood all around him. Suddenly, he knew that Hank was right. This man had no hope, and if they were going to escape, they could not bring him with them.

Another deafening roar erupted from the shadows of the jungle. This time it was louder, and clearly closer. As Cold struggled to get on his feet, a *Protoceratops* came rushing out of the jungle and it was soon followed by what he estimated to be ten more. The small, frilled herbivores were obviously frightened and trying to escape the impending doom that followed them. They threw their beaked mouths back as they ran, wailing a pitiful cry of fear as they made their escape.

"Sir, we've got to go...now," Hank barked, and he grabbed Cold by his good arm and lifted him up.

"No!" the pilot screamed, and again he tried to get up. It was at this point that Cold began to wonder if he had some sort of spinal injury that was hindering his movement.

"We leave him," Hank said coldly. "The tyrannosaur will eat him and we can escape."

"NO!" the pilot screamed louder. "Mr. Cold...please don't leave me here!"

"We should put him out of his misery," Cold suggested as he peered down at the man, unable to hide his sympathy.

Hank kept his eyes on the pilot and shook his head. "No," he suggested. "If we do that, he won't scream. If he doesn't scream, he won't attract attention to himself."

The pilot stared at both men and he began to thrash his body wildly in a pitiful attempt to move. "No!" he screamed again. "You can't leave me!"

The ground vibrated again, and now they could hear birds squawking and flapping their wings wildly as they too made their escape. Mr. Cold sighed deeply and turned away from the pleading pilot. He began jogging toward the clear valley and knew that Hank was right. If they were going to live, they had to leave now and they had to leave the pilot alive. Hank turned to follow him as the pilot shrieked a terrified scream.

"Move quicker," Hank urged as he caught up to Cold. He grabbed his good arm and pulled him along as they moved swiftly toward the jungle foliage on the opposite side of the valley. As they ran along, Hank allowed a glance back toward the herd of *Styracosaurus* and noticed they had all simultaneously turned and were looking in the direction of the burning plane.

"Keep running!" Hank shouted, and he took a quick glance over his shoulder just in time to see a massive *Tyrannosaurus rex* tear through the jungle trees and unleash its nightmarish roar.

The two men could hear the pilot screaming in terror, but Cold did not dare look back. When they arrived at the wood line, Cold kept his back turned as he did not want to see any of the carnage. Hank, on the other hand, raised a small set of binoculars to his face and focused them just as the tyrannosaur dipped its large head downward and plucked the pilot up from the ground. There was no scream to be heard as the top half of the man's body disappeared within the dinosaur's jaws. A shower of blood rained down and the man's bottom half fell to the earth as the dinosaur's jagged teeth managed to tear him clean in two.

Hank slowly dropped the binoculars from his face and turned to see that Mr. Cold was still standing still with his back turned.

"It's over," he said, still with no emotion. "He's dead."

"Good," Cold said, and he finally turned to face Hank. "He gave his life for us. I'll see to it that that man's family is taken care of."

Hank nodded, but didn't acknowledge the statement. Instead, he asked, "So what is the plan now?"

Cold stared at him curiously. "Your mission has not changed," he answered. "The only thing that has changed is you are not going to do it alone. I'm obviously going with you."

Hank nodded, but he wasn't exactly happy about it. "I had a feeling you were going to say that," he said. "Are you sure that's a good idea?"

"I don't know of another option," Cold replied.

Hank cupped his hand over his eyes and looked in the direction of the compound. He half-expected to see Harley or one of the other men heading toward the wreckage by now.

"The others will probably come looking for you," he said as he continued to look. "It may be better if you go with them."

Cold seemed to ponder the suggestion a moment before saying. "No, it's better if they think I'm dead at this point," he replied. "If they think I'm dead, and they think you're dead, they will stay focused on rescuing the others from the compound. That'll give us ample time to find the cave."

Hank scratched at the back of his neck where a mosquito had bitten him earlier. "What if we get there and this is all a farce?" he asked.

"It's not," Cold replied. "We've been gathering information for a long time. We find the cave and we will find the Fountain of Youth. And when we find that..."

"It'll change history," Hank replied.

Cold nodded. "We will locate the fountain and once we confirm its existence, then and only then, do we radio the others. We make up a story about how you rescued me and we were forced to scramble off deeper into the island to escape dinosaurs. Once we return to the mainland, we will assemble a team to return, collect water, and conduct studies to see exactly where it's coming from."

"First, we've got to make it off the island," Hank reminded him.

Cold shook his head. "No, first, I need you to help get this metal out of my arm," he complained, holding out his injured limb.

Hank glanced down at the nasty injury and breathed in deeply through his nose. "It's gonna hurt like hell," he said, glancing at Cold's eyes.

"Yes," he replied, nodding. "Just get on with it."

Hank carefully moved his rifle aside and grabbed Cold by the wrist. With his other gloved hand, he wrapped his hand around the metal protrusion and promptly jerked it free.

Cold opened his mouth to howl in pain, but somehow managed to keep his composure. He knew remaining quiet was going to be imperative to their survival.

Hank tossed the bloody piece of metal aside and placed a hand on Cold's shoulder. "Are you alright?" he asked. "Do you need a moment?"

Cold shook his head and quickly removed his torn and bloodied dress shirt. He was wearing a white, cotton, short-sleeve T-shirt underneath and though it was drenched in sweat and more blood, it was in relatively good condition. He took the remnants of the dress shirt and wrapped it tightly around the wound on his right forearm.

"I'm fine," he said. "Let's get moving before that *T-rex* finishes up and goes looking for another meal."

Hank pulled the GPS back out and took a glance at it. "Alright," he said. "I'll lead the way."

CHAPTER 16

The water was receding fast. Fortunately for Glenn Hardcastle, it was still deep enough to save him from any injury the fall may have caused. His adrenaline was pumping from all the excitement and it did wonders to help him move swiftly to dry land. Once he reached the top of a nearby hill, he dropped to his knees, removed his shirt, and promptly wrung the water out of it. Hardcastle glanced over his shoulder and peered at the Triangle Building. His plan had already gone into disarray once; he hoped it would be smooth sailing from here on out. He put his shirt back on and pulled the large knife he'd foraged from the kitchen out of his belt. As he reached for the knife, his hand brushed against the radio clasped to his belt. For a moment, he felt panic as he came to realization that the radio had become completely submerged in water when he'd fallen. He felt very relieved when he remembered the radio was waterproof. With his hand tightly gripped around the handle of the knife, he rose to his feet and carefully began his trek into the shadows of the jungle.

The shade was a welcome change. The island was always humid, but after Hurricane Simon had drenched it with a storm surge, the humidity was now off the charts. The sun was still hidden away due to the misty ceiling, but Hardcastle often wondered if that just made the heat worse. It always seemed to him that any sunlight that *did* get through became trapped, and when that condition was coupled with the constant breeze off the ocean, it made it feel as if the island was a giant convection oven. As he continued to hike along as quietly as possible, it suddenly occurred to him that he had not seen—nor heard—any sign of a bird since he'd been outside. He supposed they all left before the hurricane arrived.

Even the literal bird brains on this island had the good sense to leave, but I stayed, he realized.

He smiled as he considered the irony of his thought but kept his head on a swivel as he constantly scanned his environment in all directions. His movements were slow—much slower than he wanted to go—but he knew it was necessary for keeping his presence completely hidden. Each step taken was calculated and precise so that the risk of his footsteps being heard was minimal. The temptation to break out in a run straight for the bunker was strong, but Hardcastle had been around the dinosaurs on the island long enough to know that it would be an extremely foolish move.

He had probably made it halfway to the bunker when an unsettling sound began from somewhere beyond the thick jungle foliage on his right. Something was crashing through the woods and it sounded as if it was headed straight for him. Hardcastle stopped dead in his tracks and quickly contemplated whether he should remain still or run for safety. Whatever the animal was, it was large enough to make the ground vibrate slightly as he moved. After he thought a moment, Hardcastle figured it would be best for him to stay put and see if the approaching creature would run right by him. He gripped the knife tightly and held it out in front of him in a defensive posture as he waited.

Suddenly, a large dinosaur tore through the dense vegetation and then fell right in front of him! It had seemingly tripped over a vine and began wailing frantically. Hardcastle immediately recognized the dinosaur to be a hadrosaur. Hadrosaurs were bi-pedal herbivores that were known mostly for their duck-like bills and semi-aquatic habitats. They were plentiful on the island and it made them a favorite prey among many of the carnivores. As Hardcastle stared down at the animal, he could see panic in its eyes and suddenly he came to the realization that the dinosaur was being chased. In almost the same moment, he heard something else approaching at a high rate of speed. As the sound grew louder, it then occurred to him that it wasn't just one animal coming, it was multiple dinosaurs. He took a deep breath and immediately began to run away just as the hadrosaur began the struggle to regain its footing. Unfortunately, it would never get the chance.

Glenn Hardcastle estimated he'd only gotten a good twenty yards away from the frightened animal when suddenly three *Velociraptor*s pounced on top of it. The hadrosaur released a cry of agony and Hardcastle could only look on as the animal died while it was being eaten alive.

"Tough break," he whispered, and he turned to continue his retreat away from the carnage. He removed his hat from his head and wiped the sweat away from his brow with his forearm as he began to walk. Just as he returned his hat to his head, something powerful jumped onto his back, immediately forcing him onto the muddy ground. It was another *Velociraptor*. He could feel its large sickle claws digging into the muscles on his back.

Somehow, Hardcastle managed to hang onto the knife and he quickly began thrusting it backward, desperately trying to stab the animal so that it would get off of him. After several attempts, he finally felt the blade plunge into soft flesh and the raptor growled in pain. The dinosaur jumped backwards off Hardcastle's back and he managed to roll over just in time to see the beast leaping toward him again. This time, he was ready. As the animal came down on top of him, he jabbed the knife upward and straight into the raptor's stomach. Warm blood immediately poured from the wound and turned his once white shirt completely red. Suddenly, the hadrosaur was not the only animal Hardcastle had heard scream in agony, although the raptor sounded quite different.

Hardcastle could tell the wound was a mortal one, but the *Velociraptor* had not accepted its fate yet. The angry dinosaur dipped its head forward to sink its jagged teeth into Hardcastle's throat. He in turn twisted the knife and pushed it deeper, almost to the point that the hilt was plunging into the wound also. The dinosaur arched its back and pulled away, desperate to eliminate the excruciating pain in its belly. As it did so, Hardcastle scrambled away on his hands and knees until he finally clambered onto his feet to break into a run. He continued to sprint away until his body would not allow him to run any further, at which point he collapsed onto his hands and knees and began panting excessively. He'd had many close calls with dinosaurs on the island but he could not remember a time that he'd come so close to death.

***

Victor and Cliff moved quickly through the knee-deep water until they reached the fence surrounding the compound. They moved around the outer edge until the finally found a section that had been torn down by something that clearly wasn't hurricane related.

"What the heck did this?" Cliff asked, although he had a pretty good idea how to answer his own question. He ran a finger across one of the broken fence posts. "Just how big do these dinosaurs get here?"

Victor stepped gingerly over the razor wire that looped its way through the water like a snake. "If you'd paid attention during the briefings, you'd know exactly how big and bad they get out here," he replied gruffly. Once he cleared all of the razor wire, he said, "Could have been a *Tyrannosaurus rex*."

Cliff's eyes widened as he considered the possibility. He instinctively turned and looked over his shoulder to make sure nothing was behind them.

Victor eyed his movements and could see that concern was evident in his body language. "You're not turning yellow on me, are you?" he asked, pausing to light a cigar.

"Of course not," Cliff replied confidently. "You're confusing fear with caution. Big difference."

Victor puffed smoke from his mouth and nodded, saying nothing.

"Let's keep moving," Cliff urged as he trudged by him.

The duo made their way further into the compound and soon noticed what remained of the catwalk that had once stretched between the Triangle Building and five-story laboratory. Cliff could see similarities between the wreckage of the fence and the catwalk, but he kept the observation to himself.

"So what's our move now?" he asked, as they paused near the entrance to the office building and laboratory.

"We stick to the plan for now," Victor replied, still puffing furiously on his cigar. "Harley told us to check the compound for survivors and that's what we're gonna do. The intel we have indicated that the survivors we are looking for hunkered down in here," he added as he approached the double-glass entrance.

Once inside, both men were immediately surprised at how dark the bottom floor was. All of the windows in the office's that flanked either side of the long hallway were covered in a thin layer of mud and dirt left over from the flood water. Cliff retrieved a flashlight from a cargo pocket on his pants and promptly attached it to the barrel of his assault rifle. "I'll take the point," he said with confidence. "You watch my six and I'll check every room."

"Right," Victor agreed. "But refrain from calling out to them. We don't want to attract any dinosaurs." He then turned and began walking backwards, his rifle pointed toward the double glass doors they'd just entered.

***

Harley Cash and Jonathon Williams were already exhausted, but both of them were too stubborn to admit it. The harsh reality was that the extreme humidity and heat they were experiencing was quickly running them down. As long as they'd had a beach to hike across, the trek had been somewhat easy and uneventful. That all changed once the beach ended at a cliff face that forced them to venture into the dark jungle. Once there, the foliage was dense, wet, and riddled with thorns. Jonathon promptly retrieved his trademark knife and began slashing a path through the harsh terrain, but as sharp as the knife was, the help it provided in this circumstance was minimal. As bad as things seemed, they only got worse once the swarms of mosquitos began making a meal of them.

"I can take the thorns all day long," Harley said, panting. "Hell, I can even take the dinosaurs...but these damn mosquitoes are killing me right now." She swatted furiously at the open space in front of her in a futile attempt to rid herself of the worrisome—and painful—pest.

"It's funny you say that," Jonathon said, as he continued to hack and slash his way forward. "Mosquitoes are responsible for more deaths throughout history than any other act of nature."

"I think I've heard that somewhere before," she replied, swatting at a biting mosquito on her neck. "These can't be your ordinary modern-day mosquitoes."

Jonathon found himself trying to focus on the insects as he worked. He'd never considered the possibility that the insects on the island could be prehistoric in nature too. They certainly *seemed* to him that they were slightly larger and more painful than any mosquito he'd ever encountered before. "I've never noticed them before," he said, thinking aloud. "Although I've never been here when the weather was conducive to helping them thrive either."

"Well, I mean it, I'd rather deal with some vicious dinosaur right now than these little beasts," Harley muttered angrily.

"No, you wouldn't," Jonathon replied flatly. "Trust me on that."

Harley laughed, but there was an uneasiness to her tone as she picked up on the seriousness of Jonathon's.

The trek through the jungle took roughly an hour, but persistence paid off and they finally broke through to find a familiar sight.

"It's a road," Harley observed. "I'm assuming this will lead us to the compound?"

"Right," Jonathon replied. "Although I'm sure your intel already told you that." He noticed her arms were still slick with blood. "Are you alright?"

"Yes, I'm fine," she answered, glancing down at her arms. "Those thorns did a number on your arms too."

Jonathon suddenly noticed his own forearms were bleeding. He'd been so busy working his way through the jungle that he hadn't even felt it. All at once, he felt a wave of worry wash over him.

"We should find a place to wash this off," he said, staring at his arm. "The carnivores I've encountered here have an incredible sense of smell. I even used blood to gain the attention of some hungry pterosaurs once to make an escape."

"Well, then we need to get moving and get to the compound," Harley replied, turning her attention down the road. "There is plenty of water still there to clean up." She took one step forward when suddenly a thicket of palm trees on the opposite side of the road began moving back and forth. She and Jonathon simultaneously felt a slight vibration under their feet. Something large was moving toward them. "Jonathon, what is coming?" Harley whispered frantically. She immediately pointed her assault rifle toward the movement beyond the trees.

"Not sure," Jonathon answered, and he remained completely still.

"What do we do?" Harley asked, sounding even more panicked.

Before Jonathon could answer, a large four-legged dinosaur trampled from the shadows of the jungle and onto the dusty gravel road. The creature was large and deep gray in color—almost the same color as an elephant. There was a large frill that rose from the back of its skull adorned with two massive horns protruding horizontally from it. At the end of the dinosaur's beak-like snout, another shorter horn protruded vertically, like that of a rhinoceros. The giant herbivore that had just stepped out in front of them was none other than the well-known *Triceratops*.

Harley stepped backward quickly, still pointing her rifle at the hulking beast. "Do I need to shoot it?" she asked quickly.

"No!" Jonathon replied immediately. "It will not bother us if we stay back."

The *Triceratops* stopped in the center of the road and raised its snout to the air, sniffing. Seconds later, it bellowed a deep, guttural moan and pawed at the ground. At that moment, Jonathon noticed another *Triceratops* lumber out of the shadows and onto the road, this one slightly smaller than the first. The two *Triceratops* turned and seemed to face each other, each of them bellowing their sad songs.

"What are they doing?" Harley asked, her rifle still raised.

"I'm not sure," Jonathon whispered in response. "They seem to be communicating about something."

At that moment, at almost exactly the same time, the two *Triceratops* turned to face Harley and Jonathon. They were clearly looking at them, and for the first time, Jonathon felt an unsettling feeling creep up his spine.

"Something isn't right," he said, and both *Triceratops* seemed to respond by pawing at the dusty road. They began moaning more furiously now. "I don't understand what they're getting so worked up about," he said.

"Umm, I think I do," Harley said, glancing past him. "Look behind you...slowly."

Jonathon slowly turned and looked over his shoulder. Suddenly, it all made sense. There were three tiny *Triceratops* standing on the edge of the road munching on a large leafy shrub of some kind. The young dinosaurs seemed oblivious to their existence, but the other two—presumably the parents—were anything but.

"We've somehow stumbled our way between them and their babies," he whispered nervously.

"So do I shoot now?" Harley asked anxiously.

"They haven't attacked us yet," Jonathon responded. He was sympathetic with the animals but he was quickly beginning to wonder if killing them was going to be their only avenue of escape.

The two large *Triceratops* took a couple of steps toward Jonathon and Harley, the larger one jumped upward slightly onto its hind legs. It released a furious sound that was the closest thing they'd heard so far to a roar. Jonathon closed his eyes as he began to reluctantly accept that Harley was going to have to use her weapon on the larger beasts so that they could survive. He was just about the give the order, when suddenly the ground beneath them began to vibrate again. This time, it had nothing to do with dinosaurs.

Harley looked down at her feet. "What now?" she asked, a hint of annoyance in her tone.

"That's not a dinosaur," Jonathon replied as the vibration increased in intensity to the point of a full-fledged tremor. "This is an earthquake!"

The young *Triceratops* were apparently spooked by the shaking earth and they immediately ran toward their parents, who in turn led them away and back into the jungle to seek refuge. The ground continued to shake for almost a solid minute before stopping just as suddenly as it had begun.

Harley sighed and slowly lowered her rifle. "So not only does the island contain dinosaurs that could kill us at every turn and mosquitoes that want to suck every drop of blood from our bodies...it also has earthquakes." Harley paused and looked over at Jonathon. "Is there anything else about this island that you haven't told me?" she asked.

Jonathon held up his hands. "The earthquake is a new one on me," he replied. "I have no idea what that's all about."

Harley scratched at the back of her head. She couldn't tell if another insect was biting her or if her mind was just playing tricks on her. "I suppose it doesn't matter," she replied. "We're here and we're not leaving until we complete the mission."

"That's right," Jonathon answered as he removed his hat a moment to wipe the sweat from his brow. "Let's get to the compound, find the survivors, check on Cold, and get the hell out of here."

"Couldn't have said it better myself," Harley replied as she began jogging in the direction of the compound.

CHAPTER 17

Each crash into the door sounded louder than the one before. It had been going on almost constantly since Glenn Hardcastle had left them several hours ago.

"How long do you think that door can stand up to them?" Matt asked. He was seated at a stool near the kitchen area of the rec room. His right hand clutched a hot can of beer. In his right, he held another large knife like the one Hardcastle had left with. His face looked as if it had aged ten years since Hurricane Simon had pummeled the island and he was in much need of a hot shower.

Charlie eyed him a long moment and wondered how awful she herself must have looked. "It'll hold up as long as it needs to," she replied confidently. "Sooner or later, they'll give up and leave us alone."

Matt sighed and leaned back against the counter behind him. "I hope you're right, because it's going to be kinda hard for us to get to that door on the lower level if we can't even leave this room," he said.

Charlie looked away from him, doing her best not to let him see the doubt that was creeping into her mind. She hoped the *Troodons* would leave them alone, but truthfully, she had no idea when or if they ever would. They were incredibly intelligent creatures and if they were under the direction of Mother, it would be up to her when they stopped. She thought back to their treatment of the animals over the past couple of years and thought hard to remember if there were ever any instances where she believed the animals had been treated badly. She could think of no such instance, but she was also cognizant of the fact that the *Troodons* were being held against their will. Animals as intelligent as these would undoubtedly hold resentment toward her and Matt for that reason alone. "They'll eventually leave," she replied again, doing her best to sound genuine.

There was another large crash against the other side of the door followed by a scraping sound on the wood.

"They want in really bad," Matt said, tightening his grip around the knife.

Charlie stared at the door, as if she were expecting a hungry *Troodon* break it down at any moment.

"I suppose I should get a knife too," she said, making her way to the kitchen. She rummaged through the drawer and found one just like the one Matt had. It was quite large and reminded her of the chosen weapon of Michael Myers.

"I guess I should apologize to you," Matt said as he stood from the stool.

Charlie whipped her head around and stared at him. "Apologize? For what?" she asked incredulously.

"I should've gotten you off this island," he replied. He looked down and stared at the blade in his hand. "This thing will be useless if they break the door down."

Charlie frowned and walked over to him. She put an arm around him and squeezed his shoulder. "First of all, you *did* tell me to leave the island," she said. "It's my own stubbornness that kept me here…ironically, it was so I could be here to protect the very animals that are outside trying to break in and kill us," she added, glancing at the door. "And I know for a fact that Jonathon Williams has used a knife to kill dinosaurs on this island before so don't count us out just yet."

Matt shook his head. "Well, it's too bad he's not here," he replied with a nervous smile. "And yeah, I may have mentioned that you needed to leave until the storm blew over…but, to be honest, I didn't mean it."

Charlie pulled away from him and looked at him with bewilderment. "What exactly do you mean by that?" she asked, genuinely confused.

Matt ran his fingers through his brown hair and took a deep breath. He seemed tense and nervous. "I mean that I wanted you here with me," he said, glancing at her eyes. "I've been too chicken to ask you on a date and I thought maybe this would be my chance to get more time with you alone." He looked away and clenched his jaw. Charlie could tell he was blushing and had become very uncomfortable.

"Oh," she replied, unsure how to respond. She thought a moment and then said, "Matt, if you wanted to go on a date, all you had to do was ask."

He glanced back at her, his eyes widened. "So, you're saying you wouldn't turn me down?"

"Of course not," she replied, smiling. "But truthfully, I don't think you'd like me very much."

Matt drank the last of his warm beer and tossed the can into a nearby trash bin. "Now why would you say a thing like that?"

Charlie stared at the empty beer can Matt had just disposed of and suddenly craved alcohol too. She opened the dead refrigerator and pulled out a hot beer of her own. "I mean that there is probably a good reason why I'm still single in my mid-thirties," she answered as she opened the can and took a long swig of alcohol. When she lowered the can, she wiped her mouth with the back of her hand. "Matt, I haven't been on a date in over two years," she admitted. "Can you believe that?"

Matt walked over to her and put an arm around her. "No, I can't believe that all," he replied. "You're an attractive, intelligent woman. You've got a beautiful personality. You are kind, and—"

"Okay, okay," Charlie said with a chuckle. "I said I'd go on a date with you so you don't have to lay it on so thick."

"Well, I meant every word," Matt replied.

"And I appreciate it, but I've got a huge flaw, and if you'll be completely honest with yourself, you have the same flaw."

Matt narrowed his eyes and smiled. "Please enlighten me," he said.

Charlie smiled back at him and pursed her lips as she contemplated how to say what was on her mind. "You and I are actually a lot alike," she said finally.

"I know," Matt said quickly. "Which is why I think we're a good match."

"No, you don't understand," Charlie explained. "You and I are already in love. We're both in love with our careers. We are working together now, sure...but sooner or later, we won't be and we're both too in love with our jobs to give it up for any one person. If you and I were in a relationship and our careers began to get in the way, someone would have to bend a little for us to make it work. You and I both know that neither of us are willing to do that."

Matt laughed and shook his head. "I don't know about that," he said. "And neither do you."

"Of course I do," Charlie argued. "Think about what we're doing now," she said. "You and I work on a top-secret island in the Bermuda Triangle studying dinosaurs. Very few people on this planet even know what we're doing. What normal people do you know that live like that?"

Matt considered what she'd said but didn't speak.

"We could never have a normal romantic relationship because neither of us are normal at all," she continued.

There was a long awkward silence. Matt was unsure of how to respond. Finally, Charlie reached out and took him by the hand.

"Having said all that," she began. "I meant what I said. I'd be more than happy to go on a date with you."

Matt stared down into her blue eyes for a solid minute before leaning over and kissing her.

"I guess it's up to me to change your viewpoint," he said when he pulled back. "That was a start."

Charlie's eyes were closed and she was smiling. Matt guessed it had been a long time before she'd been kissed. Her "hard to get" attitude made him want her even more. Finally, she opened her eyes, and her smile disappeared. She immediately looked toward the door, a worried look on her face.

"What's wrong?" Matt asked. He too looked toward the door.

"They stopped," she said. "The *Troodons* haven't crashed in to the door for at least ten minutes now."

Matt thought about it and realized she was right. They'd apparently given up—at least for now. "Should we make a run for it?" he asked.

Charlie opened her mouth to respond, but never got the opportunity. Once again, the earth began to shake.

***

Cornelius Cold had wrapped his hand tightly around a small tree trunk for support. The ground shook violently and all around him he heard the sounds of panicked dinosaurs as they ran and scurried for some sort of refuge that would provide comfort.

"I didn't think it would be this intense," Hank commented as he spread his legs far apart to keep his balance.

"It's going to get worse," Cold replied. "That is why we can't abort the mission."

"Do you still think we have enough time?" Hank asked.

Cold took a breath and looked down at his watch. The ground finally rumbled to a halt and he immediately felt his body relax. "I'm not a geologist and I don't exactly have one at my disposal to discuss the matter with," he replied. "Having said that, the last forecast I heard was for three to six months. I'm starting to think that prediction is off significantly. We need to find the cave as soon as possible and collect as much water as we can. There is a possibility it won't exist a short time from now."

Hank had begun walking again and was following the GPS device in his hand. "According to this thing, we've only got a couple of miles to hike through there," he said, pointing to the other side of the wide valley.

"If we're going to cross, now would be the best time," Cold said, taking note that the earthquake had cleared the valley of all dinosaurs. He felt throbbing pain in his arm where an hour earlier a hunk of metal had been sticking through it. Hank had done a good job of getting the bleeding under control but he knew there was a high danger of getting an infection.

Maybe the water can heal me, he thought.

Hank stuffed the GPS unit in his belt and readied his rifle as he began to trot across the valley. Cold followed and grabbed his arm tightly as the shock of each step he took sent a sharp pain through his wound. He knew Hank would slow down if he complained, but he also knew the quicker they got off the open plain, the better. They'd almost reached the midway point of the clearing when Hank stopped so abruptly that Cold almost ran into him.

"What's wrong?" he asked sharply. He assumed Hank had spotted a dinosaur.

At first, Hank said nothing, he just knelt. It was then that Cold saw it.

"What does this mean for your forecast?" he asked, glancing at Cold over his shoulder.

"Oh my," Cold replied. "I don't think this should be occurring yet."

On the ground in front of them, the earth had cracked open and a ghostly appearance of steam billowed from the gash.

"So, what does this mean?" Hank asked, repeating the question with a tone that suggested genuine concern.

Cold knelt beside him and waved his hand through the wisps of steam. It was extremely hot and capable of inflicting severe burns if he kept his hand there. "I don't know," he said softly. "I'm thinking we have days...maybe hours."

"*Hours*?" Hank asked raising an eyebrow. "Look, Cold, when I signed up for this, there was no mention that the destruction of the island was even a possibility." He rose from his knelt position and offered a hand to pull Cold up.

"I told you," Cold replied as he stood. "This was not supposed to occur for another few months."

"Well, it's occurring now," Hank grumbled. "And I don't plan on being around when all of it goes down. I think we should turn back and jet out of here."

Cold glared at him with annoyance. "You've got to be kidding?" he asked, unable to hide his disappointment. "I chose you for this because you are supposed to be a man that doesn't rattle easily. You're supposed to be a man that gets the job done, whatever the cost. At least that is how you sold yourself to me."

Hank bit his lower lip and breathed deeply through his nose. "And I meant every word of it," he said finally. "But I've always performed in situations that I can control." He gestured toward the crack in the earth. "*This* is not an issue that I can control. How can I guarantee that we will succeed when you don't even know when this thing is going to blow?"

Cold shook his head. "You work for me, Hank," he growled. "Don't forget that. We have time to get this done. What are we...a mile and a half from the cave now?"

Hank retrieved the GPS unit and nodded his head as confirmation.

"So you want to give up when we're this close?" Cold asked. "The Hank Bailey I hired wouldn't come this far to just give up. He'd press on and see it through."

Hank rolled his eyes as he came to terms with what Cold was doing. He sighed and kicked up dust with his boot. "Alright, let's get on with it," he spat. "You better make it worth my while, Mr. Cold," he added, pointing a finger at the older man.

"Do your job and I will do mine," Cold replied with no expression.

Without another word, Hank spun on his heel and continued his trek toward the jungle foliage ahead.

CHAPTER 18

"Stop picking at it or you're going to regret it later," Harley said as she crouched down behind a rock with binoculars held to her face. The compound was now in view, but all her training and experience reminded her to be cautious. She would scope the location out a few minutes before they pressed on. She lowered the binoculars and looked over her shoulder to find that Jonathon had crouched down beside her, the gash on his face was causing his jaw to swell significantly.

"It itches," he complained. "I'm not picking at it, I'm just patting it. I've got to do something or I'll end up clawing my face off. I'm starting to wonder if this is going to end up like a cat scratch."

Harley scrunched up her face and raised her eyebrow. "What are you talking about now?" she asked.

"Cats are notorious for carrying all sorts of bacteria on their claws…it's the reason why a cat scratch hurts so bad. It burns and itches and easily gets infected," he explained. "I'm wondering if the pterosaurs claws can cause a similar reaction because I swear it feels like a big cat just scratched my face."

"We need to clean it," Harley replied. "Surely there is a first-aid kit somewhere in that building," she said, nodding toward the five-story laboratory and office.

"Maybe," Jonathon said. "But don't make it a priority. Let's find the survivors and get out of here. If we stumble across a first-aid kit, then we'll clean it. I'll be fine either way."

Harley wanted to argue, but knew it was pointless. She returned her attention to the compound, scanning the environment for any signs of dangerous dinosaurs. "I don't see any sign of Victor or Cliff," she said. "I'm sure that means they're already in the building."

Jonathon reached for the binoculars and looked for himself. "I don't see any signs of dinosaurs," he said. "I think we can make it." He lowered the binoculars and looked to the sky. "It's going to be dark soon. We need to be in that building before nightfall. If we hurry, we may even be able to get them out and on a boat."

"No, we can't," Harley replied, snatching the binoculars back. "You're forgetting about Hank…and I have to make sure there are no survivors at the site of the plane crash. Besides, Cold made plans for us to be picked up tomorrow at noon—although I'm sure they'll give us extra time if needed."

Jonathon let out an exasperated breath. He believed with every fiber in his being that no one survived the plane crash. However, it was impossible to convince Harley of that. As for Hank, he really didn't have high hopes for him either. Despite these strong beliefs, he tried to put himself in Harley's position and when he did so, Jonathon knew he would not be so quick to leave one of his own behind either if there was any chance they could be alive. "Alright, then it's settled. We get in that building, we find the survivors, and I assume we'll find Victor and Cliff there too. We'll remain there until morning. We get up as soon as the sun comes up and we spend no more than half the day looking. Then we leave," he said.

Harley chewed her lip a moment as she stared at the compound. She was clearly mulling over everything he had said. Finally, she agreed to his plan.

"I'm serious," Jonathon said, unconvinced that she was satisfied with an allowance of half a day of searching. "We can't afford to stay on this island any longer than that."

"I know," she snapped back at him. "I just told you that a boat is coming at noon anyway. We spend half the day looking and we leave…I got it."

Jonathon stared at her, but she didn't look back. She was clearly aggravated and wanted to argue for more time, but she stood true to her word and let him have the ultimate say.

"We're wasting time," she said, rising to her feet. "Let's get in that building."

Jonathon rose and raced after her. As the wind hit his face, he was suddenly reminded of his itching wound. He found himself really hoping they stumbled across that first-aid kit.

***

The back of Glenn Hardcastle's shirt was wet and it wasn't from sweat. The *Velociraptor* that jumped on his back had apparently cut him worse than he initially thought. That particular breed of dinosaur had notoriously sharp claws, and though he'd had many experiences with raptors, he'd never been injured by one before. He knew how the animals hunted and he silently chastised himself for being so careless. Once the hadrosaur was under attack, he shouldn't have let his guard down. More importantly, he should've retreated much faster than he did instead of standing there watching the carnage. He was unsure how much blood he'd lost, and he had no way of examining the injury for himself. The unknowns of his condition added another level of stress he really didn't need at the moment. To top it all off, there had been another earthquake. They seemed to be occurring with more frequency.

As if this wasn't already going to be hard enough, he thought.

Nightfall would come in another two hours and if he didn't make it to the bunker before then, he knew his chances of survival were slim to none. He tried to forget about his bleeding back, but the nagging stinging sensation from the open wounds would not let him. The knife that had saved his life was still clutched tightly in his hand and had now become quite sticky with raptor blood. Between the blood-stained knife, and the soaked shirt on his back, the flies undoubtedly viewed him as a dead man walking. A swarm of the flying pests hung around him now like an annoying, buzzing cloud. In his mind's eye, he could see hundreds of the filthy creatures landing on his back and the thought made him shudder.

As he trudged onward, he began to formulate a plan on how he was going to survive the night if he was unable to find the bunker in time. A fire would provide a significant amount of protection, but unfortunately everything in the jungle around him was still soaking wet. There were no rock formations that he knew of in the vicinity that might allow him to seek refuge in a cave either. What he did have was an abundance of trees. The trees in this portion of the jungle were enormous and many of the trunks were several feet in diameter. He'd noticed quite a few of them were hollowed out and large enough for a man to crawl inside. The notion of crawling inside of a dark tree trunk full of insects and worse made him shudder, but it would be better than getting eaten alive.

As a boy, Hardcastle was plagued with a terrible fear of the dark. His mother sympathized with him and allowed him to sleep with a dim light in his room. His father, on the other hand, generally gave him a hard time about the phobia and ridiculed him often about it. He'd never had a great relationship with his dad and hadn't seen him in probably ten years. Hardcastle often blamed their estrangement on the resentment he was never able to overcome due to his father's bullying him. He'd finally managed to overcome his fear of darkness shortly after he'd turned twenty years old—or so he thought. Now, for the first time in many years, the thought of being caught in the jungle at night and in total darkness began to bring him to a level of anxiety that made him nauseous.

Or does it have something to do with how much blood I've lost? he wondered.

He thought of Charlie and that imbecile Matt Walker. He had to stay focused for them. They were depending on him. The longer they remained in that building with the pack of *Troodons*, the more dire their situation grew. He found himself wondering what he'd do if he made it all the way to the bunker door that led into the office building, only to get no answer from either of them on the other end of the radio. Would he risk going back the way he came to see if they needed his help? Logically, if he somehow found himself in that scenario, the explanation would most likely be that they were dead. But how would he know for sure?

I wouldn't, he thought. *Not unless I went back to check...*

As he began to contemplate how he'd deal with such a situation, he suddenly heard rustling in the dense foliage to his immediate right. He stopped dead in his tracks and he felt his pulse quicken substantially. For nearly a minute, the jungle was still and eerily quiet. He brought the knife up in front of him and held it in a defensive posture. His eyes stayed in the direction where he'd heard the movement, unblinking. He was just beginning to think that his mind was playing tricks on him, when suddenly, he saw it. A large eye blinked slowly and then Hardcastle noticed the rest of the animal's head move slightly. It was a *Velociraptor*.

They're following me, he thought.

The raptor seemed to sense that it had been seen, and suddenly it became still as a statue. Hardcastle knew the animals well and he knew that they did not travel or hunt alone. He slowly turned his head and began to scan his environment for any signs of movement. Although he squinted and looked hard, he saw nothing. This was unfortunate in his mind because there was no way he could predict which direction the attack was going to occur. With no other options, he returned his attention to the one raptor that he had seen. Fortunately, it was still there and remained eerily still. After a moment of contemplation, he decided his only option was to remain where he was. Running, he knew, would only encourage the animals to attack—it was what they wanted him to do.

Despite every inkling of his being suggesting otherwise, Glenn Hardcastle somehow remained still. Beads of sweat rolled off his forehead and into his eyes. The burning sensation caused him to blink involuntarily and doing so seemed to spur the *Velociraptor*s attention. The animal stepped very slowly toward him, weaving its way through the surrounding foliage without making a sound. The eerie quietness around the animal's movements were not surprising to Hardcastle. He knew too well how incredibly skilled they were at both stealth and surprise attacks. He gripped the knife so tightly that his knuckles turned white, but he forced himself to remain calm and still. It was a longshot, he knew, but his hope was that if he remained still enough, the raptors would somehow lose interest and leave him be. He figured it had to be strange for them to approach prey that did not flee.

As the *Velociraptor* stepped out of the shadows and into a shaft of sunlight that pierced the jungle canopy, Hardcastle heard the sound he was dreading. From somewhere behind him, there was a subtle shuffle in the leafy vegetation that he knew was undoubtedly another approaching raptor. If this was going to be his end, he decided he was going to go down fighting. Hardcastle turned just in time to the see the raptor that had been sneaking up behind him lunge from the veil of shadow. As the animal came down over him, he heard the other raptor running toward him, apparently pleased that he'd so easily fallen into their trap.

Hardcastle raised his knife to meet the raptor that had leapt at him but missed. Instinctively, he threw his other arm in front of him for protection, but unfortunately, his forearm landed directly into the jaws of his hungry attacker. As he felt the *Velociraptor*s teeth tear into his flesh and contact bone, he threw his head back and screamed in agony.

CHAPTER 19

The most recent earthquake had been the worst yet. The shaking had become so violent that a portion of the ceiling over the recreation room had collapsed and the gaping hole suddenly allowed them another way into the floor above them. Unfortunately, they both also came to the realization that this too provided another avenue in which the *Troodons* could get to them as well.

"This building can't possibly take another beating like that," Matt said as he walked underneath the large hole and stared upward. There was quite a bit of dust still settling...so much so that he pulled his shirt tail up to his mouth to prevent breathing it in. "It's the veterinary ward," he said, his voice muffled as he spoke through the thick fabric of his shirt.

Charlie squinted and could just see the corner of the steel examination table. She thought quickly and tried to remember if there was anything that would be of use to them up there. There were scalpels and other sharp instruments used for surgery, but nothing that was better than the assortment of knives at their disposal in the kitchen area. "There are sedatives up there," she blurted out as soon as the thought popped into her head.

Matt made his way back toward her and took a moment to brush the white sheetrock dust out of his hair. "Yes, there are," he said, glancing at her. "But how could we use them to our advantage?"

Charlie raised her chin and glanced back toward the large hole that led into the veterinary ward. "There is enough up there for us to apply a lethal dosage if need be," she said thoughtfully.

Matt considered her suggestion and, though he agreed with her assessment, he wasn't sure how they could apply it.

"Yeah, I'm still working that part out," Charlie said, seemingly reading his thoughts. She paused a moment, then added, "Do you think the *Troodons* have gotten access to that room? If so, we're in big trouble."

Matt shook his head and shrugged. "Don't know," he answered, glancing back toward the hole. "I guess I could climb up there and see if they've been in there."

Charlie pursed her lips and considered their next move. As she did so, there was a loud crash against the door again.

"Oh no," Matt muttered. "Not again."

Charlie took a deep breath and closed her eyes. The more she tried to ignore it, the more overwhelming the feeling became. The entire situation, she decided, was hopeless. All they seemed to be doing at this point was prolonging the inevitable. She ran the fingers of both her hands through her hair and slowly exhaled.

How long could they possibly keep this up?

"You okay?" Matt asked.

She shook her head and though she wanted to answer him, she refrained for fear of breaking down. That was the last thing either of them needed right now.

The pounding on the door continued, but this time it was followed by a muffled voice. "Hello? Anyone in there?"

Charlie and Matt looked at each other simultaneously and then at the door.

"Yes, we are here!" Charlie replied as they both ran to the door to begin frantically moving the furniture out of the way. "Just a minute and we will get the door opened!"

It seemed as if it took a long time, but in all actuality, it took less than a minute for them to remove the barricade and open the door. As soon as she'd swung it open, two large men holding assault rifles barged in. One was tall and had a blond crewcut. There was a smoking cigar hanging out of his mouth. He eyed Charlie and Matt a long moment before finally marching into the room, right past them, the second man on his heels.

"Let's get this door closed back, shall we?" he asked, as he kicked the door shut with a large black boot. "I'm Victor, and this is my compadre Cliff," he said, gesturing to the shorter bald man.

"Boy, are we glad to see you guys," Matt replied as he immediately slid the couch back in front of the closed door.

Both of the men wore army green tank tops with camouflage cargo pants. The black combat boots each of them wore completed the ensemble and made them look as If they'd just stepped out of a *G.I. Joe* Saturday morning cartoon. The large man, Victor, seemed to be in charge and he did not even acknowledge Matt's statement.

"Where is everyone else?" Cliff asked, looking around the room.

Victor looked toward Matt for an answer.

"Glenn Hardcastle left to try and get us access through an old underground tunnel that leads to a bunker," he answered quickly.

Victor pulled the cigar from his mouth and flicked ashes onto the floor. "Now why would he do something that stupid?" he asked, his eyes narrowing.

Charlie drew near him and crossed her arms. "We were getting desperate," she said, doing her best to defend him. "He was doing what he felt would give us the best chance to make it out of this. There are dinosaurs in the building. We didn't know when help was going to arrive."

Cliff made his way toward the kitchen and began to rummage through the cabinets. "You all should've known help was coming. You were supposed to stay put," he said as he made his way toward the refrigerator.

"What happened to you?" Victor asked abruptly, staring at Matt.

Matt's eyes widened as he realized he was being addressed. "Me?" he asked. "What are you talking about?"

Victor marched toward him and grabbed his chin, turning his head slightly sideways. "Your jaw is swollen," he muttered.

"Oh, that," Matt answered, pulling away. "Yeah, Hardcastle punched me," he said meekly.

Victor grinned, and puffed smoke as he chuckled. "Is that true?" he asked, looking at Charlie.

Her arms were still crossed, and though she was glad to see the two men, she wasn't thrilled about the interrogation. "Yes, it's true," she answered flatly.

"So why did he punch you?" Cliff asked, as he pulled the tab off a hot soda he retrieved from the dead refrigerator.

"We lost a man," Matt said solemnly. "Glenn blamed me for it."

"I see," Victor replied as he ran his hand downward over his thick mustache. He seemed to be deep in thought.

"I'm sorry, and I don't mean to sound ungrateful, but when exactly are you two getting us out of here?" Charlie asked as her patience had finally expired.

Victor rubbed the back of his neck and then plopped down on the couch that was being used to barricade the door. "As soon as possible, ma'am," he replied as he took another pull from his cigar. "We've got two more members of our team headed this way and I've been given orders to locate any survivors in the compound and stay put until they get here." He paused to release another cloud of wispy gray smoke. "So, is there anyone else still alive around here besides Glenn Hardcastle?"

Charlie shook her head and looked to the floor as she again thought of George. "No, only four of us remained and now only three of us are still alive."

"Well, cheer up," Cliff said as he placed a large, callused hand on her shoulder. "We're here now and you're getting off this island very soon."

"That is music to my ears," Matt said as he hopped up and sat onto the kitchen counter.

"What about Hardcastle?" Charlie asked, glancing over her shoulder to look into Cliff's eyes.

The bald man's eyes drifted away and found Victor. "Well?" he asked.

Victor's cigar had burnt away into a small nub. He extinguished it on the tile floor between his legs as he considered an answer. Once he thought it over, he looked up and directly at Charlie. "It's not up to me or Cliff," he said. "But between you and me, Hardcastle is probably dead."

Charlie shook her head. "No, absolutely not," she replied sternly. "Do you even know him? Do you know anything about him?"

Victor swallowed and gazed toward the gaping hole in the ceiling. "What's up there?" he asked, ignoring her question.

"Veterinary ward," Matt answered for her. "We were considering going up there and getting enough sedatives to kill the *Troodons* before you showed up."

Victor and Cliff looked at each other and then back to Matt.

"What the hell is a *Troodon*?" Victor asked, raising an eyebrow.

Charlie walked over to him and said, "Medium-sized dinosaur, stands on two legs, has a few red and white feathers on top of its head."

Victor looked over toward the floor on his left as he thought. "I don't recall seeing anything like that," he said.

Cliff crushed the now empty soda can in his hand and plopped down on the couch beside Victor. "Nah, I don't remember seeing any big chickens running around either," he said, a bit of sarcasm in his tone.

"They don't look anything like chickens," Matt replied. He sounded a little annoyed. "They're extremely dangerous animals."

"They don't sound dangerous," Victor replied, glancing up at him.

"Well, trust us, they are," Charlie snapped. "They are highly intelligent—more so than the *Velociraptor*s. Some scientists have theorized that if the dinosaurs had somehow avoided extinction, it would've most likely been the *Troodon* that evolved into a humanoid."

Cliff and Victor stared at Charlie and then the both of them looked at each other. After a few seconds, they burst into laughter.

"That's a good one," Victor said as he retrieved a new cigar from a large pocket on his pants leg. "So, I guess you're saying it would've looked like us...just more scaly?"

Charlie rolled her eyes and then shook her head. "Perhaps," she said, making no effort to hide her aggravation. "I'm not saying I believe in the theory, but I'm trying to make you understand these are not your ordinary dinosaurs."

"They work harmoniously as a team more than any other species of animal I've ever studied," Matt added. "I'm warning both of you not to take them lightly."

Victor lit his cigar, filled his lungs with smoke, and then blew out a thick gray cloud. "Do they know how to use one of these?" he asked, holding up his rifle with his left hand.

Cliff snickered and muttered something no one could understand.

"Not yet," Charlie replied and she was deadly serious.

***

"What is it?" Harley asked as she crouched low behind a fallen log, her binoculars to her face.

She was staring at a smaller dinosaur, maybe four feet high in stature. The animal stood on two legs, had a long tail, and rows of sharp teeth in its jaws. The top of the animal's head was covered in small red and white feathers. Its eyes were cat-like, and set more on the front of its skull that on the sides. It was standing just outside the entrance to the office building in about two feet of water.

"It's a *Troodon*," Jonathon replied. "And it's a big one."

"Is it dangerous?"

Jonathon took a deep breath and exhaled through his nose. "I'm afraid so," he answered. "They're really smart and territorial. Getting by them will not be easy."

Harley lowered the binoculars and looked over at him. "It seems that Victor and Cliff got by it," she said. "It's just one...what's the big deal?"

Jonathon smiled and swatted at an insect buzzing around the back of his neck. "If Victor and Cliff got into that building, it's because that dinosaur let them," he countered. "And trust me, there is more than one down there."

"So, should I take that one out?" she asked, bringing the stock of her weapon to her chest.

"No, not yet," Jonathon said, pushing the barrel of the gun downward. "If you start shooting, it'll alert more of them. It'll make things worse."

"Okay," she replied, disappointment in her voice. "So what do we do?"

Jonathon adjusted his hat and stood slowly. "We need to find another way in there," he said. He glanced down at Harley. "I'm assuming you all know the schematics of the building," he said. "Is there another way in?"

Harley thought for a long moment before finally reaching into a cargo pocket on her pants. She retrieved a tightly folded piece of paper. Once she opened it, Jonathon quickly realized it was the layout of the building. She spread it out neatly over the log she'd been crouched behind.

"Perfect," he said as he studied the schematic. "This is new," he said, pointing at the catwalk that led from the Triangle Building into the third floor of the office building.

Harley again pulled the binoculars to her face and began to scan the area for the catwalk. When she found it, she slowly lowered the binoculars from her face and looked up at him, her face ashen. "Something appears to have torn it apart," she said, handing the binoculars over to him.

Jonathon looked for himself and quickly noticed what was left of the mangled catwalk. There were claw marks in the metal. The destruction was clearly caused by a large dinosaur and not Hurricane Simon as he initially thought. "Well, we can cross that idea off," he said, handing the binoculars back down to her.

He returned his attention to the blueprint and suddenly noticed an option that he thought was too good to be true.

"What about this?" he asked, pointing to what appeared to be an underground tunnel that disappeared off the edge of the page. "Where does that tunnel lead?"

Harley squinted her eyes as she studied the portion of the blueprint Jonathon was inquiring about. "That's an old emergency escape tunnel that leads to an underground bunker about a mile and half away from the compound," she answered. "We were told that it isn't structurally sound and to avoid it. It's not an option."

Jonathon picked up on the firmness of her tone but refused to give up that easily. "Well, then if the catwalk isn't an option, and the underground tunnel isn't an option, then what exactly do you suggest?" he asked, obviously annoyed.

Harley Cash clenched her jaw and weighed her options. There was a long silence and Jonathon was more than eager to give her the opportunity to mull it over as he knew eventually she'd have no choice but to see it his way. As Harley thought quietly, exhaustion began to make its worrisome presence known to her. She tried to stifle a yawn, but failed.

"Are you certain that shooting them is a bad idea?" she asked stubbornly.

Jonathon smirked, more out of frustration than amusement. "I told you," he began.

Harley held up her hand to silence him. "No, wait," she interrupted. "Just hear me out…"

Jonathon raised his eyebrows and tightened his jaw. He gestured for her to go on.

"I remember what you said…about shooting one and the sound alerting more of them making matters worse," she said.

Jonathon nodded and crossed his arms.

"So, what's wrong with that?" she asked. "We have two advantages. We are in a hidden location and we can strike from a distance," she added, glancing down at the rifle clutched tightly in her hands. "I think it would be great for more of them to come and investigate…I'd be able to pick them off one at a time from right here.

Jonathon looked over toward the *Troodon* that seemed to be standing guard outside the office building. The dinosaur paced back and forth. Its head seemed to be on a swivel as the animal frequently surveyed its surroundings for any sign of danger. Harley's idea sounded good in theory but he knew the animals would be too smart for it to work.

"Sure, you might be able to pick off a couple—maybe even three," he replied, still watching the pacing dinosaur. "But we don't know how large that *Troodon* pack is and sooner or later they'd figure out where we are, and when they do…"

"I'll be waiting here to mow them down," Harley interrupted, her voice rising.

Jonathon smiled, removed his hat, and then stared at it. He took a deep breath and shook his head as he twirled the hat around on his hand. "I admire your spirit," he muttered, still staring at the hat. "But I think this is where I respectfully remind you that I'm the dinosaur expert here." He paused and glanced over at her. She locked eyes with him. "And I'm the one that has the final say," he added sternly.

Harley's eyes narrowed and he visibly noticed her biting her tongue.

"Yeah, you'd take a few more out I'm sure, but sooner or later, they'd overwhelm us," he explained. "Trust me, it wouldn't work."

Harley finally stopped biting her tongue and returned her attention to the building schematic that was now lying on the ground beside her. "Alright, you win," she conceded. "We'll try the tunnel—but don't be shocked if it is full of water or worse. And that's of course assuming it isn't collapsed."

"There isn't any way for dinosaurs to get in the tunnel. However, I'll concede that it's possibly collapsed," Jonathon replied, returning his hat to its rightful place. "Actually, it's probable considering the recent earthquakes. But at this point, I think it's our safest option. We won't do ourselves or anyone else any good if we end up dead."

"And if we find the tunnel has collapsed?" Harley asked, rising from her crouched position.

"Then we do it your way," Jonathon said.

Harley nodded, and reached for her radio to alert Victor and Cliff of their plan.

CHAPTER 20

Mr. Cold did his best to ignore the pain in his shoulder, but the throbbing wouldn't cease. He refrained from moving his hand to his wound for fear that it would show a vulnerable side of himself to Hank. Fortunately, it was somewhat easy to hide his discomfort since Hank led the way and rarely looked back at him.

"How much further?" Cold asked as he wiped sweat away from his brow.

Hank glanced at the GPS unit he held in his hand but did not stop walking. "Looks like another mile and we'll be there," he replied.

Cold didn't immediately say anything in reply, but he looked to the sky and could see it was beginning to dim substantially. He figured they had plenty of time to reach the cave before nightfall completely enveloped the island; however, he wondered how safe the cave would be to spend the night in. From what he knew of the cave, there were dinosaurs that frequented it and even one particular species that seemed to have claimed it as their home. It probably wasn't a wise decision to sleep there.

"We need to set up somewhere to camp for the night," Cold said finally, stopping in his tracks.

Hank spun around to look at him. "You've got to be kidding me," he replied, his eyes wide. "You told me that this island could be hours away from self-destructing and you want to stop somewhere for the night?"

Cold cleared his throat and leaned against a tree to give his body a brief respite. "Either way, we're not going to be able to get off this island until tomorrow," he said. "We can't spend the night in the cave because it is usually inhabited by dinosaurs. We need to find a place to sleep, get through the night, and at first light, we'll make a mad dash to the cave. Then we continue with the plan."

Hank stared at him, panting. His mouth dropped open slowly and he finally said, "What about the earthquakes? What if it all goes to hell during the night?"

Cold chuckled and shook his head. "You worry too much, Hank. The island will make it one more night, trust me."

Hank sighed and shook his head. "And you're basing this on what exactly?"

Cold stood up straight again and walked over to Hank. "What do you want me to say?" he asked, agitated. "You want me to tell you it's a gut feeling? Fine, that's exactly what it is...does that make you feel better?"

Hank stared at him but said nothing.

Cold continued. "If something happens during the night, there is nothing we can do about it and there is a good possibility that we will die."

"That's what I thought," Hank replied angrily. "That's it, I'm out of here." He turned to walk away.

Cold grabbed his arm as he strolled past. "Hank, wait," he said, almost pleading. Hank stopped but didn't turn to look at him. "We're extremely close and as much as I don't like the circumstances, they are what they are," he continued. "We are stuck here for the night, no matter what."

Hank finally turned his head to look at him. "That's what you think," he growled and he held the radio up. "This is the point where I tell you it's time to abort the mission. I'll call Harley and tell her the whole deal. I'm sure the paleontologist you brought along wouldn't be too thrilled with what you're planning either."

Cold felt his blood pressure begin to rise. "Hank, let me remind you that I'm paying you a large chunk of money," he said through clenched teeth.

Hank chuckled and began walking away from him again. "Keep your money," he quipped. "I'll make some from someone else."

Mr. Cold watched Hank continue to walk away from him and he felt a rage overcome his entire body like a wildfire in a matter of mere seconds. He tried to stifle it, but just as he was unable to ignore the nagging pain in his shoulder, he too was unable to ignore the overwhelming rage. Without considering the issue any further, he immediately reached for the revolver he kept strapped around his calf and with no hesitation raised the weapon and pulled the trigger.

The sound was thunderous, but fortunately, Hank Bailey never heard it. The bullet tore through the back of his skull and exited from between his eyes. The explosive spray of blood, bone, and tissue was enough to confirm for Cold that the shot had been a lethal one. Hank immediately fell face first into the ground and remained motionless. Cornelius Cold squeezed the handle of the gun tightly in his hand and then screamed with fury. He'd reacted rashly and he immediately regretted his actions.

He stared at the corpse in front of him for a long time before fully accepting what he had done. When he'd finally come to terms with it all, he knelt and picked the radio and GPS unit off the ground. As soon as he put his hand around the radio, it crackled to life. It was Harley, and she immediately began telling Victor and Cliff of her and Jonathon's plan to find a nearby bunker to gain safe access to the office building. When she'd finished speaking, he thought he could hear Victor trying to respond, but there was so much static it was impossible to understand what he was saying.

I told her to avoid that tunnel, he thought. He looked down at the GPS to get an idea of just how far away from the bunker he was. When he considered the possibility of going on to the fountain alone, the more he thought about it, the more he realized it would be unwise and too risky. On the other hand, if he met up with Harley and Jonathon at the bunker, maybe he could concoct a story to convince them to join in him in going after the water. Though it seemed like a good idea in theory, he could think of no good story that he could use to entice them to follow him on the endeavor.

I suppose I'd better get to thinking, he thought.

He then slowly turned and began his trek toward the bunker.

***

The sun was almost down and the ominous mist surrounding the island made it seem that much darker. Charlie was not completely relaxed, but it was the safest she had felt since the hurricane first made landfall. Victor was not the most likeable fellow, but he was clearly there to protect them and seemed to take the job seriously. Cliff had a friendly face and truthfully looked to be on the opposite end of the spectrum from Victor where intimidation was concerned.

"So, when they call you and tell you that they've made it to the other side of that door, are we all going down there together to open it?" she asked, looking over to Victor.

The large man chuckled and breathed deeply through his nose. It seemed to be more out of exhaustion than annoyance. "Why hell no," he grumbled. "You and Dr. Walker will remain right here while Cliff and I go and retrieve them."

Charlie adjusted from lying on her back to her side so that her body could fully face Victor. "I don't think we should split up," she said. "Both of you have an extra handgun and if you each give one to Matt and me, there would be four of us armed. There is strength in numbers."

Victor smiled and shook his head. "Nah, I don't think so," he replied. "The two of you made it for quite a while with no gun, what's a few minutes while we run downstairs?"

Charlie opened her mouth for a rebuttal but Victor cut her off before she had a chance to speak.

"How about we cross that bridge when we come to it?" he asked as he pulled a cigar from his pocket.

Charlie raised her eyebrows. "How many of those things do you smoke a day?" she asked.

"Believe it or not, I don't smoke that many when I'm not working," he replied, and she thought she caught the slightest glimpse of a sadness behind his eyes. He lit the cigar and took a long pull from it before he spoke again. "When I'm home, it's booze I turn to," he added as he puffed a smoke ring into the air.

"Why is that?" Matt asked, taking a seat on a nearby stool.

Victor shook his head. "You don't want to hear about it," he grumbled. He then turned to Cliff. "It's getting late and we'll be under total darkness in a few minutes. We'll have to take shifts and keep a close watch on that," he said, moving his eyes upward to the gaping hole in the ceiling. "That's where we're most vulnerable."

Cliff nodded and instinctively pointed his assault rifle toward the hole. "Nothing's getting through there on my watch," he replied, then glanced over to Victor. "I'll take first watch...we can swap every two hours."

"Sounds good," Victor agreed, and he then walked over to the barricaded door to give it a final inspection. Once satisfied that it would hold through the night, he turned to Charlie and Matt. "Alright, all we gotta do is make it through the night and tomorrow we're out of here," he explained. "The two of you can get some sleep and Cliff and I will hold down the fort. I've got a feeling you'll both need all the energy you can muster for tomorrow."

Matt walked over to the large man and put a hand on his shoulder. "We appreciate everything you guys are doing," he said.

Victor looked over at Matt's hand and slowly removed it from his shoulder. "You can thank me when we're off the island," he replied.

"You *do* understand that the *Troodons* will be even more active during the night?" Charlie asked abruptly.

Both men turned to face her. Victor allowed a subtle smile to form on his face.

"Ah yes, I forget we're dealing with genius dinosaurs," he quipped, chewing on his cigar.

Charlie stomped toward him. "You're damn right they are," she snapped back.

"Charlie, these guys are pros, we have to trust them and let them do their jobs," Matt said.

She felt her jaw tighten and her blood pressure rise. It was bad enough that the two men she didn't know weren't taking her very seriously, but it was extremely frustrating to now find that Matt was seemingly taking their side. He drew near her and tried to put an arm around her shoulders; she pulled away.

"Don't touch me," she spat. She then retreated to a large—and rather ugly—upholstered chair in the farthest corner of the room. Once there, she curled up into it and closed her eyes. She wanted to give the appearance that she was trying to go to sleep, and truthfully, she was. However, knowing what was lurking on the other side of the door—and potentially above them—would make the task nearly impossible.

Victor and Cliff both eyed her but said nothing. Matt could see the annoyance all over their faces, especially Victor.

"She'll be alright," Matt said, trying to break the awkward silence. "She appreciates what you guys are doing, trust me she does."

Cliff allowed a slight smile to creep across his face, but it was obviously forced. Victor's expression remained stern, yet indifferent. Matt watched as he pulled his gun close to his chest and wrapped an arm around it like the weapon was an old friend.

"Cliff, I've changed my mind. I'll take the first shift," Victor said, finally pulling his gaze away from Charlie. "Get some shut-eye and I'll wake you in a couple of hours."

"You don't have to tell me twice," Cliff replied, yawning. The smaller soldier grabbed a decorative pillow from the sofa and tossed it on the nearby rug. He then collapsed to the floor and rested his head on the pillow. Within minutes, he was out like a light.

"Wow, I wish I knew his secret," Matt said as he too found a spot on the floor to retire for the night.

"When you're a soldier in the theatre of war, you learn real quick to sleep when you can," Victor said as he puffed smoke from underneath his bushy mustache. "I can check out just as quickly."

Matt shook his head and then rested his head on a lab coat he'd folded into a makeshift pillow. He then chuckled and made no effort to hide it.

"What's so funny?" Victor asked curiously.

"Nothing really," Matt replied, and he turned his head to face Victor. The mercenary raised his eyebrows and gestured for him to explain. "Well, it's just that this is exactly why Charlie got so mad," he replied, rolling over onto his back. "She's telling you how dangerous the *Troodons* are and neither of you seem to care. Cliff proves her point with how quickly he just fell asleep. He hasn't a care in the world and even if he did, it seems that the *Troodons* would be near the bottom of his list."

Victor huffed and shook his head. "Oh, he and I care plenty about the dinosaurs out there," he replied, jerking a thumb over his shoulder toward the barricaded door behind him. "But we also are here to do a job. We're being paid to come here and get you and that hellcat out of here," he further explained, glancing toward Charlie. "What we don't need is someone constantly telling us all the ways we're gonna screw up and get eaten. It's insulting, and quite frankly, we don't need that crap."

Matt was taken aback but he remained on his back and stared at the ceiling. "Well, if that's how you took her warnings, I apologize on her behalf," he said. "Please know that she meant well with everything she said."

Victor took the last pull off his latest cigar and then mashed the glowing end into the sheetrock wall over his shoulder. "Put yourself in our position," he said as he tossed what was left of the extinguished cigar onto the floor. "How would you like it if we came in here telling you how to do your job?"

"I don't suppose I'd like it very much," Matt answered.

"Right. So how about both of you shut the hell up and let us do ours," he growled. "And as far as Cliff's 'secret' to falling asleep...it helps a lot if you've got something good to snuggle up with," he added, patting the rifle he'd been hugging against his chest.

CHAPTER 21

"Is that what I think that is?" Jonathon asked as he watched Harley kneel onto one knee.

She reached down onto the sandy soil and rubbed her finger across the red liquid all over the ground. She moved her hand closer to the center of the beam of light originating from the flashlight Jonathon was holding. She rubbed her fingers together and it confirmed her suspicion.

"Blood," she muttered. "And a lot of it," she added, glancing back toward the ground around them.

"There is no way to know for sure if it's human blood," Jonathon said. "There are lots of small dinosaurs on this island that are prey for the bigger and meaner ones."

"Yeah, I'm sure that's true," Harley replied. "But, I haven't seen any that are wearing boots yet."

Jonathon moved the beam of light toward a section of sand that Harley was staring at intently. Once it was fully illuminated, there was no mistaking the imprint of a large boot. He moved the light to another boot print and then to another. Soon, it became obvious that someone was travelling in the same direction they were going.

"Someone else may be at that bunker," Jonathon said just above a whisper.

Harley considered what he'd said and then reached for her radio. "Victor, are you out there?"

There was static, and it was obvious someone was trying to respond, but it was impossible to make out what they were saying.

"Victor, I can't make out what you're saying…come again?"

More static, and more unintelligible talking.

Harley, clearly frustrated, jammed the radio back onto her belt and exhaled through her nose. "I can't make out a damn thing they're saying," she grumbled.

"So why would that be?" Jonathon asked.

She put her hands on her hips and stared up at the sky. The darkness was almost pitch black. She was certain that the stars were out tonight but she couldn't see a single one since they were all hidden by the thick veil of mist.

"It's actually a good sign," she replied. "I'm betting it's because they're in the building. Something in there is probably screwing with the reception."

Jonathon walked over next to her and continued to shine the light toward the path they were going to take. "We should keep moving," he said. "We're in a lot of danger wandering around out here at night."

"Lead the way," she said.

Jonathon began walking again and asked, "What were you radioing them for?"

"I wanted to know if everyone was accounted for," she answered.

"I see," he said. "You think the blood we found could be from one of the people that stayed behind." As soon as he said the words, he thought of Charlotte Nelson and it sent a shiver up his spine.

"I just wanted to rule it out," she replied softly.

"It could've been Hank...or a survivor from the plane crash," Jonathon said as he continued to lead the way.

Harley said nothing in response, though the thought had crossed her mind also. As much as her mind wanted to wander and speculate, she forced herself to focus on the current task at hand.

"We can't be far away," she said hopefully.

"No, I agree," Jonathon replied, though truthfully, he wasn't sure.

The two of them carried onward through the darkness and did their best to ignore the strange noises that occurred all around them. The sounds of the dinosaurs were eerie and haunting. Although it was night, a lot of the animals were active and perhaps some of them were watching them at that very moment. The thought was unsettling but Jonathon put his trust in Harley to closely monitor their surroundings while he navigated them to safety. He estimated that they'd walked for twenty more minutes—though it felt like an hour—when finally, they found a cubed structure jutting from the earth. The front of the concrete structure was fitted with a metal door painted red.

"This must be it," Harley said, sounding very relieved.

"This is definitely it," Jonathon confirmed. "Though I'm wondering how we're going to get in it."

He glanced over at keypad next to the door. "From what I remember, there is a combination that must be punched in to gain entry."

Harley smiled and walked past him. "True, but I know something you don't," she said as she pushed her hand against the door. The heavy metal door creaked as it slowly opened inward. "The power is still out and fortunately for us, that makes the door locks useless."

She suddenly paused and looked at her hand. "That's strange," she said. "The paint is wet…why would the paint be wet?" she asked looking back to Jonathon.

He shined the light toward her hand and saw the shimmering red substance over her palm. "I don't think that's paint," he said matter-of-factly.

At that moment, Harley realized it too and she immediately wiped her hand on her pants. "More blood," she muttered. "More blood means someone is probably…"

"Someone is in there," Jonathon said, finishing her observation.

Harley took a deep breath and then kicked the door open the rest of the way. She rushed down the steps with her weapon pointed ahead of her. Jonathon thought her actions were rather reckless, but he could do nothing but trail after her and keep the light directed forward so she could see.

As soon as Harley reached the bottom, he heard her begin screaming at whoever was inside to identify himself. Jonathon shined the flashlight toward the bunker's inhabitant and his jaw dropped open when he realized who he was looking at.

"Well, it took you long enough," Glenn Hardcastle said, squinting his eyes against the light.

"Who are you?" Harley asked forcefully.

"That's Glenn Hardcastle," Jonathon said stepping forward. "He's one of the survivors."

Hardcastle continued to squint. "Get that light out of my face," he snapped. "I can't see you…Jonathon, is that you—surely not."

Jonathon directed the light away from Hardcastle's face so he could see. "It's me, old friend," he replied. "Are you alright?"

Hardcastle sighed deeply and shook his head slowly. For the first time, Jonathon noticed that he looked extremely weak and seemed to be holding his left arm close to his stomach. "No…no, I'm not," he said weakly.

"There is blood on the door outside," Harley said. "I'm assuming that's yours? Are you hurt?"

Jonathon drew near him and knelt. "Glenn, what happened?"

Hardcastle looked down at him and Jonathon could plainly see that his face was ashen. "There are *Velociraptor*s out there," he said with an exhausted groan. "I was attacked and barely escaped with my life."

Jonathon allowed a smile though Hardcastle never saw it. "Knowing you, that doesn't surprise me," he replied. "I'm sure whatever raptor attacked you came out with the short end of the stick."

Hardcastle chuckled and it quickly transformed into a cough. He sounded sick and defeated. "You've got that part right," he said. "But I didn't come out unscathed."

"Well, let us help you," Jonathon replied. "Where are you injured?"

Hardcastle rolled his head around and stared at Jonathon. "I've got multiple cuts and puncture wounds," he muttered. "*That* I can handle...but *this* is a whole other ballgame," he added, and he held up his left arm.

Jonathon felt his jaw drop open and he heard Harley gasp. Glenn Hardcastle's arm was gone just below the elbow. He'd somehow managed to apply a tourniquet to slow the bleeding.

"Oh my God," Jonathon said, unable to hide his shock.

"Yeah, it sucks," Hardcastle grumbled. "Now, are you two really gonna help me or are you just gonna wait for me to bleed to death?"

***

Cliff grumbled when Victor shook him. Two hours seemed to have passed very quickly. He rubbed the sleep from his eyes and yawned as he looked around the room. He heard Charlie and Matt snoozing quietly together in a darkened corner. With Cliff now awake, Victor wasted no time setting up a place for him to lie down and get all the sleep he could manage in two hours.

"It's been quiet," he said as he closed his eyes. "If you need me, wake me. Otherwise, see you in two..."

Within minutes, Victor was sleeping as deeply as Matt and Charlie. Cliff stood and, with his rifle clutched firmly in his right hand, he stretched. He then paced the room a few times to get his blood pumping. Waking up seemed harder for him than usual and he longed for a pot of coffee. Unfortunately, without power, coffee was simply not a luxury that was available to him. He instead took a seat on a nearby stool and sipped on another warm soft drink he retrieved from the fridge.

Things remained quiet for a full hour and Cliff found himself struggling to stay awake. He shook his head rapidly in an effort to stay alert but it was becoming increasingly difficult. Sitting still was boring and boredom made him even more tired. He needed something to do to pass the time. Cliff took a deep breath and allowed his eyes to drift upward toward the ceiling. He remembered Matt Walker saying something about their being powerful sedatives in the veterinary ward above.

Well, I'm not doing anything else, he thought. *Maybe those sedatives will become useful later...*

Without considering the matter further, Cliff carefully and quietly moved the stool he'd been seated on directly underneath the hole. He then climbed upon it and felt around the edges of the ragged opening until he found a suitable grip to pull himself upward. Within seconds, he found himself on the fourth floor and inside the veterinary ward. The room was far darker than the one he'd just left and if it wasn't for the illuminated red EXIT signs above the two doors, he doubted he'd even be able to see his hand in front of his face.

Without further contemplation, Cliff switched on the light affixed to the barrel of his rifle and then surveyed his surroundings. The room seemed to be in relatively good condition. In fact, he'd have guessed it had been untouched since before the hurricane if it weren't for one glaring exception. In all directions, the floor was covered in three-toed foot prints. The prints clearly belonged to a dinosaur, though he wasn't sure what kind. If the presence of the prints were not sinister enough, he soon came to the realization that they were all red—red as blood.

Did an injured dinosaur come in here?

The discovery prompted him to look toward the doors and he immediately noticed one of them had been forced open, evidenced by the splintered door jamb. His awareness was heightened and suddenly his head was on a swivel. Experience had taught him to trust his gut and always plan for the worst. In the moment, he was expecting a hungry dinosaur to jump from a darkened corner at any moment.

Once he was satisfied that the room was indeed clear, Cliff glanced through the hole and into the recreation room below. He knew that if Victor woke up to find him gone, there would be inevitable hell to pay. The thought made him begin to regret his decision and he began to make his way back toward the hole. Suddenly, he remembered the whole reason he'd climbed up there to begin with.

The sedatives, he thought. He paused a moment and shook his head. He'd been so busy looking for dinosaurs in the room that he'd lost his focus and forgotten his objective. *I've gone this far, it would be stupid to go back down empty handed,* he considered.

With the light on his rifle showing the way, he began to open cabinet doors and drawers. He wasn't even sure what exactly he was looking for, but he guessed they would be in a medicine bottle with a label of some kind. As bad as he wanted to rush through the search, he was also cognizant of the fact that he needed to remain as quiet as humanly possible. The door was open and he had no idea if the intelligent dinosaurs Charlie and Matt had spoken of were out there or not.

Cliff had reached the final cabinet and as he rummaged through it, the sound of soft whispering pulled his attention toward the broken door. He whipped his head around quickly and the assault rifle moved quickly with him. He kept the light on the door for a long moment and listened intensely. He saw nor heard anything.

Cliff's heart raced and he felt the hairs stand up on the back of his neck as he anxiously awaited on any sort of indication that something was just outside the door. He didn't get one.

Your mind is playing tricks on you again, he thought. *It's the exhaustion...it must be the exhaustion...no one could possibly be out there.*

He slowly moved toward the broken door and carefully moved into the hallway. He took his time and discreetly surveyed both directions before he actually stepped out of the room. Once in the hallway, Cliff held his weapon pointed in the direction of the stairwell. Just as his pulse was beginning to return to a normal pace, Cliff suddenly heard a voice that startled him.

"Need me...wake me," the voice said, just above a whisper. It was obviously Victor.

Cliff smiled, lowered his rifle, and turned to face his counterpart. He knew he was probably about to face the consequences of leaving his post.

"Victor, you just scared the hell out of me," he said with a slight quake in his voice.

Only Victor wasn't standing there when he turned around. Cliff was instead greeted with a flash of movement in front of him followed quickly by intense pressure and pain in his throat. He opened his mouth to scream but his vocal cords had been severed. Cliff instinctively began furiously striking the attacking *Troodon* on the side of its skull, but the animal only responded by gnashing its teeth deeper into his flesh. Blood spurted from his wound and Cliff lost consciousness in mere seconds.

CHAPTER 22

"It's an absolute miracle that you didn't bleed to death," Harley said as she examined the bloody mess that remained of Glenn Hardcastle's left arm.

"I'm too stubborn to die," he replied with a weak smile. "I knew sooner or later one of these bastards was going to get the best of me, but if they're gonna kill me, they have to do better than this."

"They'll just take you a piece at a time if need be," Jonathon quipped as he knelt down next to him. "Let me look at that again," he said, reaching for Hardcastle's arm.

Though they'd done a great job of slowing the bleeding, there was still blood oozing from the wound. It was just a matter of time before Hardcastle would lose consciousness and succumb to his injuries. Jonathon bit his lip and inhaled deeply through his nose as he came to terms with what needed to be done. He glanced over at Harley.

"It's better, but he's still bleeding," he said. "Infection is a concern also."

Harley could see the concern on Jonathon's face and she knew he was right. Hardcastle, for his part, sat motionless with his eyes closed and his head back. He was clearly in pain and the loss of blood had left him extremely weak.

"I've got a Zippo in my pocket," Hardcastle murmured, as if he'd suddenly developed the ability to read minds.

Jonathon looked at his old friend with sad eyes. "I think it's the only way to make sure we keep you alive," he replied.

Hardcastle kept his eyes closed and said nothing.

"However," Jonathon said with a smirk, "I'd be fine with you dying and getting out of our way. I don't need you slowing us down."

Hardcastle sighed and opened one eye to look at him. "So, this is what you've been doing the past couple of years? Becoming a comedian?"

Jonathon continued to smile but did not respond. He instead reached into Hardcastle's pocket and retrieved the lighter. Harley had discovered a small propane stove and had set it up on the counter against the back wall. Jonathon tossed her the lighter and she promptly lit it. She then placed a frying pan on top and allowed it to begin heating up.

"Well, since you brought it up, what exactly have you been doing these past couple of years?" Jonathon asked him.

Hardcastle shifted in his chair. "You wouldn't believe me if I told you," he grumbled.

"Let me take a guess," Jonathon replied. "You've been training dinosaurs as if they're circus dogs...am I right?"

"Apparently, you've been talking to Cornelius Cold," Hardcastle answered.

"And he's probably wishing he'd never listened to me," a new voice called out from the stairway.

"Mr. Cold?" Harley replied as the man limped into the light.

"Yes, it's me," he said, sounding relieved and tired. "Thank God I found you."

Jonathon rose to his feet. "You survived the plane crash?"

Cold nodded and leaned against a wall to take the weight off his sore legs. "You almost sound like you're disappointed," he replied with an exhausted smile.

"Did anyone else survive?" Harley asked.

Cold's expression turned grim. He bit his lip and shook his head. "I'm afraid not," he said. "I barely escaped before the fuselage became engulfed in flames." He then turned his attention to Hardcastle. "How is he?" he asked, glancing at his gruesome injury.

"I'll live," Hardcastle mumbled. "You all can chit-chat later...how about we get on with this?"

"Get on with what?" Cold asked, looking at both Jonathon and Harley.

"We've got to cauterize his arm or he could get an infection—or slowly bleed to death," Harley answered.

Cold winced as he imagined what Hardcastle was about to experience. He then limped over to him and put a hand on his shoulder. "What happened to you?"

"*Velociraptor*," Hardcastle answered weakly.

"Well, you're a lucky man," Cold replied. "I'd venture to say that a raptor usually doesn't allow its prey to escape."

"Well, it's not often that a man survives a plane crash either, pal."

Jonathon handed Hardcastle a rag he'd found on the counter. "You're gonna want to stick this in your mouth and bite down hard on it," he suggested.

After taking the rag, Hardcastle eyed it a moment then looked back at Jonathon. "I don't have any idea where this rag has been," he said.

Jonathon smiled and looked to Harley. "Are we ready?"

"I'm ready if he is," she answered, looking at Hardcastle. Cold squeezed his shoulder tightly.

"Let's get on with it," he growled and he then shoved the rag into his mouth.

Harley gave Jonathon a *hold him down* look and without further delay pulled the scorching hot pan from the stove. Hardcastle closed his eyes tightly and Jonathon grabbed his injured arm. He could feel Hardcastle's muscles tense up in anticipation of the unbearable pain that he was about to endure. Mr. Cold grabbed his right arm and the two men prepared themselves to keep their friend as still as possible.

Harley firmly pushed the flat bottom of the frying pan against Hardcastle's wound. He screamed but the sound was muffled by the rag in his mouth. Surprisingly, he didn't jerk or thrash his body as badly as Jonathon had anticipated. He'd always known the man was tough as nails, but the way he was handling the current situation made the respect he had for him grow.

"You're doing great, bud," Jonathon said, doing his best to offer encouragement.

Hardcastle offered no response of any kind and suddenly his body went completely limp.

"Oh my God," Harley said, surprised. "I think he just passed out."

"Probably for the best," Mr. Cold said with little empathy. "If he's unconscious, you'll be able to take your time and do the job right."

Harley looked closely at the burned flesh and waited to see if there were any places where blood continued to ooze. Jonathon took the moment to ask Mr. Cold more questions about what he'd been up to the past few hours.

"So, what happened to the plane?" he asked.

Cold looked away from Hardcastle and locked eyes with Jonathon. "Pterosaurs," he answered. "There was a swarm of them that seemed to come out of nowhere...we were overwhelmed. There was nothing the pilot or anyone else could do."

"You see these gashes?" Jonathon asked, pointing to his face.

Cold nodded.

"A pterosaur attacked us when we were floating down to earth. I'm not sure why so many of them were in the air at the same time. Must've had something to do with the hurricane." He paused for a moment and then asked, "The crash site didn't seem so far away...what took you so long to get here?"

Cold shifted his feet and crossed his arms. "Well, the pilot didn't die immediately," he said rather sadly. "I dragged him from the plane but he was too injured to walk." He paused and shook his head. "I think he had a spinal injury."

Jonathon felt a knot form in his stomach. "You stayed with him until he died?"

Cold nodded somberly. "I did," he replied. "I kept hoping someone would show up to help, but unfortunately no help came."

Harley shot Jonathon an icy stare. He remembered when she'd wanted to go check on the crash site but he'd talked her out of it.

"I'm sorry," Jonathon said softly, turning shamefully away from Harley.

Cold turned his head and seemed to stare somewhere beyond the solid concrete wall in front of him. "It wouldn't have mattered," he said with a nervous laugh. "There was nothing anyone could've done."

"That should do it," Harley said, tossing the frying pan aside. "He still lost a lot of blood…I'm not sure if he's going to be okay or not."

"He'll be fine," Jonathon replied quickly, and Mr. Cold nodded in agreement.

Harley looked at both men skeptically.

"Trust us," Cold said flatly. "You don't know him like we do."

Suddenly, Hardcastle began to moan softly and his head rolled forward.

"See there," Jonathon said. "He's already coming back around." He knelt down in front of him and asked, "Are you alright, bud?"

Hardcastle swallowed and nodded his head. His breathing was heavy. "I think I just need to lie down for a little while," he whispered.

Mr. Cold and Jonathon pulled him to his feet as Harley prepared a place on the concrete floor for him to lie. She found an old dusty jacket hanging from a hook in the wall and quickly fashioned it into a makeshift pillow. Once he was settled onto the floor, it only took a few minutes before he drifted off to sleep. Harley continued to look at him with a skeptical glance. Clearly, she was still unconvinced that he'd somehow survive his injuries.

"So, this is one survivor," Cold said, looking down at Hardcastle pitifully. He then turned his attention to Harley. "What about the other three?"

Harley sighed and put her hands on her hips. "I don't know yet," she muttered. "Victor and Cliff made it to the compound but there's a lot of static when we try to communicate with them on the radio. I think the building is creating some sort of interference that is screwing with the signal."

Cold nodded. "The building is mostly made of metal so that's a possibility." He paused and glanced back at Hardcastle. "Why in the world is he way over here and not inside the compound?"

Jonathon shrugged. "I never even got the chance to ask him," he said. "We were so concerned with keeping him alive, we just didn't get around to it."

"I see. So, the two of you are going to try and get access to the compound using the tunnel?" he asked, changing the subject.

Harley was rummaging through the cabinets, but when she heard Cold's question, she stopped suddenly. "How could you possibly know that?" she asked with a raised eyebrow.

Cold reached toward the small of his back where he'd clipped the radio. He pulled it free and held it up so they could see it. "I heard you tell Victor and Cliff," he explained.

Harley walked over to him and took the radio. After examining it a moment, she asked, "Where did you get this?"

Mr. Cold's face turned a lighter shade and he became visibly uncomfortable. "Well," he said, shuffling his feet. "I didn't want to tell you just yet...but, I found Hank."

Harley took a step back and squeezed the radio tightly. "Oh no," she said very quietly.

Cold nodded. "I'm afraid he didn't make it."

For a brief moment, Jonathon thought that she was going to cry. However, her expression quickly turned from sadness to anger and he could see the muscles in her neck tighten. "Did he suffer?" she asked.

Cold shook his head. "I don't think he did," he answered.

Harley lowered her head. "Okay," she said. "Will we be able to retrieve the body?"

Mr. Cold's Adam's apple bobbed as he swallowed. "No, I don't think so," he said flatly.

Jonathon walked over to Harley and put a hand on her shoulder. "We'll try to find him before we leave," he said. "That's a promise."

"I'm afraid we won't be able to do that," Cold interrupted.

Harley and Jonathon whipped their heads around in surprise. They both stared at him wide-eyed.

"Excuse me?" Harley said. She made no effort to hide her anger.

Mr. Cold held up his hands apologetically. "Let me explain," he said. "It's not that I don't want to search for him—believe me, I do. But unfortunately, we've got bigger problems than just dinosaurs I'm afraid."

Jonathon drew closer to him and rubbed at the soreness in the back of his neck. "Cold, I can't think of anything worse that would keep us from looking for Hank than these blasted dinosaurs. So, if there is something worse than that, please spit it out."

Mr. Cold smiled slightly and seemed to open his eyes wider. "Alright, I'll get right to it," he said. "The truth is I've been holding something back from the two of you—well, from everyone actually."

Harley crossed her arms, the rifle dangled from the strap and rested against her waist. "Oh, is that right?" she snapped and then took a step toward him. "What exactly have you been holding back?"

"Don't you both want to know what is causing all the earthquakes we've experienced since we got here?" he asked with a chuckle. He seemed to relish the opportunity to let them in on his secret.

"Go on," Harley urged and she took another step closer.

"This island probably won't make it another full day," Cold said. "We're standing on a ticking time-bomb and if we don't hurry up and get out of here, we're going to blow up with it."

"What the hell are you talking about? What is going to happen to this island?" Jonathon asked bitterly. "Explain."

"I will," Cold replied. "But before I do, we need to discuss another matter," he said. His eyes danced from Harley to Jonathon. He seemed almost maniacal and Jonathon had never seen him act that way before.

"What other matter?" Harley asked, taking yet another step toward him. She was a mere three feet from him now.

Cold's eyes finally stopped on Jonathon. "He can tell you all about it," he said.

Harley turned to look at Jonathon. "What is he talking about?" she asked.

Jonathon shrugged his shoulders and adjusted his hat. "I don't have a clue," he grumbled. "But I'm growing tired of this game. Cold, if you've got something to say, spit it out."

"If this island is destroyed, what will be lost with it?" Cold asked still staring intensely at Jonathon.

Harley quickly answered, "The dinosaurs."

Cold nodded but kept his eyes focused on Jonathon. "What else would be lost forever?"

Suddenly, Jonathon picked up on what Cold was referring to. He felt his pulse begin to race and he immediately began to try and figure out how he could've possibly found out about the fountain of youth.

Jonathon took a deep breath and exhaled slowly. He then closed his eyes and pinched the bridge of his nose as he began to sense a headache on the horizon.

"How do you know about that?" he asked, his eyes still closed.

"The department I work for has its ways," he answered slyly.

Jonathon shook his head and clenched his jaw. "That's not the answer I want," he snapped back. "Tell me how you found out."

Mr. Cold raised his eyebrows and pursed his lips a moment as he thought. "Very well," he said finally. "I don't suppose it really matters at this point since the proverbial cat is out of the bag."

Harley let out an exasperated sigh. "Someone please tell me what is going on."

Cold ignored her and kept his attention on Jonathon. "Let's just say your friend Silas Treadwell has loose lips," he said.

Jonathon frowned and walked over to the counter. He placed both hands on the top and leaned forward, his head facing downward. "Silas told you," he muttered quietly, clearly disappointed.

"He did," Cold confirmed. "And the sad thing is that he still has no idea that he did."

Jonathon kept his back turned to Cold and he continued to face the countertop. "What the hell does that mean?" he growled.

"You still don't fully grasp the value of this island and its inhabitants," Cold replied. "Myself, and the department I work for, were willing to take all and any avenues at our disposal to find out as much as we could about this place."

Jonathon finally stood up straight and turned to face him. Suddenly, he began to understand. "Did you bug his phone?" he asked as he thought back to his conversation with Silas about his aspirations of writing a tell-all book.

Mr. Cold stared at him and nodded slowly.

Harley had been patiently watching the two men speak cryptically at one another and had finally had enough. She charged between them. "Alright, I'm going to ask one more time," she said, clearly angry. "Tell me what is going on here or I may shoot both of you."

Jonathon smiled. "If I tell you, you won't believe me," he replied.

"Tell me," she demanded.

Jonathon sighed and crossed his arms. "Alright," he said. "Cold here is referring to the fountain of youth...it's on this island."

Harley narrowed her eyes and cocked her head to the side. "You're kidding."

"He is telling you the truth," Cold answered for him. "It exists and he's seen it."

Harley stepped toward Jonathon and locked eyes with him. "Tell me he's crazy," she said, jerking a thumb toward Mr. Cold. "There is no such thing as the fountain of youth."

"I wish I could say that were true," he said genuinely. "If it were true, none of this would be happening and many people that have died here would still be alive."

Harley nodded slowly and then began pacing the room. "So, if this is true, I'm guessing you're also going to tell me that it's got something to do with why there are dinosaurs still roaming around here."

"I think it's the logical explanation," Jonathon answered.

"Okay, then where is it exactly?" she asked, still pacing.

"It's in a cave a couple of miles from here," Cold said. "It's not that far, but the terrain is somewhat difficult to get through."

Jonathon turned and walked to where Cold was standing. They were almost nose to nose. "Are you telling me you've seen it?" he asked.

Cold looked him up and down and then gently pushed him back. "No, I have not seen it," he snapped. "At least not in person. When we found out about the existence of the fountain, we began taking geological thermal scans of the island from the air. We were looking for an area that would register temperature signatures consistent with caves—and more importantly, water."

"So, you located it?" Harley asked, finally stopping next to Jonathon.

Cold nodded. "Yes, but that's not all we found," he replied. "As fate would have it, our search for the fountain also brought a more sinister natural presence to light."

Jonathon gestured for him to continue as his anxiety level increased.

"There is an underground volcano here," he explained. "And the shallow underground fractures coupled with the extreme heat signatures made our geologists jump right out of their chairs. It was clear that time was running out on this island. They estimated we had months before the volcano pushed through the crust, but it seems their calculations were off pretty significantly."

"And just how long do we have?" Harley asked, wide-eyed.

Mr. Cold popped his knuckles and shifted his weight...clearly his injured arm was bothering him. "It's hard to say," he said. "Could be days, but most likely we have hours."

"*Hours*?" Jonathon replied, dumbfounded.

Cold inhaled deeply through his nose and nodded. "Probably so," he said. He paused and then approached Jonathon, once again bringing the two men almost nose to nose. "And if we don't act now, the fountain will be destroyed."

"Act?" Harley asked. "Act how? We can't stop a natural occurrence like the one you're describing."

Cold waved her off with a dismissive gesture. "No, of course we can't," he replied. "We're not going to stop anything. But what we *can* do is gather some of the water and take it back to the states where we can do extensive research on it. If we can duplicate—"

"No," Jonathon interrupted firmly. "Why would we want to do that? If you know about the fountain, then you probably know that not long ago a 500-year-old man finally died and was grateful to do so. He felt that the magical powers of that water were a curse, not a gift."

"Ah yes," Cold replied. "We know all about Chief Macuya—or Osvaldo, whatever you wish to call him. And just because one man told you it was curse does not mean that it could not be a tremendous benefit to mankind. Think of all the good that we could do with it," he paused and closed his eyes as if he were watching a movie in his mind's eye. "There is no telling what sort of medical advancements we could discover that would make the quality of life longer and better for everyone. Remember that your wife was a benefactor of the miracles of modern medicine."

"You keep Lucy out of this," Jonathon quipped, and he poked a finger into Cold's chest.

Cold glanced down at his chest and then shot a fiery look at Jonathon. "Who are you to deny the world of the benefits of what that water could bring us?"

Jonathon chuckled and turned away from Mr. Cold. He walked toward the opposite end of the bunker and leaned against the cool concrete wall. "You said the same thing about these dinosaurs," he said, smiling rather maniacally. He then glanced over at the unconscious Glenn Hardcastle. "You told me two years ago that studying these animals would be beneficial to mankind. But all I've seen so far is that the people that continue to meddle with this island continue to die. When are you going to get that through your thick skull?"

"I will get the water with or without your help," Cold spat in disgust.

Jonathon shook his head. "You're not even supposed to be here! Exactly when and how was this water going to be collected?"

"Hank Bailey," he answered quickly. "Hank was the man I hired to confirm the cave's existence and to retrieve a sample of water. All the while Harley, Victor, Cliff, and yourself searched for, and then worked to extract, the survivors from this island. Hank was never a part of that plan."

Jonathon noticed a brief expression of anger wash over Harley's face. "So that explains why I was left in the dark when he was hired," she said bitterly.

"Yes, I'm sorry, but this was top secret and I wanted you to focus on the task of locating the survivors," he replied somewhat apologetically. "The plan was for him to report back to us and at a later date a larger team would come back to gather a significantly larger sample."

"And then your plane went down unexpectedly," Jonathon said.

"And once we were all on the ground, the earthquakes threw you another curveball," Harley added.

Mr. Cold nodded and bit his lower lip. He stretched both of his arms outward on either side of his torso, palms up. "I've got no choice but to complete the mission," he said. "I'd be grateful for some help."

Jonathon scowled at him. "We've still got people in that compound that need our help," he said, pointing toward the tunnel door.

"And they've got Victor and Cliff there to help them," Cold countered.

"We hope they do," Jonathon rebutted. "We haven't really been able to speak to them since they've been in that building."

Cold sighed and closed his eyes. He was clearly agitated but was doing his best to control his emotions. "Harley, I think if you joined me, we could make it in a matter of hours. We could be back to the beach by noon and join the others when it's time to leave."

"Absolutely not," Jonathon said, stepping toward him. He positioned himself in between Cold and Harley as if he were trying to keep her from even hearing the suggestion. "I've been in that cave and as I remember it, it was full of *Troodons*. Those are dangerous animals that—"

"I know about the *Troodons*," Cold replied. "Do you really think that the only reason I've had Dr. Nelson studying that particular species of dinosaur was for military reasons?"

Jonathon felt his heart race. "You've been studying them so that you can get past them in the cave?"

Cold shrugged. "Partially," he admitted. "I wasn't lying when I told you that the animals were being trained for use in warzones. However, learning their behaviors was an added bonus once we began this quest to find the fountain."

"Well, I don't care how much time you've spent studying, or what sort of technology you've used to find the cave," Jonathon said. "But me and Harley are going to focus on the reason we were dropped onto this wretched island to being with. If you want to go kill yourself to get a bottle of water, then you go right on ahead."

Jonathon turned to look at Harley and was stunned by the expression on her face. It was not a look of someone that agreed with his position. She stared at him wide-eyed and her expression slowly turned to something that resembled a child begging for forgiveness.

"Oh no," he said softly.

She smiled slightly. "Jonathon, you and Glenn get to the compound," she said. "I'm going to help him get the water."

He marched toward her and grabbed her forearm. He then pulled her toward a far corner of the bunker. "Please don't do this," he whispered.

"I'll be fine," she said, and her tone suggested she believed it. "I know that you've had some bad experiences here, but I get what he's trying to do," she added, glancing past him to where Cold was standing.

"You haven't seen what I've seen here. There are monsters on this island that can kill you before you even know what's happening. And don't think that gun hanging around your neck is going to keep you alive either," he said. "You shoot that thing at a tyrannosaur and it'll just smile at you and keep coming."

"Trust me, I won't be relying on my gun," she replied, sounding somewhat insulted. "And by the way, I've kept your butt alive since we jumped out of that plane."

Jonathon took a step back from her. It was clear that nothing he could say was going to sway her to stay. "Please," he said softly.

Harley grabbed him by the back of the neck and pulled his face toward hers until their foreheads touched and she was looking directly into his eyes. "Look in my eyes," she said. "When I tell you I will be fine, I mean every word of it. I'll get him to the cave, we will collect the water, and we will meet you at that beach by noon tomorrow."

Jonathon pulled away from her and stomped toward Cold. "You know I've never trusted you since the first day I met you," he growled. "You remind me of an old man I used to know."

Mr. Cold stared at him, perplexed.

"His name was Angus Wedgeworth and his bones are somewhere wasting away on this island as we speak. He became obsessed with finding that fountain too," Jonathon said. "It didn't work out too well for him and you're making the same mistakes he made."

"Maybe I am," Cold shot back, and then glanced over at Harley. "But did he have a heavily armed combat soldier by his side?"

"I'm pretty sure he did not," she said.

Jonathon could only watch in awe as she now stood beside her employer. She was now fully on board with his plan and there wasn't a single thing he could do to stop it.

CHAPTER 23

The moment that Victor awoke, he felt panicked. He glanced at his watch and was surprised to see that nearly four hours had passed since he and Cliff had changed shifts. Daybreak was mere minutes away and Cliff was nowhere in sight. Victor scrambled to his feet and readied his rifle. He paused a moment to check on Charlie and Matt. He was pleased to see that they were still asleep.

I got enough to worry about without babysitting them right now, he thought.

As he surveyed the environment, Victor quickly noticed a stool had been placed directly under the gaping hole in the ceiling. It seemed to him that for some unknown reason Cliff had decided to climb up to the fourth floor. With careful consideration to each and every step he took, Victor quietly crept toward the hole with his rifle pointed the same direction as his line of vision. He refrained from calling out to his partner, though every fiber in his being currently wanted to.

In his mind, the best-case scenario would be that Cliff had decided to do some exploring, took a seat, and fell asleep. As angry as it would make him, Victor sincerely hoped that was what he was going to find. Worst-case scenario would obviously involve him being dead, and then there was something in between that would probably involve Cliff bleeding out and in desperate need of help.

After gaining the confidence he needed to believe the upper floor was clear of dinosaurs, Victor quietly climbed upon the stool and then pulled himself upward into the room above. Due to the lack of windows, the room was quite dark. Victor flicked on the light mounted on the barrel of his rifle and began to scan his surroundings for any sign of movement.

The first thing he noticed was the bloody prints all over the floor. They were three-toed and most likely left there by a *Troodon*. Victor reminded himself of the warnings Charlie and Matt had given him concerning the dinosaur's intelligence. There was a knot forming in his stomach and it continued to grow with every passing second that he did not find Cliff. With as much stealth as he could muster, Victor continued with soft footsteps toward the hallway. Once he reached it, he cautiously peered both directions for any sign of movement. The light originating from the barrel of his weapon picked up something shiny smeared all over the floor. It was more blood and it looked much fresher than the dinosaur prints in the veterinary ward.

Victor felt the knot in his stomach tighten even more and his pulse began to race. He looked on as the blood trail seemed to slither its way toward a nearby stairwell where it eventually disappeared altogether. Victor took a deep breath and then reached for another cigar in his pants pocket. He then placed it in his mouth but refrained from lighting it. He was afraid that the smell would potentially attract unwanted attention to himself. With great reluctance, he began to venture further into the hallway until he eventually found himself moving down the stairs.

Once he was back on the third floor, Victor continued to follow the blood trail down the hallway until it finally ended in front of a door. Also in front of the door were the remains of Cliff Gordon. His mouth was open, an expression of pure terror etched on his face. His entrails had been taken and there was a nasty wound to his throat. Victor instinctively whipped his head around in all directions. As he did so, his light followed, and there was a brilliant flash of illumination in all directions.

He could not be sure but he thought he saw a shadowy figure disappear around the corner at the far end of the hallway. Every fiber in his being told him he should retreat back to the recreation room below, but Victor knew the feeling was fueled by fear. The fact that he felt a bit of fear scared him even more than the possibility that there was a deadly dinosaur just around the corner. He took a deep breath and, with little effort, replaced the fear with anger. Most people would feel sadness upon the discovery that someone they were working with was now dead, but for Victor, it enraged him. Cliff was a soldier and had served his country just as he had. He didn't deserve a death as cruel as the one he'd just been dealt. Victor had to make whatever was responsible pay for it. He snorted, and with his rifle leading the way, he began to walk toward the end of the hallway.

"Alright, I'm coming for you," he growled through clenched teeth. "I know you're used to people running from you, but you'll get no such pleasure from me."

He moved ahead with purpose and as soon as he reached the blind corner, he darted around it and opened fire. The barrel of his rifle spat fire and the bullets that spewed from it tore through sheetrock and wood that covered the walls all around him. Within seconds, he realized there was no dinosaur waiting for him...the small corridor was completely empty. Victor noticed a staircase that led down to the lower floor and realized the animal had narrowly escaped death. With determination fueling him, he trudged onward and marched down the stairs.

Once again, he found himself on the third floor. The hallway was still quite bloody from where George Powell had been killed hours earlier. His vision remained contained to wherever the light on his rifle was pointed. It was not an ideal situation and he knew that he was at a severe disadvantage to the dinosaurs that had been operating in the darkness of the building for days now. Since his eyes were of little use to him, he strained hard to listen with his ears for any sign of movement within the veil of black around him.

"I know you're out there," he said, frustrated when he heard nothing at all. "Come on out and see if I'm as easy to kill as Cliff."

Again, he listened intently, and he thought he heard the subtle sound of breathing somewhere just behind him. He whipped around, expecting to see a dinosaur mere feet behind him, ready to pounce and kill him.

Again, he saw nothing.

Victor shook his head and for the first time, he relaxed. Perhaps the shadow he'd seen on the fourth floor hadn't been a dinosaur at all. He guessed his eyes were now playing tricks on him. As he felt his heart rate begin to return to normal, he rested his back against the wall and then reached into his pocket for another cigar. After planting it between his lips, he then retrieved his lighter and his face lit up a golden orange color as he lit the cigar. He took a pull from it and blew the smoke out softly as he contemplated what his next course of action should be. With Cliff gone, it was just him and the two scientists that were depending on him. Luckily, the sun was now up, and with the water fully receded, he'd changed his mind. It would indeed be far safer to take Charlie and Matt downstairs with him, despite what he'd said earlier about them continuing to wait in the rec room. The way he saw it, the sooner they got out of the building, the better.

He'd just about decided to make his way back up the fourth floor so he could return to the room through the hole in the ceiling when he began to hear screaming. It was a woman—it was Charlie. Panicked, Victor ran toward the door that led into the recreation room. The screaming intensified and now he could hear Matt also.

"What is going on?" Victor yelled. "Open the door!" he shouted, as he desperately tried to push his way into the room. The barricade they'd placed in front of the door was obviously a good one because he was unable to get it to budge at all.

He could hear Charlie screaming for help and then he heard another sound—a more sinister sound. It sounded like a dog's bark, but the sounds were strange and resembled words though he could not understand exactly what was being said. Desperation began to overcome him, and he shouted a warning for them to steer clear of the door.

Without further hesitation, he squeezed the trigger on his rifle and again the barrel spat fire and lead that quickly weakened the heavy wooden door significantly. Once satisfied that he'd done enough damage, Victor then raised his heavy combat boot from the floor and pushed it with all his might against the door. As expected, it gave way, and he then quickly barged his way into the room, knocking chairs out of his way as he moved forward.

"What happened?" he asked as the dust began to settle. It was then that he saw Matt lying on the floor. He was bleeding profusely from a gash on his leg.

"She took her," he rasped, wincing. "The evil bitch took her!"

"*Who* took her?" Victor asked, kneeling beside him.

"The *Troodons* came in here," he replied, and he then reached for the gash on his leg. "Oh my God, am I going to die?"

Victor again glanced at the wound and then snatched up the lab coat that Charlie had been using as a pillow. He took a knife from his belt and began cutting the coat into long strips. Then he took the strips and began tying the tightly around Matt's wound. "You'll live," he said flatly. "Now tell me what happened."

Matt shook his head and licked his lips. "I'm not sure...I woke up, and they were in here," he said, wide-eyed. "She was telling them to take Charlie," he said. "I mean, I couldn't understand them but—"

"Wait," Victor interrupted. "You keep saying *she*...who are you talking about?"

"Mother...the big one," Matt said. "She's the leader, they do what she says."

Victor shook his head in disbelief. "You call her Mother?" he asked.

Matt nodded. "Charlie named her that," he replied. "...when she realized that she was the pack leader. She is the biggest, and I believe the most intelligent. And now she's taken Charlie," he said. "She pulled her straight up through that ceiling."

Victor glanced up at the gaping hole that he'd crawled through about a half-hour earlier. "Stay here," he said, still looking up at the hole. "I'll see if I can find her before it's too late."

Without further hesitation, Victor charged back into the hallway and made his way to the staircase. He figured if the *Troodon* was making an escape with Charlie, it would have to come down the stairs. The only problem was that there were stairwells on both ends of the hallway and Victor was forced to choose one or the other. As he contemplated with direction he would go, he paused and again strained his ears to hear any sound. When he heard nothing, he decided on the stairwell to his left. Victor quickly shuffled down the stairs and did not stop until he reached the ground floor. He then stormed outside and began scanning his environment for any sign of the *Troodons* or Charlie. Suddenly, he saw what he was looking for.

On the opposite end of the building, three *Troodons* were running toward the jungle. The one in the lead was much larger than the others, and cradled in that dinosaur's arms was Charlie. She appeared to be unconscious. Victor raised his rifle toward the fleeing animals but thought better of it. The risk of hitting Charlie was too great. Defeated, he looked to the misty sky and was thankful to see the daylight again. He didn't feel that the odds were very good for Charlie, but it was his mission to come here and get the survivors home. Until hope was all lost, that objective would remain the same.

He snatched the radio from his belt and opened the mike. "Harley, are you out there? Over."

Seconds later, the radio crackled to life. "Victor, I'm here…everything alright? Over."

Victor sighed, took a deep breath, and prepared to give her the bad news.

TERROR IN THE MIST

CHAPTER 24

Harley felt her mouth drop open when Victor told her what all had transpired during the night. She looked over at Jonathon and saw a similar response.

"I don't know what to do," she said, as she slowly pulled the radio away from her mouth. She looked to Mr. Cold. "I don't have any idea what to do now."

It was the first time Jonathon had seen her look vulnerable and it scared him. For the first time ever, he'd been able to share some of the leadership with someone else on the island and it had made things significantly less stressful than his prior trips. The look on Harley's face now suggested that the full burden was once again on his shoulders. He knew full well what they should do but the challenge would be convincing Mr. Cold.

"Getting Charlie back is our first priority," he said, determined.

"I agree," Cold said. "But she could already be dead...you have to know that."

Jonathon shook his head. "No, if the *Troodons* wanted her dead, she'd be no different than Cliff," he argued. "They took her for a reason."

"What reason?" Harley asked, dumbfounded.

"They want a fight," Glenn Hardcastle said suddenly.

They all looked over at him and was surprised to find that he'd been awake and paying attention to their conversation.

"Glenn, are you alright?" Mr. Cold asked.

He nodded, and slowly sat up. He used his remaining hand to rub his forehead. "I feel more alert than yesterday," he rasped. "But the pain is significantly worse."

"That's good," Harley said. "That's a good sign. Once we get back to the mainland, we'll get you the medical attention you need and you'll be back on your feet in no time."

"What do you mean they want a fight?" Jonathon asked. It seemed he was the only one in the room that remembered what Hardcastle had said.

He sighed and looked over at Jonathon. "Charlie and Matt have been poking and prodding those animals for two years now," he said. "I don't have to tell you that those *Troodons* are smart, but I don't think I'd be wrong if I told you that they're much smarter than you probably ever imagined."

"Yes, I'm starting to see that," Jonathon muttered in response.

"They know we're on the island, and they want us gone," Hardcastle said. "People have been here since you and Angus Wedgeworth stumbled across this island almost ten years ago. My guess is that they want that to stop now. We go after Charlie, they'll kill us all."

"All of us won't be going after her," Harley said. "We don't even know where she was taken."

Cold stepped forward. "Oh, I think we know exactly where they took her, right, Jonathon?"

Jonathon nodded slowly. "The *Troodons* have always lived in and around the cave with the fountain," he said.

"Fountain?" Glenn looked at each of them for some sort of explanation.

"Long story," Mr. Cold said. "We'll tell it to you later."

"So now I guess we have an additional reason to go to the cave," Harley said. "We're not going just for the water anymore."

Jonathon closed his eyes and clenched his jaw. "Our time is very short here," he said, and he looked over to Cold. "You said this island is going to basically self-destruct at any moment now."

"Right," Cold replied. "So, we'd better get moving."

"What are you going to fight them with?" Hardcastle asked.

"She's heavily armed," Cold replied, pointing to Harley. "And I've got this," he added, holding up the handgun he'd taken from Hank.

Hardcastle began to laugh and it quickly evolved into an awful cough. When he regained his composure he said, "That's not going to be enough. You're severely underestimating them."

"Well, it's all we've got," Cold replied.

Hardcastle shook his head. "No, it's not," he said. "There is an armory on the first floor of the office building at the compound."

"The first floor was recently underwater," Harley reminded him.

"Yes," Hardcastle acknowledged. "But some of the weaponry we have is locked away in waterproof cases. We'll be able to find something in there that we can use to fight them, I'm sure."

"Well then that settles it," Jonathon said as he approached the doorway that led into the underground tunnel. "Hardcastle and Cold can stay here while Harley and I use the tunnel to get to the compound. We'll get Victor and the other survivor, find weapons at the armory, and then we'll come back here."

"Then we'll go get the water and Charlie," Cold said. "Yes, I think that's a good plan, Jonathon."

Jonathon noticed that Cold had placed getting the water before Charlie in his phrasing but decided to ignore it. "He is not in any condition to join us," he said, pointing to Hardcastle.

"Don't worry, I won't be. I would just slow you down," Hardcastle said. "How exactly will we be getting off this island?"

Harley looked at her watch. "There is a boat coming for us in four hours."

"That's not going to be enough time," Jonathon said. He pulled his hat off and ran his fingers through his hair as he thought. "Someone is going to have to meet the boat and get them to wait on us."

"Let me handle that," Hardcastle said.

Cold and Jonathon immediately looked at each other as if each of them wanted the other to say what they were all thinking.

"I'm not sure that's a good idea," Harley said, doing the dirty work for them.

"No, it's not the best idea," Hardcastle agreed. "But it's all we've got. You'll need all the numbers you can get if you're going to go into the *Troodon* den. I'll get to the beach…don't worry about that."

Suddenly, Harley's radio crackled on. "So, what is the plan?" Victor asked. Harley slapped her head as she realized she'd forgotten all about him. She pulled the radio from her belt and said, "Victor, get to that door and get ready…we're coming your way."

"Alright, so now we've got a plan," Cold said. "We just need to execute it."

"And hope the island holds out," Jonathon added. He glanced over at Hardcastle. "We should be back in an hour. Don't leave here until we get back. I'm going to get you something to protect yourself with while we're in the armory."

Hardcastle nodded, and held out his hand. "Good luck," he said, as Jonathon shook it.

Jonathon then took a deep breath, and opened the door that led into the tunnel. Harley tossed him the flashlight and he took a peek inside.

"Do you see any obstructions?" Hardcastle asked.

Jonathon shook his head. "No…but I can see water a good way down there…probably ankle deep."

"Alright, well let's get moving because a little water will be the least of our worries if another earthquake happens," Harley said.

Jonathon took a deep breath and stepped inside. He didn't know exactly what he was afraid of, but there was an unmistakable feeling of dread that overcame him as he walked. There would be no dinosaurs in there, but still the ominous feeling loomed. Though his stomach was in knots, Jonathon said nothing, he just kept walking. He'd estimated they were roughly halfway through when he noticed a large crack in the ceiling of the tunnel. Dirt had poured through and it was clearly a weak spot that was probably caused by the earthquake.

"One more shake and it'll collapse right there," Harley said, a slight tremble in her voice.

"Try not to think about it," Cold said. "We have to keep moving."

***

Once Victor had gotten the order, he was more than eager to throw Matt over his shoulder if need be and get to the tunnel. He'd had all he could take of the relentless attacks they'd endured from the *Troodons*. He ran up the stairs and into the recreation room where Matt was still lying on the floor.

"I don't suppose there is any chance at all that you can walk?" he asked.

Matt winced as he sat up. "I can try, but I don't know how fast I can move."

Victor rolled his eyes as the answer he got was exactly the answer he expected. Without discussing the matter further, he knelt, pulled Matt over his shoulder, and then stood to leave. As he stood, he heard a voice from somewhere behind him.

"*Walk? Walk?*"

"Who the hell was that?" Victor said, as he quickly looked behind him.

"I don't know, but it sounded just like you," Matt replied with a stammer.

Victor saw no one behind him, but as he was about to turn back, a dangling piece of sheetrock fell from the hole in the ceiling. As his eyes drifted up, it was then that he saw it. There were two *Troodons* standing in the veterinary ward above and they were peering down at them.

"Did that thing say that?" Victor asked. He felt a chill run up his spine as he realized there could be no other explanation.

"It...it mimicked you," Matt said, awestruck. "I've never heard one do that before."

Victor didn't wait to see if the animal did it again, he turned and began to jog toward the door. "Keep an eye on our six," he said as he stepped into the hallway. "If those things start to chase after us, you better speak up!"

He began to make his way down the stairwell when he heard a loud crash that originated from the recreation room. It sounded as if more of the ceiling had collapsed and in his mind's eye, he could see both *Troodons* jumping down on the third floor and giving chase after them.

"Do you see anything?" he asked, frantic.

"No...nothing yet," Matt replied.

As they reached the ground floor and rounded the corner that led to the door of the tunnel, Matt began to hear the unmistakable sound of the dinosaur's large three-toed feet padding down the stairs. It seemed to echo loudly down the hallway. Victor heard it too and he immediately turned, pointed his rifle in the direction of the sound, and opened fire. The gunfire was loud, and echoed so loudly that both men's ears rang. However, the pursuing *Troodons* seemed to have stopped.

"They'd better hurry up," Victor grumbled as he released the locks on their side of the door.

***

"I see the door!" Jonathon said with obvious relief.

As soon as they reached it, he frantically released the locks and turned the lever to open the door. As soon as it swung open, Victor and Matt charged in.

"Victor!" Harley said excitedly. "I never thought I'd be so glad to see you!"

Victor, rather carelessly, dropped Matt to the floor and then leaned his body against the wall. He was out of breath and clearly exhausted. "I could say the same about you, Cash," he replied. "There are two dinosaurs out there," he added, pointing toward the open hallway.

Jonathon pulled the door closed slightly and looked at Matt. "What are they?" he asked.

"*Troodons*," Matt answered, as he rubbed the shoulder he'd landed on when Victor dropped him. "They're in the stairwell right now, but they're clearly stalking us."

Jonathon closed his eyes and shook his head. He wasn't counting on having to deal with any dinosaurs in the building. "We've got to get to the armory," he said to Matt. "How far away from us is it?"

Matt closed his own eyes as he seemed to be mapping out the first floor in his head. "It's only three doors down on the right," he said confidently. "The room is unlocked...you'll need to be quick."

Jonathon nodded, then looked to Victor. "Can you cover us while we go and get what we need?"

Victor checked his rifle. "Yeah, I've got a little bit of ammunition left. Just hurry up...I want to get out of here."

"We all do," Harley said, patting the large man's shoulder.

"What should I do?" Cold asked.

"Stay here with Victor in case he needs some assistance," Jonathon said. "Me and Harley will be back in five minutes tops."

"Alright," Victor said, determined. "Let's get on with it." He barged through the door and immediately opened fire.

Jonathon and Harley didn't wait to see if there were any dinosaurs on the receiving end of his rifle. They just ran for the armory. It was just as Matt has said, three doors down on the right. Jonathon pushed the door open with his shoulder without stopping. Once inside, they immediately began to grab cases of guns, ignoring any weapons that had been left in the open and once submerged in water.

"Here, use this," Harley said, finding a flat, blue cart in the corner of the room.

She wheeled it over and they began piling cases on it, not really taking the time to see what they were grabbing. The gunfire in the hallway had ceased and with the cart full, they hurried back to the tunnel entrance where the others were waiting.

"Any sign of the *Troodons*?" Jonathon asked as they rushed through the door.

"They were standing at the end of the hallway when I started shooting," Victor answered. "Not sure if I hit them or not, but they retreated back into the stairwell and I haven't seen them since." He eyed the cart and immediately reached for a small case on top. "I'll take these," he said, opening the case and pulling two grenades from inside.

"Grenades?" Mr. Cold said in amazement. "Why are there grenades?" he asked, looking at Matt.

Matt shrugged. "That's Glenn Hardcastle's department," he said. "You'll have to ask him. But for what it's worth, we've always stressed to him that we want non-lethal weapons used whenever possible."

"I will ask him," Cold grumbled. "I thought I made it very clear that these animals are huge assets that needed to be protected. I understand the need for some of the firepower but grenades seem to be a little excessive."

"It doesn't matter right now," Jonathon said, sounding agitated. "What matters is that we need to get moving before the *Troodons* come back." He pulled the door closed and then began to turn the deadbolt back into the locked position.

It wouldn't turn.

"What's the problem?" Cold asked, noticing him struggle.

"I can't get it to lock back," he said through clenched teeth.

"Move and let me try," Victor said, reaching for the lock. The big man twisted with all his might but the lock would not turn. "The moisture down here has done a number on it," he grumbled. "It's rusty and I think when you opened it, something may have broken loose inside."

"Well, that's just great," Harley said. "What's going to keep the *Troodons* from chasing after us now?"

Victor rested his back against the closed door and took a moment to light a cigar. "I'll watch your six," he said. "Get moving."

Jonathon looked at Harley and could see the concern on her face. "He's right...we've got to get moving." He began pushing the cart.

"You're gonna have to get up and walk," Cold answered, pulling Matt to his feet. "No one here is carrying you any further."

Matt looked at Victor as if he was expecting him to offer to carry him again. "I'm holding this door until you all get a good head start," he said. "Get moving...I'll be right behind you."

Matt took a deep breath and began to walk. He grimaced as he put weight on his injured leg but moved as quickly as he could manage. Jonathon and Harley led the way with Jonathon pushing the cart, and Harley holding the flashlight. The tunnel sloped downward and made pushing the cart effortless, but Jonathon knew once they passed the halfway point, the incline would begin the other direction and it would get significantly harder. Mr. Cold was right on their heels. He occasionally looked over his shoulder to check on Matt's progress and found that the injured man was falling further and further behind.

"Matt isn't keeping up," he said aloud.

"Victor will carry him again if need be," Harley said. "We've got to hurry."

Victor had held the door as long as he could stand it. He hadn't heard any sound at all on the other side of it and decided that the *Troodons* had most likely retreated. He started to walk away, but then paused. Curiosity of where the dinosaurs were was killing him. Against his better judgement, he slowly cracked the door open and peeked out into the hallway. What he saw made his heart skip a beat and his cigar dropped out of his mouth. What had once been only two *Troodons* had suddenly swelled into what he guessed was about ten or twelve now.

Did they go and get reinforcements?

Victor slowly pulled the door closed again and decided his best course of action now was to run. If they tried to push the door open, there was nothing he would be able to do to stop them from coming in now. He picked up speed as he ran down the incline and in no time at all, he'd caught up to Matt.

"Oh, for crying out loud," he grumbled. He stopped and again threw the injured man over his shoulder. "If we make it out of this, you owe me a box of Cuban cigars," he said.

"That's a deal," Matt said, relieved to be getting help.

Victor was practically running in darkness, but he could just make out a bit of light ahead originating from Harley's flashlight. The slope under his feet began to end and as the concrete walkway flattened out under his feet, he estimated they were roughly halfway through the tunnel. Unfortunately, as Harley and the others began to make their way up the incline, they disappeared from sight and for the first time, he and Matt were completely enveloped in total darkness.

Suddenly, without any warning, the ground began to rumble under his feet.

"Oh no," he said, panting.

"Oh no what?" Matt asked, concerned.

Before Victor had a chance to reply, the rumbling intensified into another strong earthquake. The ground shook so violently that he fell to the ground, and Matt tumbled down beside him. As Victor tried to get back on his feet, he heard a loud crashing sound ahead of him. It sounded as if the ceiling of the tunnel had collapsed. He fumbled around for the button that would turn on the flashlight mounted to his rifle. When he found it, his worst fear was confirmed. The tunnel ahead of them had indeed collapsed and they could go no further.

"This can't be happening," Matt said in disbelief. "I can't believe this!"

Victor wiped the sweat from his brow and leaned over, resting his hands on his knees as he panted. "Well believe it," he said softly. "We're trapped."

"No," Matt argued, and he struggled to get on his feet. "We'll just have to fight those *Troodons* and get back into the building…we'll find another place to hide."

"As much as I admire your fight, we're not going to be able to do that," Victor said, still panting.

Matt clenched his jaw and limped over to him. "What are you talking about?" he asked, sounding somewhat angry. "There are only two of them!"

Victor chuckled as he remembered that Matt hadn't seen what he'd seen in the hallway. "I'm afraid it's a little worse than that," he said.

Matt stared at him, confused. "So, we're just going to wait here and hope they don't come into the tunnel?"

As if on cue, the sound of *Troodons* barking echoed loudly through the tunnel behind them.

"I guess that's not an option either," Victor said, sounding defeated. He then allowed his back to rest on the wall and then he slowly slid to the floor.

"What are you doing?" Matt asked, staring down at him in disbelief. "Get up...we have to fight!"

"I'm afraid we're not going to be able to do that," Victor replied. "There are probably twelve of those things coming for us and I don't have enough ammunition to stop that many before they overtake us."

Matt hobbled closer to him and then dropped down beside him. "So, you're just going to sit here and let them kill us?"

The *Troodons* were getting louder which meant they were getting closer.

"I didn't say that," he said, sounding very calm. He then reached into his pocket. "I've got two left," he said, holding up two cigars.

Matt suddenly understood what was happening. Victor saw no other way out. They were going to die right where they were, but it was going to be on their terms. As his eyes began to well up, he reached for a cigar. Victor then pulled the Zippo from his pocket and lit both of them up.

"You're alright, Doc," he said as he returned the Zippo to his pocket. "If it was gonna go down like this, I'm glad it's going down like this with you." He then laid the two grenades he'd gotten from the cart in front of them.

"Will this hurt?" Matt asked, tears now streaming down his face. "I don't want it to hurt."

Victor took a long pull from the cigar and shook his head. "Nah...it's not gonna hurt."

The *Troodon* barks grew louder and he estimated they were only another minute away now.

"Quick, get on the other side of me," Victor urged, and he helped Matt move around him. He then reached down and picked up the grenades. "They'll jump on me first and as soon as they do, it'll all be over," he said as he pulled the pins from both grenades.

Matt watched with horror as Victor slowly turned the light on his rifle toward the oncoming horde of *Troodons*. Victor released both grenades just as they pounced on him. He was right...Matt never felt a thing.

CHAPTER 25

It took both Jonathon and Mr. Cold to pull Harley out of the tunnel. She was just as strong as she looked and Jonathon did not think he'd have been able to get her out on his own. As soon as the earthquake began, he feared the worst for Victor and Matt. The loud crashing that soon followed just confirmed it.

Harley was not as willing to give up as he had been. She immediately began running back toward the middle of the tunnel, even as it continued to collapse. Jonathon had to sprint after her and tackle her to the ground to stop her. He was afraid that if he didn't, she too would become entombed and die there.

"There is nothing we can do," he said, doing his best to calm her.

"How can you say that?" she screamed, still trying to pull herself free. "We won't know if we don't go and check!"

"He's right, Harley," Mr. Cold said. "There is nothing we can do for them now."

Harley looked at both of them coldly. "If you don't let me go, I swear to God I'll kill both of you," she hissed. "I mean it." And at that moment, she began to struggle for her gun.

"Let her go!" Cold shouted, and he released her.

Jonathon wasn't so willing. "Harley, please!"

But it was too late, she wrenched herself free and began running back into the tunnel. She'd probably taken ten steps when suddenly an explosion erupted from somewhere beyond the rubble. The blast was strong enough that she lost her footing and fell to the ground. She stayed there, on her hands and knees, her head down.

Jonathon ran up behind her and as he reached her he realized she was sobbing. Not knowing what to say, he knelt and put a hand on her shoulder. "Come on," he said softly. "We can't stay here...it's not safe." He looked up at the tunnel ceiling. "This thing could collapse the rest of the way at any moment."

For a moment, he didn't think she was going to get up and he contemplated attempting to drag her out yet again. But fortunately, much to his relief, she finally wiped the remaining tears out of her eyes and she stood.

"Let's go get Dr. Nelson and get out of here," she said in a tone just above a whisper.

Jonathon grabbed her arm and steered her back toward the bunker. "That's exactly what we're going to do," he said. "You head on back, and I'll push the cart out."

Once back in the bunker, Jonathon began rummaging through the cases of weapons. "What all do we have here?" he asked, glancing at Hardcastle.

"Do you see any of the cases labelled *sonic cannon*?" Hardcastle asked, peering over his shoulder.

"As a matter of fact, I do," Jonathon replied, pulling one of the two large cases on the bottom of the cart free. "What is it?"

"That is a powerful weapon that hasn't been fully tested," Mr. Cold said.

"Actually, it has," Hardcastle rebutted. "I had to use it on the *Spinosaurus* during the hurricane…it worked beautifully."

"What does it do?" Jonathon asked as he opened the case. The weapon inside was long and shaped similar to a bazooka, but the end of it had a large bell with a speaker of some sort embedded inside it.

"It can transmit a sound as high as 200 decibels…enough to kill you," Cold said. He then turned to Hardcastle. "How did the *Spinosaurus* react?"

Hardcastle shrugged. "Well, before I answer, keep in mind that the *Spinosaurus* is the largest animal on the island," he began. "But to be honest, it seemed to piss it off more than anything else."

Cold frowned. It wasn't the answer he was hoping to hear.

"But," Hardcastle continued. "For a dinosaur as small as *Troodons* or raptors, it'll do the job easily."

"Great, then you should take it," Jonathon said.

Hardcastle was surprised. "Me? I don't think so…you guys will need it more than me," he said.

"But you've used it before, and you're alone," Jonathon replied.

Hardcastle stared at him a moment and then laughed. "But you're forgetting that I've got one arm now," he said. "To use that properly you need two."

Jonathon felt his face flush red from embarrassment. The weapon *was* quite large and would be very difficult for Hardcastle to use. "Well, what do you want to take?" he asked. "You get first pick."

"Give me a good handgun and I'll be alright," Hardcastle replied. "I don't intend on fighting any dinosaurs at all. I'll stick to the shadows and get to the beach as soon as I can."

Jonathon loaded a gun for him and then handed it over. He then looked at Mr. Cold. "Better give him your radio," he said. "We'll need to stay in contact."

Cold nodded and then clipped his radio to Hardcastle's belt. "It's on, but the volume is turned down very low," he said.

Hardcastle nodded. "Do me one more favor," he said, turning back to Jonathon. "What's left of this arm is useless...I want it taped against my side."

"Are sure?" Jonathon asked, surprised by the request.

Hardcastle nodded. "It already hurts like hell and I'm still having to remind myself that I don't have the hand to use. Trust me...I need it taped up so I won't be tempted to use that arm."

Harley had been listening to the conversation and without saying a word, walked to him and began fulfilling his request. Hardcastle looked over at her; he could see the mixture of sadness and anger in her eyes.

"I'm sorry for what you've had to go through," he said softly as she worked. "This island has a way of driving you mad."

Harley glanced at him and smiled. "Yeah, hopefully it'll all be gone in a few hours."

Hardcastle glanced over at Cold. "What is this I'm hearing about the island being destroyed?"

Mr. Cold sighed, remembering that Hardcastle had been unconscious when they'd all discussed it the night before. He went on to quickly relay what he'd learned from the geologists that had been studying the island. As Harley finished the taping job, he said, "It sounds like an underground volcano is going to push through the surface."

Jonathon and Harley looked at each other and then to Cold.

"Is that a possibility?" Jonathon asked.

Before he could answer, Hardcastle spoke again.

"I think it was February 1943 when a family in Mexico noticed a little patch of land on their farm suddenly swell upward and a tiny fissure formed. They noticed smoke coming from the fissure and a short time later a crater developed. Twenty-four hours after that, a 170-foot cone had formed and flames began to erupt from it during the night. In a matter of days, the valley surrounding it became covered in ash," he said. "Basically, a volcano formed on a family's farm in one day."

Jonathon's eyes narrowed as he tried to imagine what Hardcastle was describing. He again looked to Mr. Cold. "Is this what's happening here?" he asked.

Cold breathed deeply through his nose. "I don't know," he said, sounding somewhat annoyed. "Maybe...probably."

"The earthquakes have been going on for days now," Hardcastle said. "It's just a matter of time."

"Then we need to stop talking," Harley said, agitated. "Time is running out. We need to go now."

Hardcastle nodded. "She's right. I'll meet you all at the beach—and Charlie better be with you."

"She will be," Jonathon replied, sounding determined.

Hardcastle headed for the door, with the gun in his hand. As he walked by Jonathon, he paused, leaned over, and whispered in his ear. "That other large case has a flamethrower," he said. "If I were you, I'd take that. All animals fear fire."

Jonathon smiled and nodded. "Get to the beach," he said, patting him on the back.

Hardcastle clutched the handgun tightly in his remaining hand and left the bunker without another word.

Jonathon immediately followed his suggestion and retrieved the flamethrower. Mr. Cold and Harley looked on in amazement as he placed the tank onto his back.

"Don't look at me like that, I don't even know how to use it," he admitted sheepishly.

Harley smiled and walked over to him. "Well, it's a good thing that I do," she said. She then spent the next several minutes giving him a crash course on how to use the weapon.

"Harley, why don't you take the sonic cannon?" he suggested after she'd finished. "Cold, take the rifle and bring extra ammunition. I think we've got what we need."

"Let's do this," Harley said, and she led them out of the bunker.

"Remember that we may encounter dinosaurs between here and the cave," Jonathon reminded her. "Be alert and if either of you hears anything, speak up before it's too late."

They nodded in agreement and began the trek toward the cave. There were still reminders everywhere they looked that only days ago Hurricane Simon had torn across the landscape. Trees were bent over and uprooted in a fashion that reminded Jonathon that although the dinosaurs on the island were massive and terrifying, Mother Nature was capable of wiping them all out whenever she saw fit. And it seemed she was going to do just that but instead of a storm, a volcano would be her weapon of choice. As they walked across the beautiful prehistoric landscape, Jonathon felt a sadness come over him as he realized it would soon all be over. Ever since he'd discovered the island, he'd felt a great need—no responsibility, to take care of it and keep it hidden from the outside world. It had become painfully obvious that he'd failed miserably at the task, but now it seemed it would've all been for naught anyway.

Mr. Cold had taken the lead and seemed to be using a handheld GPS to chart their course to the cave. Jonathon said nothing, but he occasionally glanced over at Harley to see how she was doing. She'd been very quiet since they'd lost Matt and Victor. It seemed to have had a much greater impact on her than the loss of Hank or Cliff. He wasn't sure why that was, but guessed it had something to do with the fact they'd just become reunited, and once they were reunited, he figured she felt more responsible for their safety. He wanted to talk to her, to remind her that it wasn't her fault. But he was unable to muster the courage to do so.

"How much further?" he asked as he glanced down at his watch. The ship would be arriving in another two hours.

"We've got another mile or so and we should be there," Cold answered.

Truthfully, they could've gotten there even faster but Cold purposely took them along a somewhat longer route to avoid finding the remains of Hank Bailey. That, he knew, would cause complications he simply did not want to contend with. The task at hand was simple: Get the water, and get off the island. Dr. Charlotte Nelson was, in his mind, as good as dead. Trying to venture deep into the den of the *Troodons* was a careless risk that he had no intention of taking.

In the distance, across the valley, they all watched in awe as a herd of sauropods marched majestically toward the large lake in the middle of the clearing. They seemed to have not a care in the world, and certainly knew nothing of their impending doom.

"They really are amazing," Harley said as she walked casually alongside Jonathon. "There can't be very many animals here that would be able to harm them."

Jonathon nodded as he too stared at them appreciatively. "No, just tyrannosaurs and the *Spinosaurus*...that's pretty much it," he answered. "The young ones have to worry about smaller predators, but usually the adults are there to protect them if need be."

"Speaking of tyrannosaurs," Harley said. "I haven't seen one since we've been here."

"You don't want to," Mr. Cold said quickly.

Jonathon chuckled. "He's absolutely right about that," he said. "Trust me, you don't want to be in the vicinity of one of those."

Harley looked around her, scanning the environment. "So where are they... I mean, how close are we to their territory?"

"Too close," Jonathon answered. "They frequently hunt in this valley, which is why I'm eager to get away from it."

"Not that much farther," Cold said, hearing Jonathon's concern. "Once we reach the jungle, we've got another half mile to go and we should be there."

"Wait, something is wrong," Harley said suddenly, pointing toward the herd of sauropods. "They're running away from the water."

Jonathon looked in the direction she was pointing and noticed that the mammoth animals were indeed galloping away from the water. His first thought was that Harley was going to get to see her first tyrannosaur, but seconds later, he realized that wasn't what spooked them at all.

"Not again," Cold said, stopping.

The ground began to shake and there was an audible rumbling sound that they could hear underneath the earth. "That doesn't sound good," Harley said. "Our time must be really short now."

The three of them stood still, waiting on the shaking to stop, but it intensified to the point of causing Cold and Harley to fall to the ground. Jonathon almost went down also, but barely managed to keep his balance. All around them, the dinosaurs of the island bellowed and wailed their frightened cries. It was a sickening sound and Jonathon thought it would never end.

Just as he thought things could get no worse, a terrifying roar rolled across the valley from the opposite side.

"What was *that*?" Harley asked, immediately pointing the rifle toward the dark jungle where the sound originated.

"*That* is the sound of a scared *Tyrannosaurus rex*," Jonathon said. "We need to leave...now." He turned and began to jog toward the cover of the jungle.

Harley and Mr. Cold scrambled to their feet to do the same. The earth continued to shake and it made running an awkward and clumsy task. It was Jonathon's turn to fall over, and Mr. Cold fell again as well. Harley paused to try and help both men up. She looked over her shoulder and at that moment, she finally understood what Jonathon meant about not wanting to see the tyrannosaur in person.

"Oh my God," she said, her eyes wide with terror.

Jonathon immediately recognized the fear in her expression and knew what she was seeing. He looked behind him and found two large tyrannosaurs lumbering across the valley, each of them taking turns throwing their heads back and releasing their deafening roars.

"What are they doing?" Cold asked in amazement.

"They're scared," Jonathon answered. "They're just as confused as everything else is on this island."

"Does that mean they won't bother us?" Harley asked.

Jonathon stared at the massive creatures and desperately wanted to give Harley the answer she wanted. However, their current trajectory and speed didn't make him very confident. The earth finally began to settle down and the shaking ceased. Jonathon immediately scrambled to his feet.

"Run! Now!" he said, unable to hide his fear.

Harley and Mr. Cold chased after him with all the speed they could muster.

"If we make it into the jungle, we'll have a chance," Jonathon yelled over his shoulder. He could hear the tyrannosaur's large three-toed feet slamming against the earth loudly as they continued to chase them.

They were almost to the jungle when suddenly the nightmare they were experiencing turned from bad to worse. Immediately in front of them, another monstrous dinosaur stormed out of the jungle with an explosive fury made evident by the creature's own nightmarish roar. It was the lone *Spinosaurus* on the island. The beast's roar seemed full of pain and rage. Jonathon immediately noticed that the animal's slender skull was torn and bloody. One of its eyes appeared to be gouged out, and each time it opened its jaws, he could see that the roof of the animal's mouth appeared to be burned and blackened.

What on earth happened to you? Jonathon wondered as he stopped dead in his tracks.

"Oh my God, what do we do now?" Harley asked.

"The sonic cannon, I think it's time to use it," Jonathon answered, pointing to the strange weapon strapped to her back.

Harley frantically reached for the weapon and prepared to aim at the *Spinosaurus*.

"There is no time for that!" Cold said, and before Jonathon had a chance to talk him out of it, he began to open fire on the approaching *Spinosaurus*.

The giant beast immediately felt the bullets pelt the tough flesh on its chest, but the gunfire did little to no damage. The angry dinosaur roared again like a medieval dragon and before Cold had any time to react, he was plucked from the ground and tossed aside like a Frisbee. Harley and Jonathon watched in horror as the man flew at least fifty yards through the air and they simultaneously winced as they heard his body slam to earth with a sickening *thud*.

Harley finally readied the sonic cannon, but it was too late, the *Spinosaurus* was upon them. She screamed as she placed her finger on the trigger. The animal was just about to trample over her when she instinctively rolled to the right. Jonathon was forced to run in the opposite direction and in doing so, tripped and hit his head hard on a rock. He laid on his back and felt himself on the verge of losing consciousness.

No! he willed himself. *Get up!*

As he struggled to remain awake, he suddenly realized that the *Spinosaurus* wasn't targeting them at all. It clearly was after what had been approaching from behind them. The two tyrannosaurs roared with fury as they crashed into their larger adversary. The *Spinosaurus* wasted no time in snapping its jaws closed onto the neck of the one that met it first. The other tyrannosaur sunk its sharp teeth onto the *Spinosaurus's* right arm, but the furious creature clamped its jaws even tighter onto the throat of the first victim.

Jonathon watched in awe as the tyrannosaur that was trapped in the *Spinosaurus's* mouth thrashed wildly in an effort to wrench itself free, but as more and more blood began to ooze from the wounds where the needle-like teeth had pierced deeply into its throat, the animal's movements became more lethargic until the point of no movement at all. The first tyrannosaur had been strangled to death.

Jonathon felt warm blood running down the side of his head and into his ear. He knew that if he and Harley were going to escape, now was their moment. He got on his hands and knees and immediately began looking for her. She'd rolled across the ground on the other side of the *Spinosaurus*, but after he'd hit his head, he'd lost sight of her. He felt his heart rate pick up significantly as the two remaining dinosaurs continued their fight to the death. As soon as there was a victor, he was very cognizant of the fact that he and Harley would become the prize. As he moved behind the *Spinosaurus* in search of Harley, he curiously looked up and noticed that the remaining tyrannosaur had all but ripped the right arm of the larger dinosaur completely off. It was a bloody mess and would never be used again. Returning his attention to the task at hand, Jonathon crawled over to where he'd last seen Harley. She was nowhere to be found.

For a moment, he wondered if perhaps she'd run into the jungle. He certainly hoped that was the case, but as he was just about to turn away, he noticed something troubling on the ground another ten feet away. The now broken sonic cannon was lying there, but perhaps more troubling, there was quite a bit of blood spattered on the grass around it.

As the *Spinosaurus* began to get the upper hand on the now bloody tyrannosaur, Jonathon used his hand to clear the blood off the side of his head. He then wiped it on his pants as he stood. He took one final moment to look around for any sign of Harley. When he saw none, he gripped the large flamethrower in his hands and began to sprint toward the shadowy jungle.

Just as he took refuge under the canopy of the trees, he glanced over his shoulder just in time to see the other tyrannosaur fall lifeless to the ground. The victorious *Spinosaurus* stomped its large clawed foot on top of its kill and released a furious roar that rattled every bone in Jonathon's body. The monstrous beast then began to feed on its new meal, completely unaware of Jonathon's narrow escape.

CHAPTER 26

Glenn Hardcastle had moved through the jungle with a great deal of stealth. It wasn't hard because there was a part of him that couldn't shake the feeling that the *Velociraptor*s could still be nearby and waiting for their moment to finish him off. He was more than willing to take his time and move at as slow a pace as necessary to keep him from getting attacked again.

His injured arm ached so badly at times that he worried he would pass out, but it was the fear of the *Velociraptor*s again that seemed to motivate him to remain conscious. Multiple times, the sounds of twigs snapping in his vicinity made him pause and search his surroundings for any sign of the vicious pack hunter. No matter how much he tried to push the thought that he was being watched aside, it seemed his mind would refuse to cooperate.

As if his terrible injury and his mind weren't making things hard enough, there had been another earthquake. This one had probably been the worst of all. The earth shook so violently that he was forced to kneel on one knee to keep from falling over. Not only was it the most intense, but it seemed to last longer than any of the ones before it. Hardcastle didn't know how long they had, but he was beginning to wonder if the ship was going to be too late to rescue them.

He had estimated that he was roughly halfway to the beach when once again he heard the sound of movement somewhere beyond a crop of tropical flowers to his right. As he'd done countless times before, Hardcastle paused and watched intensely for any sign of movement. He was just about to take another step forward when he spotted exactly what he'd feared the most. About sixty yards to his right and just beyond the colorful flowering vegetation, Hardcastle spotted two raptors walking slowly in the same direction that he was going.

He glanced at his watch and realized he only had an hour before the ship was scheduled to arrive. It was very important that he was on the beach when their help emerged from beyond the wall of mist. Obviously, he was powerless to do anything if the island began to turn into an erupting volcano before it arrived, but he had to assume that would not be the case. If he got himself killed, it could be catastrophic for Jonathon and the others that were depending on him. If no one was there when the ship emerged, it was very likely that they'd all be feared dead and in turn, the ship would probably leave. The presence of the *Velociraptor*s made things significantly more difficult, but he had to find a way to succeed.

***

Jonathon had entered full-fledged panic mode. Harley was absolutely nowhere in sight and there wasn't the slightest sign of where she'd been. The only thing he knew to do now was to continue the trek toward the cave. It was his hope that maybe Harley had escaped the fighting dinosaurs before him and was now somewhere ahead. With any luck, they'd both meet up at the entrance to the cave and enter it together.

The panic and uncertainty he was feeling had given him a boost of adrenaline. As exhausted as he was, he continued to run. Jonathon felt if he could just reach the cave he could not only put his attention on finding Charlie, but it would also probably let him know Harley's fate. It was the unknown that was driving him crazy. The last thing he wanted to happen was for him find both women dead and be forced to return to the beach alone. If that happened, he didn't know how he'd be able to live with himself.

It had been almost ten years since the last time that Jonathon had entered the cave. He kept thinking he'd come across something that looked familiar and reminded him that he was on the right track. Unfortunately, due to years of new growth and fresh storm damage, he saw nothing that jogged his memory. Jonathon was on the verge of thinking that perhaps he'd missed it, or gone the wrong direction altogether. In his haste to escape the dinosaurs that were fighting, he'd forgotten all about the GPS unit that Mr. Cold was using to guide them on the right path.

His head ached from the abuse it had taken over the past two days. The gash on his face still burned to the point that he was almost certain infection had set in. The new wound he'd sustained when his head hit a rock half an hour before certainly wasn't helping. The blood on the side of his face was now dried, and his hat now felt glued to his hair. If it weren't for the adrenaline, he wondered if he'd even be able to continue under the circumstances.

Just as he was beginning to lose hope of finding the cave at all, he tore through a thicket of ferns and suddenly he saw it. At nearly thirty feet wide, and twenty feet tall, the mouth of the cave was black and ominous. Just as he'd remembered, there were curtains of vines and other leafy vegetation that hung from the top of the opening providing perfect camouflage that would make it hard to notice for the unobservant passerby. There was no sign of Harley. As he stood in front of the entrance, he paused a moment, panting. His outer shirt was soaked with sweat and blood. In an effort to reach some tolerable level of comfort, Jonathon ripped his shirt open and tossed it aside as the buttons bounced off the rocky ground under his boots. His sleeveless white T-shirt was dirty and bloody also, but considerably less so.

Jonathon knew practically nothing about the military-style flamethrower but thankfully Harley was a good teacher. She'd taught him how to light the pilot flame and explained that once he pulled the trigger, a valve would open and release the pressurized flammable liquid. Once it crossed over the pilot igniter, the flames expelled could reach targets up to one hundred feet away. She also cautioned him to be precise and conservative since the flammable liquid would run out quickly. He also had a handgun at his disposal tucked away in the back of his pants. Part of him wished that he'd grabbed a rifle also, but the weight of the flamethrower and its tank was tough enough for him to handle in his exhausted state.

With the weapon readied and his anxiety level through the roof, Jonathon began walking into the darkness of the cave. Once fully enveloped in the darkness, Jonathon waited patiently for his eyes to adjust. It was tempting to fire a burst of flame ahead of him just so that he'd see what he was walking into, but Harley's advice of using the weapon conservatively weighed heavily on his mind. Despite the darkness, the cool and damp environment was a welcome change from the typically hot and humid conditions outside.

Just as his eyes finally began to adjust, Jonathon came across several shafts of light that shone down from the ceiling of the cave and directly into a pool of water on the stone floor. The water was the bluest he'd ever seen and sparkled majestically in the light. It was the fountain of youth, the object on the island that had indirectly caused so many deaths. Jonathon had forgotten how the water seemed to beckon whoever was around to come and take a drink. There was no doubt a supernatural element about it and it seemed that this time the temptation to drink from the fountain was even stronger than before.

He stared at the water for a long moment and almost felt as if he'd entered some sort of trance. There was a presence in the shadows behind him watching intensely. The presence paced slowly but made sure to stay within the shroud of the shadows. The animal's cat-like eyes provided it with excellent night vision and the cover of darkness was its preferred environment for hunting. Jonathon did not sense the stalking *Troodon* as he continued to stare at the enchanting blue liquid.

Suddenly, he heard a soft groan from the opposite wall of the cave from the hidden *Troodons*. It was a woman's voice and it immediately pulled him from the spell the water had temporarily placed him under. He turned away from the fountain and jogged over to a large, darkened crevice in the cave wall. It was there that he found Harley. Jonathon was immediately overcome with a strong sense of relief.

"Are you alright?" he whispered.

She was seated on the stone floor and was bleeding badly, but he was unable to tell from where. She looked up at him when she heard his voice and her eyes had a glazed look about them that scared him. She'd apparently lost a lot of blood.

"J-Jonathon," she stammered weakly.

"Yes," he said. "It's me...I'm getting you out of here." He knelt down and attempted to pull her up.

With what seemed to be almost all of the strength she could muster, Harley pushed him away. "No," she groaned a little louder than he'd have liked. "Get Dr. Nelson."

Jonathon's heart leapt. "Charlie? She's alive?" he asked as he pulled away from her.

Harley swallowed and nodded. The small amount of illumination that originated from the shafts of light was enough for him to see the glistening sheen of sweat all over her face. She didn't look good and he found himself wondering how he'd even get her to the beach. He shook the thought from his head and decided he'd carry her if that was what it took.

"Where is she?" he asked her with desperation in his voice.

She licked her lips and turned her head to look further into the darkness of the cave. "T-they go b-back and forth through there," she said weakly. She gently raised her arm and pointed past the fountain.

Jonathon had never been past the pool of water in the cave and he'd never really given it much thought. Obviously, there had to be another chamber where the *Troodon* pack's actual den was located. As he squinted his eyes and tried to see beyond the veil of darkness, Harley suddenly prodded him with something. He looked down and realized she was trying to give him a flashlight.

"Alright," he said leaning down to whisper in her ear. "I'm going to go after Charlie but I will be back for you as soon as possible."

She smiled at him. Her breathing was labored and the longer he stared at her, the more worried he got. He took the light from her and pushed a few dangling strands of brown hair out of her face. He knew she was a warrior and he also figured if he'd sustained whatever injury she was now suffering from, he probably wouldn't be able to hang in there as well as she was.

"You better be here when I get back," he said, smiling. "Don't head to the beach without me or I'll never make it back."

She nodded slowly and then rested her head against the rock wall. Jonathon then rose and turned to face the unknown dangers that lurked beyond the darkness ahead of him. He flicked the flashlight on and the bright beam revealed a narrow passageway. With soft steps and the flamethrower readied to unleash hell, he entered the passageway. He estimated the walls were around six feet wide when he entered, but as the floor began to slope downward, the gap narrowed to three. As the beam of light continued to show him the way, the passageway abruptly ended and Jonathon found himself in a much larger chamber than the one that housed the fountain of youth. The walls seemed to form a circle and it reminded him of a small amphitheater.

As he shined the light around the chamber, he noticed various tunnels that apparently led even further into the cave. The tunnels, however, were much smaller...too small for him to stand up in. If he had to, he could crawl through them but it would be a tight fit with the tank for the flamethrower on his back. It was disheartening when he realized there was no sign of Charlie in the chamber. Not only because he *still* had no idea where she was, but also because he was seriously beginning to think he'd have to crawl through a tunnel—and if he did, which one?

Jonathon took a deep breath as he contemplated what to do. Time was still not on his side and he had to make a decision quickly. He began walking toward the tunnel straight ahead of him. When got nearly halfway there, he took a step and felt the stone floor disappear beneath his foot. He tried desperately to fall backwards, but unfortunately, his other foot slipped on loose rock. With no idea of what he was falling into—or how far he would fall—Jonathon instinctively tried to fall sideways as he reached for anything available to grab onto. His hand found nothing, and seconds later, he tumbled downward.

Fortunately, the rocky ground was sloped and Jonathon managed to roll and slide into the strange pit instead of falling. Once he reached the bottom, the ground seemed to turn sandy. The flashlight had escaped his grasp and Jonathon immediately scrambled to find it. In his mind's eye, he could see multiple *Troodons* emerging from the walls and closing in around him. The thought made him panic and he grew more frantic. As he searched and clawed his way along the sandy ground, his right hand found something unexpected. It felt like a leg—a human leg. The leg was smooth and cool to the touch. Jonathon felt his way up the leg and as he made his way up to the person's head, he came to the conclusion he'd found Charlie.

She was unconscious and the coolness of her skin troubled him. For a brief moment, he feared that she was dead, but once he placed an ear near her nose, he was relieved to hear her breathing. With the flashlight still lost, he sat down and pulled her over and onto his lap.

"Charlie," he whispered. "Charlie, I need you to wake up."

He shook her gently and she began to groan softly.

"That's it," he said as he strained his eyes to see anything in the blackness around them. "Wake up. We've got to get out of here."

Charlie continued to groan and she turned her head slightly. It was as if she was trying to emerge from a very deep sleep. Jonathon lightly slapped her face and shook her again.

"Wh-what?" she muttered groggily.

Jonathon smiled and hugged her tightly to him. He kissed the top of her head. "That's it," he said. "Wake up."

Still very much aware of the impending danger around them, without further hesitation, Jonathon pulled Charlie to her feet. She wobbled a moment and leaned heavily against him.

"Can you walk?" he asked.

She swallowed hard and slowly nodded. "Yes," she said. "But I haven't been able to find a way out."

Still blinded by darkness, Jonathon felt the wall closest to them and realized it was impossible to climb. The slope he'd slid down was narrow and it occurred to him that it was probably the only way in or out.

"I found the way in," he replied. "There is an incline somewhere in that direction," he added, pointing—though he knew she couldn't see him.

"I'll follow you," she said as she clutched his shirt.

"Alright, hold on tight," he said as he began to move.

He'd taken only four steps when suddenly an eerie sound startled him. Somewhere to their left, a low growl was heard. Jonathon stopped in his tracks and though his heart rate began to increase, the flamethrower in his hands comforted him.

"It's one of *them*," Charlie said, her voice quaking.

Jonathon stood completely still a long moment, doing his best to control his breathing and stay calm. He kept the flamethrower pointed in the direction where he'd heard the growling and contemplated what his next move would be. Just as he was about to take another step forward, he heard another sound. This time, it was the guttural barking noise the *Troodons* seemed to make when they were communicating. It definitely sounded to Jonathon as if the animals maybe had their own sort of language as Silas had described to him.

"They're everywhere," Charlie said as she heard the sound too.

"Stay close to me," Jonathon replied. He held the flamethrower tightly in his hands and moved a finger to the trigger that would unleash death ahead of them. He could hear eerie breathing all around them and could sense a sinister presence closing in like a vice. "Alright, this is going to get nasty," he muttered to Charlie.

Before she even had a chance to reply, he squeezed the trigger and an angry burst of flame exploded from the end of the nozzle. The resulting orange light immediately illuminated the pit in which Jonathon and Charlie had found themselves. All around them, there were at least twenty-five *Troodons* lurking along the pit walls, stalking them in the darkness, and waiting for their moment to pounce. The flame had clearly frightened them and Jonathon looked on as three *Troodons* directly in front of them became engulfed in fire.

The burning dinosaurs wailed and shrieked pitifully as the remaining *Troodons* began barking furiously and hissing toward Jonathon. All of them had teeth bared and seemed to agree in unison that their moment to kill had arrived. Jonathon sensed the danger and instinctively began throwing flame to his left and continued the rotation until he'd engulfed every *Troodon* in the pit into a fiery blaze. The high-pitched screaming of the burning animals around them was sickening. When Jonathon would be able to take the time to reflect, he was sure he'd be able to feel pity for the vicious creatures. But in the moment, all he wanted was to get out alive.

CHAPTER 27

Hardcastle's pace had slowed considerably. He'd practically kept one eye on the terrain ahead of him, and one eye on the raptors that moved roughly sixty yards away and parallel to him. Though he was grateful, Hardcastle was very puzzled that they had not noticed him and also that there had been no sign of any other raptors in the vicinity. He continued onward until he finally began to hear the surf ahead of him. Before he reached the beach, Hardcastle decided that he'd stay hidden away in the shadows at the edge of the jungle until help arrived. He figured it would be unwise to trounce out onto the sandy beach where he'd be vulnerable to the nearby *Velociraptor*s. The thought made him again glance over to see what the raptors that had been alongside him were doing. When he did so, he instantly felt his jaw drop and he again stopped dead in his tracks. Suddenly, there weren't just two *Velociraptor*s there, but six…and they were all feeding on something on the ground.

***

Jonathon was practically pushed up the sloped incline by Charlie Nelson as the screaming *Troodons* continued to burn and die in the pit behind them. The flaming dinosaurs supplied plenty of light and visibility had improved significantly for Jonathon. As he made his way back in the direction of where he'd left Harley, he caught a glimpse of both his and Charlie's tall shadows dancing on the cave wall ahead of them. As he followed the shadows upward, he was surprised at exactly how tall the cave ceiling was. He estimated it had to be at least one hundred feet high and he could clearly see that it was peppered with clusters of large bats. The sight made him shiver as he entered the narrow passageway that led back into the large chamber where the fountain was located.

The incline seemed to be steeper than he remembered and his legs began to ache. Jonathon quickly realized it wasn't the incline so much as it was Charlie clinging tightly to his shirt and weighing him down. He resisted the urge to tell her to let go because it was the only way he knew for sure she was still with him. Once they'd made their way out of the passage, Jonathon made a beeline straight for the crevice in the wall where he'd left Harley.

"Harley," he whispered. "Harley, are you there?"

There was no answer. He turned toward Charlie and said, "She was right here before a few minutes before I found you. I'll watch the passageway if you'll get down low and check the crevice. I can't see her at all."

Charlie nodded and knelt down as Jonathon turned and readied the flamethrower for more destruction if needed. She felt nothing, and eventually got down on her hands and knees to make absolutely sure.

"She's not here," she said frantically.

Jonathon sighed deeply and cursed under his breath. Beads of sweat rolled out from under his hat, down his forehead, and dripped off his nose and chin. As he stood there, wondering what to do, he glanced over his shoulder at the passageway behind him. The sounds of dying dinosaurs continued to echo from the pit but their numbers were far fewer. Jonathon turned his attention back toward the mouth of the cave and just as he was beginning to accept the possibility he'd have to go on with only Charlie, he spotted a silhouette step into the frame of the cave's exit.

He clearly heard Charlie gasp when she spotted it too. The *Troodon* that stood between them and their freedom was far larger than the others. It stood nearly two feet taller and the feathering on top of its skull was a deeper shade of red—almost purple. The dinosaur's teeth were bared and a silver strand of saliva dripped from its chin. The creature turned its head sideways and snarled loudly at Jonathon. At the animal's feet was an unconscious woman—Harley.

"It's the one we call Mother," Charlie whispered from just behind him. "She's the leader of the pack—and the most intelligent animal I've ever known."

"And I just killed most, if not all, of her pack," Jonathon said, trying to stay calm.

Charlie swallowed, unsure what to say.

As Jonathon stared at the angry *Troodon*, he said, "Alright, here is how this is going to go down. Clearly, she only wants me, and I don't intend on going quietly. When it all begins, you get out of here."

She clutched his arm tightly. "I can't just leave you here," she snapped at him. Though she was afraid, he could sense remarkable bravery too.

"You can," he replied with a smile, "and you will. Do you think you can get Harley out of here?"

Charlie bit her lip as she began to accept that she was not going to change his mind. "I'll find a way," she answered. Reluctantly, she released his arm.

"Alright," he said, taking a moment to adjust his hat. "Move into that crevice and no matter what happens, don't try to help me. Your focus should be on getting yourself and Harley to the beach. Glenn Hardcastle will be waiting on you there."

Charlie stared at him and considered arguing but ultimately knew it would only prolong the inevitable. With great reluctance, she backed away toward the crevice. Jonathon stepped toward the center of the cave and in front of the fountain. The flamethrower was still clutched so tightly in his hands that his knuckles were white.

"I'm here," he said, looking at the terrifying prehistoric reptile in front of him. "I'm the one you want."

The large *Troodon* stared at him curiously but remained right where she stood. Had it not been for Harley lying at the animal's feet, Jonathon could've easily lit the beast on fire and lived to fight another day. He locked eyes with the *Troodon* and for a long moment, he waited to see if the creature would move away from Harley so he'd be able to kill it. Mother just continued to stare at him. There was a coldness in her eyes that made him very uneasy. It also angered him.

"What are you waiting for?" he yelled. The dinosaur blinked once and continued to snarl angrily but otherwise remained right where she stood.

Jonathon tightened his jaw and glanced over at Charlie. She was still tucked away nervously in the crevice, waiting for her moment to scramble after Harley. With frustration mounting, Jonathon began to approach the *Troodon*.

"Come on," he shouted. "Come and get me!" He casually released his grip from the flamethrower and spread both his arms outward. As soon as he did so, the *Troodon* lurched forward and snapped its jaws.

The movement startled Jonathon and he immediately snatched the flamethrower back into his grasp and moved his finger toward the trigger. The dinosaur responded by immediately pulling back and again planted itself behind Harley. Suddenly, Jonathon understood.

She's not going to move as long as this thing is in my hands, he thought, looking at the weapon in his grip.

"Alright," he said, glancing back up at Mother. "I get it now." He then allowed the nozzle to drop to the ground. Jonathon then reached for his sternum and unbuckled the leather strap that held the metal tank in place on his back. It fell and clanged loudly on the stone floor behind him. At that moment, the *Troodon* stepped over Harley and began approaching him. Jonathon began taking a step back and as he did so, he glanced over at Charlie. He gestured for her to get Harley and his eyes reminded her to leave without looking back. She stayed put for a moment staring at him, clearly struggling with what she had reluctantly agreed to do.

"I'll be fine," Jonathon said finally with a smile. "Get Harley and get out of here...she only wants me."

Without further hesitation, Charlie nodded and began to slowly move out of the crevice. She kept close to the cave wall and the *Troodon* didn't so much as glance in her direction. Mother was watching Jonathon, and he was staring right back at her. He could see the intent in her eyes and it was obvious that she knew he was responsible for killing all of the other *Troodons* in the pit. She wanted him dead...she wanted to taste his flesh.

Jonathon continued to step backward, and momentarily allowed his eyes to look past the *Troodon*. Charlie had briskly moved to Harley and was now dragging her toward the bright daylight outside the cave. The *Troodon* kept her eyes locked onto Jonathon and it was clear that she cared about nothing else but killing him. Jonathon allowed himself a moment to breathe a sigh of relief as he knew that no matter what happened now, he'd at least given Charlie and Harley a chance to get off the island.

The large *Troodon* snarled again as if she was trying to get Jonathon's attention back on his impending doom. He continued to walk backward and a sinking feeling began to overcome him as he began to understand that he was now getting further and further away from the exit of the cave. Finally, he took another step back and his foot caught a rock ledge. He nearly toppled backward, but managed to regain his balance. He glanced over his shoulder and saw that his foot had caught the rock wall of the fountain. Despite the dire situation he now found himself in, Jonathon still felt a deep temptation to take a drink of the attractive blue water.

He turned back to see where Mother was just in time to see the angry *Troodon* open her mouth and leap for him. Jonathon instinctively rolled out of the way just in the nick of time. Mother sailed past where he'd been standing and fell into the fountain. Jonathon knew that if he was going to make it out, now was his best shot in doing so. He immediately scrambled to his feet and prepared to run out of the cave as quickly as his legs could carry him. Unfortunately, Mother was faster. In almost one fluid motion, she'd crashed into the water, rolled back onto her feet, and then used her powerful legs to propel back into Jonathon's path.

"You've got to be kidding me," he said awestruck.

The dinosaur snapped at him and released a sinister growl in response. Jonathon glanced over to where he'd dropped the flamethrower. It was only twenty feet away and in his mind's eye, he could see himself making a beeline for it, snatching the weapon up, and torching the *Troodon* just as she got to him. Mother seemingly sensed what he was planning and wasted no time with another attack. She lunged for Jonathon and again, he managed to dodge her advance. This time, however, Mother was ready. As he dove out of the way, the *Troodon* spun in response and slapped him hard with her powerful tail. Jonathon took the blow in his ribs and immediately felt all of the air rush from his lungs. The handgun that had been in the back of his pants was jarred loose and clattered away from him, lost in the darkness.

He rolled over onto his hands and knees, gasping desperately for a gulp of air. Mother, noticing her prey now seemed injured, again moved in for the attack. Jonathon sensed her bearing down on him and though he still struggled for air, he instinctively pulled the large knife from his belt and met the bloodthirsty beast as her jaws snapped at his neck. He plunged the knife into her chest, but the blade met bone and glanced awkwardly into her shoulder. Though he'd been unable to reach his intended target, Jonathon still managed to inflict enough pain to make the dinosaur pull back, at least for a moment.

With air now returning to his lungs, Jonathon began to frantically crawl to where the flamethrower lay mere feet away. Mother, again amazingly cognizant of what he was doing, roared angrily and though blood poured profusely from the wound in her shoulder, she again darted after him. Jonathon managed to grab the weapon just as the *Troodon* caught him by the foot with her jaws. Jonathon kicked at the dinosaur's snout with his other foot, but she held on tightly.

As he felt the *Troodons* teeth begin to pierce into the top of his foot, Jonathon howled in pain and then, fueled by pure adrenaline, he grabbed the flamethrower hose, rolled onto his back, and then used the hose to swing the heavy fuel tank hard against the dinosaur's skull. The metal tank connected perfectly and it was enough to make the *Troodon* release his foot. As the stunned animal pulled back from him, Jonathon then noticed that the rock floor next to him was suddenly wet. For a moment, he wondered if it was blood...possibly from his foot, or from the *Troodons* injured shoulder. But then the strong smell of propane entered his nostrils and he came to the realization that he'd inadvertently yanked the hose loose from the tank as he'd swung it at the dinosaur.

Propane was all over the ground but Jonathon had somehow avoided getting any of it on himself. As Mother regained her composure and returned her devilish gaze upon him, an idea popped into his head.

"Come on!" he shouted anxiously. "Come and get me, I'm right here!"

Mother opened her mouth and barked furiously at him. She then began to trot toward him. Her mouth opened revealing every single one of her needle-like teeth along with her long, thin reptilian tongue. As she approached, Jonathon took his knife and swung it with a slanted motion, eventually contacting the stone floor. The blade glanced off the hard surface and the result he was looking for didn't occur. Mother continued her approach with no regard for his strange new behavior. Jonathon again swung at the stone floor, and again nothing happened. The *Troodons* was only seconds away from raining teeth and claws over him.

Third time is the charm, he thought as he came to the realization that if this attempt failed, he'd most likely be unable to survive another attack. For the final time, he struck the stone floor with purpose. This time, sparks flew and Jonathon quickly scrambled to his feet as the propane ignited just as Mother stepped into it. The large *Troodon* was immediately engulfed in fire just as Jonathon had planned. What he had not planned for, however, was that the animal's momentum would continue toward him. He stepped backward to avoid the burning *Troodon*, but for the second time, his heel caught the ledge of the fountain behind him. This time, Jonathon made no effort to stop his fall. He fell into the magical water and Mother fell in over him.

CHAPTER 28

Charlie dragged Harley several yards away from the mouth of the cave before finally collapsing from exhaustion. She knew there was no way she'd be able to drag the larger woman all the way to the beach. After she took a moment to catch her breath, she rolled over and began to frantically shake the woman she'd just met. Though she didn't know her, what she did know was that this woman was involved in trying to rescue her. She owed her.

"Wake up," Charlie pleaded.

Harley's eyes flickered for a moment but otherwise, there was no response. Now that there was significantly more light, Charlie began to examine her. The vast amount of blood on her shirt and matted in her hair probably had a lot to do with her lethargic state. Charlie looked her over closely and finally discovered a nasty gash in her scalp. She was acutely aware that head injuries bled profusely and medical attention was needed immediately if Harley was going to have the best chance for survival.

Charlie glanced over toward the cave and desperately hoped she'd see Jonathon strolling in her direction. He wasn't there, but suddenly the shrieking sound of another *Troodon* in pain echoed loudly from inside. Despite his insistence that she move on without him, Charlie ran back toward the cave. Even if she wanted to leave him, she'd be unable to get Harley back to the beach alone. Her best chance—Harley's best chance—would require Jonathon's help and if he died, she figured so would they.

Just as she made it to the cave entrance, Jonathon emerged. He was soaking wet and limping, but very much alive.

"Oh my God, what happened?" she asked. "Are you alright?"

He nodded and gave her an exhausted thumbs up. "I'm afraid all the lab work you've been doing on the *Troodons* has been cancelled indefinitely," he said.

Charlie sighed. "I know," she replied. "And I for one am glad."

Jonathon winced as he tried to put more pressure on his injured foot. "I was hoping you'd say that," he groaned.

"Do we need to look at your foot?" Charlie asked as she kneeled to take a closer look.

Jonathon shook his head. "No," he answered quickly as he pulled his foot away. "If I leave the shoe on, it'll help control the swelling." He looked over to where Harley was laying, still unconscious. He began limping toward her. "Come on, let's go."

Charlie followed after him and prepared to help him lift Harley onto his shoulder. Just as they reached her, the earth began to shake again. Jonathon, already unsteady on his feet, lost his balance and stumbled to the ground. Charlie managed to keep her footing but could tell this was the worst tremor yet. Again, she felt a responsibility to look after Harley. She knelt down beside her as the earthquake rumbled even harder.

Suddenly, the ground began to rip apart and Jonathon had to roll out of the way to avoid falling into the zig-zagging crevice that aggressively formed between him and the two women. Steam billowed from the crack and the heat was so intense that it singed his arm. It quickly became apparent to him that their time on the island was up…it was time to leave. As the ground continued to shake wildly underneath them, Jonathon jumped over the crevice and, with Charlie's assistance, they carefully placed Harley over his shoulder. Just as they began to trot away, the cave that had contained the fountain of youth for millions of years collapsed and a plume of dust enveloped them. Seconds later, a swarm of bats burst from the rubble, their numbers so vast that for a few seconds it seemed as if dusk had come early. Charlie screamed as the thick cloud of bats glanced off her in all directions. She began waving her arms furiously in all directions, especially around her head, as her primary fear was that one of the winged mammals would get caught in her hair.

As the swarm of bats finally began to dissipate, Charlie looked over at Jonathon, her blonde hair now messy and visibly dirty. "Are we going to make it to the beach in time?" she asked, her tone more angry than fearful.

Jonathon didn't answer because he didn't want to give her false hope. He just gritted his teeth and began to move as fast as he could.

***

Glenn Hardcastle was becoming quite impatient and the curiosity was killing him. The six *Velociraptor*s were clearly eating something but he was still unable to see what it was. As if that weren't frustrating enough, he was mere feet away from the beach but refrained from stepping onto it for fear of being seen by the ravenous carnivores. As he listened to the surf roll in from the Atlantic, another sound hummed from beyond the wall of mist. It was obviously the boat that Cornelius Cold had assured them all was coming. Hardcastle glanced over his shoulder as if Jonathon and the others would be there, ready to board with him and leave the wretched island again. As expected, he saw nothing.

When he again peered toward the wall of mist, he was relieved to see that the boat had indeed emerged. It was a sleek military ship of some kind, small and painted gray with a large American flag billowing majestically in the wind above the bridge. Concerned that the *Velociraptor*s would also hear the boat, he quickly glanced over in their direction. The dinosaurs had all stopped eating simultaneously and seemed to sense that something was wrong. At first, Hardcastle assumed it was the boat, but then he began to feel a steady vibration under his feet. It was another earthquake.

The *Velociraptor*s scattered as the tremors became more intense, leaving their unfinished meal right where it was. Hardcastle had a hard time standing but he was drawn to see exactly what the raptors had been feasting on. Using palm tree trunks to steady himself, he hurried toward the spot where the carnivores had been eating. What he found made his stomach lurch. It was a human body and very little was left of the man's torso. Hardcastle held a hand over his mouth and turned his head in an attempt to stifle away the urge to vomit.

As the ground continued to rumble, he glanced back toward the water to check on the boat. He could see men on deck with binoculars watching the island intensely; they were clearly aware of the earthquake. At that moment, Hardcastle contemplated making a mad dash for the beach where he could be rescued and begin receiving the medical attention he desperately needed. However, the remains of the man that lay before him seemed to beckon him to look again.

With great reluctance, Hardcastle again turned his attention to the deceased man and this time he tried to focus more on his face. Something looked awfully wrong about it, and for a moment he wondered if the raptors had nibbled away at some of his features. Hardcastle then noticed that the man seemed to be wearing military garb similar to that of Harley Cash...he even had dog tags. Suddenly, he felt even more responsibility in investigating the man's remains further and since there were dog tags, he would probably even be able to identify him. As he snatched the dog tags from the man's neck, he looked closer at his face and the realization set in that the nasty injury was a result of a gunshot wound to the back of his head. He glanced down at the dog tags and read the name. *Henry Bailey*.

***

"Just keep running!" Jonathon shouted as he did his best to ignore the pain in his injured foot.

The ground continued to shake, though not quite as intensely as it had been moments earlier. For the first, and perhaps the only time, Jonathon was grateful for his multiple visits to the island. He'd become quite familiar with the terrain and knew exactly where they needed to run to make a straight shot back to the beach. Unfortunately, he knew that they'd have to cross the large clearing in the center of the island and the point where they'd exit the jungle would be near the spot where he'd narrowly escaped while the *Spinosaurus* and two tyrannosaurs had battled to the death.

Jonathon considered warning Charlie about the possibility of the *Spinosaurus's* presence, but decided against it. He hoped that the earthquake had scared it away to retreat wherever the animal called home. As they entered the clearing, he knew it was imperative that they crossed it as soon as possible. One thing he'd learned from his numerous visits to the island was that everything was much more vulnerable in the clearing than in the shadows of the jungle. As he stepped out of from under the tree canopy and into the bright light, he immediately noticed the two corpses of the tyrannosaurs that had lost their fight against the *Spinosaurus*. While there, he could not resist the urge to make a passing glance at Mr. Cold's body. He felt a tremendous amount of guilt for having to leave the man behind, but it was all he could do to carry Harley out.

His eyes scanned the spot where he'd last seen Mr. Cold, but much to his surprise, there was no body to be seen. For a moment, he considered the possibility that he was looking in the wrong spot, but as he thought about it, he was certain that was not the case. He wondered if perhaps a dinosaur—maybe the *Spinosaurus*—had taken the body elsewhere. However, that possibility made no sense because the large carnivore had more than enough of a meal between the two dead tyrannosaurs. As much as he wanted to investigate the matter further, he simply didn't have the time.

"Something is burning!" Charlie shouted in disbelief.

Jonathon slowed just enough so that he could turn his body to see what she was referring to. When he did so, he saw a massive plume of smoke billowing from an area he estimated was at or near the collapsed cave. When he turned back to focus on the terrain ahead of him, he noticed another strange phenomenon. For a second, he'd have sworn that it was beginning to snow. He soon realized, however, that what he thought was snow was actually ash.

"It's a volcano," he told Charlie, doing his best to sound calm. "That's what's been causing all the earthquakes. A cone is probably forming near the cave. We've got to hurry."

Charlie responded by picking up her pace to the point of passing him—*or had he slowed down?* As they crossed the center of the clearing, his shoulder burned intensely, so much so that he seemed to completely block out all the pain in his foot. After they'd entered the jungle on the opposite side of the clearing, they continued on for what Jonathon guessed was probably another twenty minutes. His side ached to the point that he had to slow to a trot and Charlie began to pull further and further away from him. She ran so fast and so far ahead that he completely lost sight of her. Jonathon's trot eventually evolved into a walk and before he knew it, the exhaustion he'd been doing his absolute best to ignore, finally overtook him. He collapsed, but did his best to make the fall as soft as possible for Harley.

He laid on his back, panting profusely, and he wondered how long he'd need before he could gather the strength to continue. Jonathon feared that Charlie would notice he was no longer behind her and come back to look for him. He truly hoped she ran into Hardcastle before that happened because he knew he'd stop her. As tired as he was, he still believed he could get himself and Harley to the beach if he could just take a few minutes to collect himself. After a couple of minutes of lying on his back, he finally turned over and prepared to stand again. The earth had ceased shaking again but the ash continued to fall. He knew that the cone that had formed would begin spewing more fire as the hours ticked by. It seemed there would be little hope for most of the dinosaurs on the island. This thought saddened him, but when he thought of his wife Lucy and daughter Lily, it was easy to refocus on what was most important. He took a deep breath and again stood up. His injured foot instantly reminded him that he was hurt as soon as he put weight on it.

Jonathon reached down to pull Harley over his shoulder yet again. She stirred briefly and muttered something that he was unable to understand.

"Hang in there," he whispered. "We're almost there."

As he stood up straight, a sound behind him made him jump and spin around to see what was there. What he found made his heart stop and nearly made him collapse again.

"You've got to be kidding me," he said in disbelief.

Standing nearly ten feet behind him were three raptors. He was unsure how long they'd been there, but he guessed they'd been sneaking up on him for quite some time. And knowing raptors the way that he did, he began to look around in all directions for more. *Velociraptor*s were cunning hunters that were notorious for using a combination of stealth and precision in their attacks. He knew that if there were three out in the open, there was probably at least one other hiding nearby, ready to pounce. No matter the odds, Jonathon also knew he was in absolutely no position to outsmart or fight them.

As the three raptors began to draw near him, their teeth and claws exposed and obviously ready to rip and tear him apart, he closed his eyes and accepted the fact that his luck had finally run out. He'd dodged death so many times on the wretched island in the mist that he knew it should not have come as any surprise to him. He considered Harley Cash, still unconscious on his shoulders, and part of him envied her. It was probable that she would not be aware of the terrible moments leading to her death. Jonathon, on the other hand, would spend his last breath thinking of his wife and daughter. He remembered drying Lucy's tears when she'd come to the realization that he would be returning yet again to the island. He'd promised her that he would be back—and now it wasn't going to happen. With his eyes still closed, he dropped to his knees and waited for it all to be over. He silently prayed that it would be as quick and as painless as possible.

The raptors, though momentarily confused by the strange behavior of their prey, wasted no time in beginning their attack. Seemingly in unison, they all leapt into the air in a frightening display of their power and ferocity. Though Jonathon kept his eyes closed tightly, he sensed what was happening. In his mind's eye, it all seemed to happen in slow motion. The three carnivores would come down upon him and they'd use their sickle claws to slash open his abdomen in one cruel, merciless movement. For what seemed like an eternity, it became eerily silent, and then—the sound of rapid gunfire erupted from somewhere behind him.

The furious barrage of bullets that whistled over his head made Jonathon immediately open his eyes. He instinctively fell forward and did his best to cover and protect the still unconscious Harley. He looked up just in time to see the powerful projectiles tear through the three *Velociraptor*s, instantly halting their trajectory through the air. Just as they'd all leaped at once, they all fell lifeless to the ground in unison as well. Once it was obvious they were no longer a threat, the gunfire immediately ceased. Jonathon quickly looked in both directions for another raptor attack, but he saw none. Most likely if there were any other raptors nearby, they'd have fled as soon as the report of the assault rifles began.

After he was satisfied there were no more raptors on the way, Jonathon whipped his head around and saw a trio of soldiers approaching from the direction of the beach.

"Are you alright, sir?" the man in the middle called out.

Jonathon rolled over on his back and smiled. His foot hurt, the gashes on his face burned, he was hungry, and beyond exhausted...yet he seemed to feel the best he'd felt since he had landed on the island. Once again, he somehow cheated death.

"I feel awesome fellas," he replied gratefully. "What took you so long?"

EPILOGUE:

It turned out that Jonathon's saving grace was all due to Charlie running ahead and reaching the beach before he did. He was later told that as soon as she stepped onto the sand, she began screaming for someone to go in and help him get Harley out of the jungle. Had she stayed behind to help him, they would've most likely all died together only fifty yards away from rescue. After thanking her—and the soldiers that came to his aid—profusely, he regretfully let Charlie know about the deaths of Victor and Matt. The news hit her much harder than he originally anticipated. She immediately collapsed to the floor and began to sob uncontrollably. He wanted to console her, to say something that would help ease her pain. However, he knew that was a lost cause. She'd apparently been much closer to Dr. Matthew Walker than he had known and her reaction to his death was heartbreaking.

Once Jonathon had to the courage to leave Charlie to grieve, he turned his attention to Harley Cash. Her condition reminded him a lot of Silas Treadwell and how close to death he'd come on Jonathon's previous adventure on the island. The medic on the ship told him that she was in excellent health and that had it not been for that, there would be no hope. As encouraging as that evaluation was, he cautioned Jonathon that she was nowhere near out of the woods yet. The medic suggested that if Jonathon believed in prayer, Harley could certainly use some.

Next, Jonathon checked on Glenn Hardcastle and miraculously, he seemed to be doing remarkably well for a man that had lost an appendage just hours earlier. As soon as he saw his old friend, the two of them embraced and both swore they'd never return to the island again. Hardcastle soon noticed that Mr. Cold was nowhere to be found and Jonathon explained what he'd seen happen to their former mysterious boss. He'd been certain that he had witnessed the man's death, but after never seeing a body, he began to wonder.

It was then that Hardcastle informed Jonathon of the gruesome discovery he'd made regarding Hank Bailey's body—and his strong belief that Mr. Cold had murdered him. At first, Jonathon tried to repudiate the claim, but as hard as he tried, he could think of no other explanation. The more he argued with Hardcastle on the matter, the more he began to slowly change his opinion. Finally, he concluded that as hard as it was to believe, Cold was the only logical suspect responsible for

Hank's death. He certainly didn't shoot himself in the back of the head. They figured his body had probably been dragged away and brought to be shared among a pack of hungry raptors. Hank Bailey certainly deserved better, and suddenly Jonathon found himself hoping that Cold was indeed dead.

"Of course he's dead," Hardcastle assured him.

Jonathon nodded, and wanted to believe it. However, for some reason that he could not explain, he just could not allow himself to accept it—at least not until he saw a body. And unfortunately, with the newly formed volcano threatening all life on the island, he wondered if he'd ever be able to get the closure he needed on the matter. By the time they'd escaped the island, the cone was nearing 200 feet high and a geologist on board the military ship explained that it would be triple that height in a week's time. The future did not look good for the dinosaurs that had somehow managed to escape extinction for over 65 million years. Part of that fact made Jonathon quite sad, and another part of it made him happy.

The dinosaurs on the island in the mist simply did not belong in the present day. Part of what had led to their resilience and ability to thrive for so long had been their seclusion and separation from man. As with most things on planet earth, when man became involved, somehow some way, they found a way to exploit it and ultimately destroy. The recent formation of the volcano almost seemed like nature's way of making sure that the island and the dinosaurs that inhabited it were handled on its own terms. There was no room for man there and, for better or worse, it seemed that nature was making sure it would stay that way.

Once the shipped docked again on the mainland, Jonathon, Hardcastle, and Charlie were all taken to a large semi-truck parked nearby with steep stairs that led to a door on the back of the trailer. The three of them were ordered inside and were surprised to find some sort of mobile military unit, though Jonathon was unable to tell exactly which branch. He looked to both Charlie and Hardcastle for answers since he was aware that they'd both had a much closer working relationship with Mr. Cold than him. Instead of answers, all he got was blank stares and shrugs. They seemed to be as much in the dark about what was going on as he was. The trio of survivors were ushered toward the front of the trailer and into a tiny interrogation room with no windows. Nothing was said or explained to any of them, despite Hardcastle's insistence that someone tell them what was going on. A pitcher of water with three paper cups was left in the room, and they sat alone side by side on the same side of the table. Jonathon guessed they remained there for at least half an hour.

Finally, the door swung open and a man in a black suit stepped inside. His dark hair was combed neatly and he was clean shaven. He reminded Jonathon a lot of Cornelius Cold, only younger. The man had a file folder tucked under his arm and he pulled the chair out from the opposite side of the table and took a seat. He then pulled out three pieces of paper—along with three pens he retrieved from his coat pocket—and placed the items in front of each of them.

"I'm truly sorry for all that you've been through over the past few days," the man said, and he offered a friendly smile. "I'm also cognizant of each of your relationships to Cornelius, and because of that, I'm willing to make a deal with each of you."

"A deal?" Jonathon asked as he leaned over to look at the document in front of him.

"That's right," the man replied. "A deal. Basically, all I want is for each of you to go away..." the man paused, took a deep breath through his nose, and then flashed another smile at the three of them. "I'm sorry," he said carefully. "I worded that wrong...please forgive my rudeness."

"Please get to the point," Hardcastle said angrily. "In case you haven't noticed, I need a hospital," he added, holding up his gauze-wrapped stump.

"Right," the man agreed. "I will get to the point." He reached for the piece of paper in front of Hardcastle and pointed to a line at the very bottom. "I want you each to sign your respective agreement and you can all be on your way."

"And what exactly does this say?" Charlie asked, picking up the piece of paper to read it.

"It says that if you speak to anyone about what you know of that island or its...er, inhabitants, you will each be charged with treason, and essentially, you'll spend the rest of your life locked away so that you will be unable to tell another soul."

The man's tone was very matter-of-fact and he didn't so much as blink when he spoke. Jonathon stared at him a long moment and then finally snatched the pen up. He quickly scrawled out his signature and shoved the piece of paper back across the table. The man took it and gave an appreciative nod.

"You do understand that this includes your friend Silas Treadwell?" he asked. Clearly, he was involved in the bugging that Cold had spoken of. Jonathon wondered if he'd been forced to sign the same agreement.

"Silas and I will still be friends, but we'll stick to talking about things that a lot of older guys like to talk about like football and how many times we get up to take a piss at night," he replied. "Is that okay?"

The man smiled. "Yes, that will be okay."

"Good," Jonathon replied, crossing his arms. "Now I'd like to go home to see my wife and kid if that's alright with you."

"That sounds like a very good idea," the man agreed cheerfully. He then returned his attention to Charlie and Hardcastle. He glanced down at their respective agreements and then his gaze returned to each of them, his eyebrows raising slightly.

The two of them signed also and as soon as the man in black had the documents back in the folder and under his arm, he stood, opened the door, and motioned for them to exit.

"There will be a car waiting outside," he said. "Mr. Hardcastle, you will get the medical attention you need and deserve. As for Mr. Williams and Ms. Nelson, I trust you've each already gotten the medical attention and drugs you needed. The two of you will now be taken to an airport and put on a plane. Once on the ground, a car will be waiting to take you home. I want to thank you on behalf of the United States of America for your cooperation. You're all patriots."

Jonathon looked at Hardcastle and he got a smirk in reply. Jonathon then shook his head, rolled his eyes, and made his way out of the trailer. As promised, a black car was waiting outside.

"You gonna be alright?" he asked Hardcastle as he prepared to get in the car.

Hardcastle smiled and offered his remaining hand. The two shook hands and he said, "Don't talk like you'll never see me again...you haven't seen the last of me, Williams."

Jonathon nodded. "You know where to find me. Let me know how Harley is as soon as you can."

He nodded and then Charlie gave Hardcastle a hug as she followed Jonathon into the car.

They talked almost the entire drive to the airport and even more so on the airplane. Charlie asked Jonathon questions she'd never asked before. She wanted to know all about his wife and his new baby. The two of them exchanged stories of their experiences in paleontology and the most exciting finds of their careers. When they finally reached the moment where they had to go their separate ways, Charlie suddenly reached out and hugged him tightly.

"I haven't thanked you for saving my life," she said.

"Twice," Jonathon replied.

She pulled back and looked at him. "What?"

"Technically, I've saved your life twice," he said. "Once in the cave and once a couple of years ago when we were both locked in a cage with a hungry tyrannosaur knocking at the door."

Charlie pursed her lips and thought a minute. "As I remember it, your father revived me after I'd drowned."

Jonathon shook his head and laughed. "So, you assume it was all unicorns and rainbows while you were knocked out and the cage we were in was—" he paused. "You know what, never mind."

Charlie laughed with him and the two of them shared another embrace.

"Take care of yourself, Charlotte," he said as he pulled away and turned to leave.

"We're going on a dig this summer," she called after him. "You already promised!"

"Absolutely," he agreed. "I sorta miss the days when the only dinos we encountered were all bones."

***

By the time Jonathon arrived at his home, the sun was just beginning to rise. It was the start of a new day, and the fact that he had somehow arrived at his home at that particular moment was symbolic for him. It was the start of a new chapter in his life. A new chapter that did not include running for his life from prehistoric monsters on a faraway island. As he approached the front porch, Rex, his Golden Retriever, greeted him. Jonathon thought that was odd since the dog had become overly protective of Lucy. He rarely left her side.

"It's about time," a female voice called out from the shadows on the porch. It was Lucy. She had been sitting on one of the two rocking chairs that they'd spent many early mornings sitting in together to watch the sunrise. "You're just in time," she said, glancing toward the east.

Jonathon smiled widely at her and then jogged up the steps to greet her as she stood. They kissed for a long moment and when they finally broke apart, he watched her eyes as she began to study the gashes on his face.

"Did it improve my looks?" he asked, trying to ease the tension.

She took a deep breath and he could see tears beginning to well up in her eyes.

"Please don't do that," he said softly. "You were doing that when I left. How is Lily?"

"Oh, she's fine, sleeping like a brick," she said, making an effort to stifle her emotions. "I'm just so thankful that you're back. Please promise me…"

"I'm not going back," he said reassuringly. "That's a promise." He pulled back to look at her again and was glad to see her smiling. "How did you know I was on the way? I wanted it to be a surprise."

"I received a call from that man you told me about…Glenn Hardcastle," she said. "He apologized profusely when I answered the phone and told me that the only reason he was calling was because you'd made him promise to let you know immediately when he found out the condition of Harley…" she paused. "Who is Harley?"

"I've got plenty of time to tell you that," he quipped. "Just tell me how she is."

"He said she is awake. She is awake and wants to speak to you," Lucy replied. "What would she want to speak to you about?"

Jonathon sighed and answered, "I think you'd better have a seat," he said, gently pushing her back into the rocking chair.

"Was it that bad?" she asked. Her tone suggested that she wasn't sure if she wanted to know the truth or not.

"I'll tell you all about it," he said as he took a seat in the other chair. "But first, we're going to watch the sunrise. After all, it's a new day."

THE END

SEVEREDPRESS

CHECK OUT OTHER GREAT DINOSAUR THRILLERS

WRITTEN IN STONE
by David Rhodes

Charles Dawson is trapped 100 million years in the past. Trying to survive from day to day in a world of dinosaurs he devises a plan to change his fate. As he begins to write messages in the soft mud of a nearby stream, he can only hope they will be found by someone who can stop his time travel. Professor Ron Fontana and Professor Ray Taggit, scientists with opposing views, each discover the fossilized messages. While attempting to save Charles, Professor Fontana, his daughter Lauren and their friend Danny are forced to join Taggit and his group of mercenaries. Taggit does not intend to rescue Charles Dawson, but to force Dawson to travel back in time to gather samples for Taggit's fame and fortune. As the two groups jump through time they find they must work together to make it back alive as this fast-paced thriller climaxes at the very moment the age of dinosaurs is ending.

HARD TIME
by Alex Laybourne

Rookie officer Peter Malone and his heavily armed team are sent on a deadly mission to extract a dangerous criminal from a classified prison world. A Kruger Correctional facility where only the hardest, most vicious criminals are sent to fend for themselves, never to return.

But when the team come face to face with ancient beasts from a lost world, their mission is changed. The new objective: Survive.

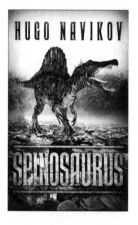
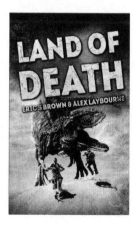

CHECK OUT OTHER GREAT DINOSAUR THRILLERS

JURASSIC ISLAND
by Viktor Zarkov

Guided by satellite photos and modern technology a ragtag group of survivalists and scientists travel to an uncharted island in the remote South Indian Ocean. Things go to hell in a hurry once the team reaches the island and the massive megalodon that attacked their boats is only the beginning of their desperate fight for survival.

Nothing could have prepared billionaire explorer Joseph Thornton and washed up archaeologist Christopher "Colt" McKinnon for the terrifying prehistoric creatures that wait for them on JURASSIC ISLAND!

K-REX
by L.Z. Hunter

Deep within the Congo jungle, Circuitz Mining employs mercenaries as security for its Coltan mining site. Armed with assault rifles and decades of experience, nothing should go wrong. However, the dangers within the jungle stretch beyond venomous snakes and poisonous spiders. There is more to fear than guerrillas and vicious animals. Undetected, something lurks under the expansive treetop canopy . . .

Something ancient.

Something dangerous.

Kasai Rex!

Made in the USA
Lexington, KY
06 February 2019